Reac

'The book starts as a co … into a thriller. The first time I caught my breath was in the final coda.'

Paul, 54, consultant psychiatrist

'*Taboo* is an intellectual farce, which looks at the current emptiness at the heart of today's conceptual art world and questions what's important in art, as in life . . . There are very funny one-liners throughout.'

Jean, 50, writer and management consultant

'The book sent my imagination and memories back to art college vividly, showing up the pain and vulnerability of art college as you place into the world that which is so personal and raw. Paul's slightly worrying [lack of] knowledge of contemporary art is a constant source of amusement through the book.'

Luci, 31, artist

'I absolutely loved *Taboo.* It is witty and funny – particularly the History of Art references. [It brings out] both the humorous aspect as well as the surprising beauty of conceptual art. The descriptions are vivid yet simple. I almost cried when reading the last chapter . . . very human as well as entertaining and thought-provoking . . . A wonderful read.'

Bethan, 18, student

Also by the author

More than a bookshop: Zwemmer's and art in the 20th century

Taboo

Nigel Halliday

First published in Great Britain in 2025
Published by nrvhbooks
nrvhbooks@gmail.com

www.taboothenovel.uk

ISBN 978-1-068-28050-4

Typeset in Goudy by Falcon Oast Graphic Art Ltd.
www.falcon.uk.com
Printed and bound by ImprintDigital.com

1 3 5 7 9 10 8 6 4 2

For Sue

Contents

Prologue

On the television Paul and Jan watched the young reporter advancing along a cobbled street, his curly hair blowing in the cold wind. A row of bricked-up railway arches lined the left-hand side of the street. Opposite, at the far end, was a forlorn, two-storey, pre-war factory building.

The reporter, wrapped inside a heavy coat, spoke as he walked, his voice dripping with condescension: 'Farlane Street – to you and me just a familiar, grim relic of a bygone industrial era. But today, the scene of an artistic disaster.'

He stopped outside the old factory. Flakes of lime-green paint still clung to the metal window frames, and the dirt of years obscured the glass.

'This is the studio of controversial artist Stephen Meriton, who is preparing for his first major retrospective right here in his home town of Clayforth. But when the municipal gallery came calling earlier today to collect his latest bizarre work, the project came to an unexpected halt.'

The scene cut to a longer shot from back down the road. A white van was waiting outside the studio. Its engine could be heard revving angrily. A motto 'Earlier today' appeared at the top of the screen.

'We were filming the preparations for the exhibition here earlier today,' the reporter continued as a voiceover, 'when this happened.'

The van was now advancing at speed towards the camera when, from a side road, a car emerged without due care or attention, and the van came to an abrupt halt.

The reporter's face reappeared: 'Thankfully, no one was hurt and no damage was done – except that the work of art itself . . . disappeared. "How can a work of art disappear?" you ask. Well, in the arcane world of contemporary art, nothing surprises us any more. In this case, the work simply did not exist in the first place – as you can see from our footage taken at the time.'

The picture now cut to the studio front doors, which were being opened from inside. A short, fleshy man, clothed entirely in black, emerged backwards, slowly feeling with his feet for the steps as he descended towards the pavement. His attention appeared to be fixed on a large box that he was carrying. His left hand was cupped under a corner at the base; his right hand was raised to steady the side. But his hands were empty. He seemed to wobble slightly as he reached the second step. As he did so a second man, taller and thinner but identically dressed, was coming into view through the doorway. From the position of his hands he was evidently grasping the other end of whatever it was that was not there.

They progressed with what appeared to be telepathic coordination, tilting their hands in response to the angle of the steps, and then to the pavement, preserving a consistent distance between the two of them.

Watching the television from the vantage point of the kitchen doorway, Paul stopped his unconscious twisting of the tea towel in his hands. His mouth fell slightly open as he stared in bewilderment, oblivious to Jan's snort of derision. He noticed that the men's faces were painted like clowns, an impression that was strengthened when the shorter one turned his head, wiped his brow slowly with his sleeve as if relieved to have got safely so far, and winked solemnly at the camera, before grasping the edge of the shape again with delicate precision. But his face was not the bright white of a traditional clown, but bore the pallor of death.

The two figures shuffled off the pavement into the road, then round to the back of the van, where a ramp was in position. Paul noticed Meriton appear on the edge of the picture, scowling. The two men swapped their hand positions smartly to hold the shape from the bottom, then edged up the ramp, ducking their heads in turn as they disappeared from view.

'The work, says Meriton, exists in the shape,' the reporter explained.

The driver slammed the van doors.

'Which is OK. But what happens if you forget where you put it? Or, in this case, if you have to make an emergency stop?'

The camera was now back at the end of the street, showing the two vehicles in the middle ground, nose to nose. The picture shook in anticipation as the film crew ran to the scene of the confrontation. The camera moved more smoothly down the side of the van to the rear where the doors had been opened again. Sprawled on the floor at the far end of the van's interior were the two mime artists. With exemplary professionalism they had forborne to use their hands to protect themselves in their forward flight. Each still very clearly held the bottom corners of the shape, their hands the correct distance apart. Both looked at the camera with an air of pathetic eagerness, as if the situation might yet be retrieved. But as one was lying across the other, it was evident that the shape was no longer intact.

'So: problem.' The reporter assumed a magisterial air, as he spoke to the camera, an image of the now-empty van interior behind him. 'Somewhere in the back of this van is a work of art. But where is it? Has it disappeared into thin – or even thinner – air? Is the van now a permanent art gallery? And will the owner be applying for an Arts Council grant?'

The programme cut back to the newsreader, who smiled: 'And in case you are wondering: yes, it is still only January. April Fool's Day is yet to come.'

'Serves him right,' Jan snorted derisively, her hair swirling as she tossed her head and lay back on the sofa, holding the newspaper at an uncomfortable angle above her. She had been paying only part-attention to *News at Ten* when the newsreader had mentioned the name that now haunted their home: 'And finally, controversial British artist Stephen Meriton appears to have lost one of his creations. Charles Fairbright reports.'

At the mention of Meriton's name, Jan had shouted to Paul in the kitchen: 'It's your nemesis again. He's on TV.'

Paul had appeared in the doorway holding a tea towel, which he was already winding into a corkscrew. Even when safely mediated through a television, any confrontation with Meriton was likely to convulse him with anxiety and resentment. The familiar ache had returned to his arms and legs. Pains were creeping into his shoulders. His skull seemed to be contracting against his brain.

But as he watched, he was again overwhelmed, however unwillingly, by a sympathy and respect for Meriton as an artist, for his vision and courage. To have the confidence to create a non-physical work was almost overpoweringly impressive. To have it transported by grim, white-faced clowns showed a degree of wit that Paul had not previously suspected.

He stroked the thin strands of his beard. He needed no prompting to intuit the significance of this creation. Indeed, he was more than ever convinced of the connection between his own art and Meriton's, of the parallel nature of their quest. For all the drab mundaneness of Farlane Street and the rude glibness of the television, he knew that something great had been lost.

Once more he was moved. He was impressed. And he was jealous.

But at least now, he reflected as he returned to the kitchen, he had something to fight back with: a weighty creation – very weighty – that he was sure of. Wrapped and ready in the garage was a work of his own, deceptively simple and yet powerfully innovative and emotionally rich. This, he knew, would finally shut the scummy faces of the mockers and make them jealous in their turn.

Four months earlier

1

September

Clayforth College of Art basked in autumn sunshine as Paul made his way through the black iron gateway. He walked cautiously to avoid being jostled by other students who were still caught up in the ebullience of the start of term. He carried his satchel in front of him, like a baby in a sling, his arms wrapped around it for protection.

The new atrium had been completed over the summer. Its bright red metal framework around large panels of glass struck a wilfully discordant note against the grey Victorian school building that the college had inherited. It beckoned the students to enter upon their work with the same spirit of bright-eyed irony and undirected defiance. The automatic sliding doors were already smeared with the handprints of the more athletic students who, running full tilt up the steps, had reached the doors before they could fully retract.

No such modernising had taken place among the support staff. Miss Grimm – only the Pay Office knew her real name – sat stiffly in her new cubicle, positioned in the centre of the foyer, whence, in keeping with the college's diversity policy, she could glare at all comers equally. However, the students, who daily filled the building with joyful noise and eager invention, were not easily put off, and over the years had periodically returned at night to festoon her space with Valentine's cards and proposals of marriage.

Paul walked slowly up the curving staircase round the inner wall of the atrium, behind a group of students who were precariously clutching bags, portfolios and cups of coffee whilst shouting loudly to make themselves heard over their Walkman earpieces. As he kept pace with them, not wanting to risk pushing past, the prospect of his new project set a familiar fantasy playing at the edge of his mind, as though someone had turned up the volume on an unattended television. He was bounding confidently up the steps to a podium to receive a shiny award, which on close inspection might have looked like an Oscar, or possibly the FA Cup, because he had never watched the Turner Prize awards. With the trophy was a discreet envelope containing a cheque that would solve his and Jan's financial needs. Behind him was a confusion of noise from the audience, amongst whom somewhere were his parents, overawed by the scale of the acclaim and finally convicted for their lack of belief. But what he particularly noticed was the wary look on the faces of the cultural illuminati ahead of him on the stage. They too were, one by one, rising to their feet as they applauded. But behind the polite smiles he could discern an uneasiness, a recognition that they were in the presence of an artistic genius whom they did not fully comprehend and who, if the truth be told, slightly alarmed them.

At the top of the stairs they trudged along a corridor to which, with the limited resources left after the construction of the atrium, a coat of battle-ship grey had been administered indiscriminately to every wall, door and frame, electrical wire, redundant junction box, and light switch. Verbal Corner, an area dedicated, in the interests of equality and irony, to the more verbally-challenged output of the previous year, had been left intact. A poster of Lord Kitchener, fiercely pointing the wrong finger at passers-by, announced: 'Your country kneads you.' Next to it a text-based offering asked in loud capital letters: 'Do you read me? The answer is ever yes or no.' The walls were otherwise bare of decoration, awaiting the new year's festival of originality.

Over the swing doors at the end of the corridor were inscribed the words *Painting Department*. To those in the know, the first word was framed by invisible inverted commas, like the teeth of a trap set for the unwary. For, as an institution at the cutting edge of artistic innovation, the college did not demean itself with anything as traditional as paint. There had been a moment in 1994, as the principal was preparing to rebirth the college as the seethingly visionary eye-of-the-storm of the visual arts in the north, when he had raised the possibility of changing the name of the department. However, the desultory debate that ensued had quickly established that the honest, indeed confessional, approach, *Department of Conceptual Art*, would more likely act as a deterrent than as an attraction. *Department of Creative Arts* was vetoed by the other departments as a slur on themselves; whilst their counter-proposal, *Department of Useless, Mindless Baboonery*, was never likely to get through unsuspected. So, along with the proposed atrium, they had embraced the irony and stuck with *Painting Department*.

Paul turned deftly to catch the door with his shoulder, as it was left to swing at him by the preceding group. They, meanwhile, although energised to the very highest point of creative determination by their extra-shot coffees, had stopped inside as they caught the mood.

✎ ✎ ✎

The studio was unnaturally quiet. Even the radio had been turned down. Early though it was in the term, Meriton was making his rounds, seeking whom he might devour.

Paul edged past the stationary group and made for his workspace. He received even less than usual in the way of acknowledgement from other students, as each was giving an impressive display of industrious engagement or at least of profound reflection, as they mentally followed Meriton's progress round the studio. Paul could see the top of Meriton's bald head several rows away at the far end of the room.

He opened his bag and gingerly set a plastic phial on the work surface. He took out a series of drawings, which he propped against the grubby chipboard partition that separated his space from Bridget's. Finally, he eased out a large book about Michelangelo, which he had stumbled across in the college library, and set to work.

The warmth of the day brought out the lingering scent of industrial floor cleaner applied during the holidays. Through the open windows, which stretched the length of the studio, the high-pitched monotone of a tutor's voice from the textile department downstairs wafted up like the whine of a distant chainsaw. Inside the studio, at a lower register, the monotonous metallic rhythm from the radio and the hum of the fluorescent lights echoed off the creamy white walls. Here tired safety notices and posters for long-departed exhibitions had been joined by a portrait of Kurt Cobain made entirely of used chewing gum, a group work by the class of 1996. Careless dusting during the summer had dislodged several pieces of gum, shortening the stray quiff of hair that hung fashionably across his left eye and down to his chin. This act of unwitting iconoclasm had robbed him of the air of cool sympathy with which for two years he had gazed down on the students. Now he seemed to be sucking the ends of his hair, awkward and embarrassed, bereft of any ability to offer either encouragement or solace to those who looked up to him.

Paul opened the phial, wrinkled his nose, then dipped his narrow pen in the red fluid. He peered at the book propped in front of him and began to draw. It was difficult to focus at first, as he anticipated the arrival of Meriton, whose black shoes could be heard squeaking on the lino as he advanced down the second aisle. Any hopes that the long summer break might have lightened his mood were quickly dissipated as his acerbic tone washed up over the partitions around the workspaces, and conveyed to everyone his general opinion of an individual's work, even when the words themselves failed to carry. The students had heard about his wife's accident, which could only have made him worse.

The prevailing pedagogic method of art-school tutors had not prevailed upon Meriton. For many in the profession their role was limited to the heaping of unqualified affirmation upon their charges, an approach that at least made for genial relationships and easy marking. But Meriton was a celebrity artist, who bore the scars of a successful career. For him every encounter was a battle to be won, and no artist should be allowed to think more highly of their work than it merited. Fortunate students were passed over in silence, but those that caught his attention received the full weight of his judgement.

Unknown to the students, who had implored the college principal, Julian Curridge, to grant an end to this torture, Meriton had made the same request. But the principal was charged with the most sacred of all responsibilities within the college: the finances. Continuity of funding depended on inspectors' reports, and these in turn depended on there being paperwork sufficient to demonstrate that at least some form of teaching was being delivered. But teaching was another concept with which the college struggled. 'Artists are born, not taught' was a motto often quoted within its walls, and might have helpfully been written as a warning over the gates to the college grounds. Like its buildings and the medium of oil paint, teaching seemed to belong to an earlier, less sophisticated age. For most of the time, in an atmosphere of supervised neglect, students were left free to develop their own work, albeit on the unwritten understanding that their freedom must necessarily take them beyond the boundaries of traditional practice, materials and values, into the realms of perpetual innovation, subversion and, if possible, outrage. And yet the idea of teaching could not be entirely sloughed off. Like a Darwinian vestigial organ, it lingered within the institution, serving no recognised purpose but still capable of causing discomfort, usually when external assessors brought it up. The paper trail showing Meriton making the rounds of the Painting Department once a month, and his colleague, Eric Horton, delivering a series of lectures, was an essential component in safeguarding the institution's finances. Thus Curridge contrived as ever to appear sympathetic to both parties, but granted relief to neither.

Paul poked his tongue between his lips in concentration, confidence slowly returning. As the work took shape, the trepidation at Meriton's imminent assessment began to give way to the pleasure Paul felt in the surprise that awaited the viewer. They would look from drawing to label and back again; they might even recoil in shock as realisation dawned. Yet Paul could envisage them then being drawn back in, fascinated and admiring of this transformation, so concise and coherent: subject and material of the same substance; outer appearance and inner reality united. Art and life.

Two years previously Paul had been among the unwary who had enrolled to study in the Painting Department on the assumption that the words meant what they said. Already aged twenty-five, he had arrived full of impatience and relief that he could at last fulfil his ambition to become a painter. But as the true status of painting within the department became clear, any prospective joy of self-actualisation had been lost in a career so far marked only by confusion, ridicule and dismay. For the first year he had determined to hold true to his goals. Paints and canvas had been found in a college oubliette, where studio assistants had been hoarding them against the day when fashion might come full circle. He had produced a number of dark townscapes in which sallow residents struggled vainly up dark streets that flouted the laws of perspective and sometimes those of gravity. But his single-mindedness had been to no avail. In a college devoted to individualism the herd instinct is overwhelming. Paul's efforts were derided in equal measure by students and staff. Half a decade older than most other students, married, and apparently clinging to the sensibilities of a previous century, he found himself marginalised from discussion, omitted from social events, and subject to a steady flow of low-level mockery and open condemnation, which slowly eroded his confidence in both himself and his work. For just as the most expert diver must finally surface for air, so even the most obstinate of artists in the end needs the affirmation of others.

The experience of his first year had slowly ground down Paul's ambition and had led him to formulate, reluctantly, a simple syllogism: his hopes of a successful career in the fine arts depended on his success in obtaining a degree; such success lay solely within the gift of the examiners; therefore, it was according to the parameters by which the examiners defined success that he would finally be judged. You can only win by their rules. He had therefore determined to put painting aside, and to step into the perpetual revolution of conceptual art. As he sat now hunched over the drawing within the confines of his workspace in the Painting Department, even his use of a pen seemed to him like an act of defiance against his tormentors.

The narrow neck of the phial required him to aim carefully as he dipped the pen. He was copying one of Michelangelo's drawings from the library book. But to add further layers of complexity, the Michelangelo was itself a copy from another artist called Masaccio, a drawing of the apostle Peter. Fortunately for Paul, drawing was a skill he had acquired as a teenager, since, along with painting and teaching, the college did not concern itself with anything so obviously outmoded as drawing, or indeed skill.

In the frustration of those first two years at the college, Paul had frequently fallen into dark moods, scolding himself for not having more thoroughly researched the college before applying. But such investigations would have made little difference. For there would never have been any realistic alternative to his attending the local institution. Paul's parents had prevented him from going to art college when he was eighteen and had coerced him into what they regarded as the marginally more useful study of English literature, on the strength of which he had obtained a job as a barman. Following graduation and marriage, it was Jan who earned the serious money and her first job as a trainee solicitor had brought them to Clayforth. Drifting into his mid-twenties, Paul had been given direction only by the unexpected terms of his great-aunt's will. This sparkle-eyed lady had mischievously determined not to risk unsettling the complacency of Paul's parents with an inrush of inherited wealth, and had left their share directly to Paul and his sister. Paul and Jan had used most of his legacy as a deposit on a shoebox of a house up the side of the valley overlooking the town. But Jan had insisted, as much out of realism as out of love, that they keep back enough to pay the fees for Paul to go to art college. They still needed her income for daily living, however, so there had never been any serious possibility that he might go to college anywhere but in Clayforth.

But then, why would he have wanted to? For, at the same moment that his prospects were being so miraculously transformed, Clayforth College of Art had blinked eagerly in the glare of national publicity with the high-profile appointment of Stephen Meriton, Clayforth's only famous artist, or famous anything. Meriton in the

1970s had been one of Britain's leading minimalists, and his serene, contemplative works were fêted internationally. But as the 1980s progressed he had found himself drowned out by a brash, upstart generation. The attention of the art world was wrenched away, along with invitations to exhibit. After a few years of increasing disappointment Meriton had moved back to his roots in Clayforth, to reconsider the second half of his career. There he had worked in seclusion until Curridge enticed him out with the prospect of sharing his experience with a new, even younger generation.

A year later the college had blinked again in an even brighter spotlight, as the national tabloids picked up a second appointment, that of Eric Horton, 'the one that ate the babies'. Horton had never actually eaten a baby, but in an interview he joked incautiously about having done so. The ensuing scandal in the media, accompanied by generous illustrations of his sculptures of deformed foetuses and barbecued saints, had been so effective in establishing his reputation and income that he had subsequently posed for photographers with his mouth open and ominously close to a baby's head, sparking another round of lucrative exposure. His new position of authority to influence the students of Clayforth had afforded the tabloids an excuse to rerun their horrified headlines across double-page spreads.

Although Paul knew nothing about the work of either Meriton or Horton, he had understood that providentially he was living within a bus-ride of the very centre of the British artistic maelstrom. Here, finally, he would start life for real. Here he would find release for the gnawing creative urge that, since his teenage years, had so often made its presence known, usually in the form of a yearning void just behind his breastbone. He would create images never before seen in all the history of humanity, and ones that would last beyond his own lifetime. He would explore and strive to grasp after the very nature of reality, which at times seemed so distant and so unnecessarily opaque. He would make paintings that would distil moments of human experience and capture them in a crystalline purity. He would create art that would change lives, and that would bring him satisfaction, fulfilment and recognition.

✎ ✎ ✎

Paul finished the apostle's outstretched arm, closed the book, put the top carefully back on the phial and returned it to his bag. He propped the new drawing against the partition of his workspace, and lined it up with the other half-dozen in the series, including an expressionist head by Matisse and a copy of a figure from van Gogh's *Potato eaters*. Paul had used his finger on the latter to drag through the liquid to imitate the impasto of the oil paint. They had all dried to the same russet hue. He was not sure where he was going with the art-historical references, but he could sense with the Michelangelo that a copy of a copy had the potential to add extra layers of uncertainty that could be explored in high-sounding obfuscation in the statement he would write to go with them. He would get Nick to help him with that later. But above all there was the shock of discovery, that initial disgust followed by the slow realisation of the power of the idea: this was what would overwhelm and convince the viewer.

He leaned back on the plastic chair, its grey metal legs still encrusted with oil paint from an earlier age. Resting his feet up on the edge of his desk, swinging backwards, hugging his arms round his knees, he was smiling. After two years of torment he had at last found a direction, an original idea, a foothold in the vastness of the art world. From now on he would be making objects that were authentically his own, exciting and provocative. For these drawings were only a preliminary exercise before the great idea, the magnificent hammer-blow with which he would silence the jeering. No more the poor, hopeless, old, know-nothing Paul Blythe. Instead, a serious player whom they would admire, even if they didn't like him. He would be acknowledged as the edgiest, most daringly out-there member of the student body, and by the time of the degree show in the summer they, and others beyond the college, would realise that his was a genuine voice of the time, articulating the anxieties of the day, challenging the taboos, exposing the murky truths. The name of Paul Blythe would be known, and they would respect him.

The clip of the black shoes sounded behind Paul, and he sat smartly to attention, biting his tongue as the chair legs jarred on the ground. Fractionally preceded by the smell of aftershave, Meriton leaned past Paul without a word and appraised the drawings. Paul instinctively stood up and backed away, taking the chair with him as a defensive barrier, but with a quivering anticipation at what lay to be discovered within the work. Meriton's head turned slightly to the right as he scanned along the line, then to the left, and then back to the right. It took scarcely ten seconds, and yet the intensity of his attention left no doubt that he had sucked from them every moment of interest. Paul ran his hand along the back of the chair, like a peasant fingering his cap in the presence of gentry.

'Blood,' Meriton said wearily, his eyes fixing on the van Gogh.

Whatever electric spark maintained Paul's sentient existence seemed suddenly to run to earth. His body swayed under the brutal impact of Meriton's one word, and Paul gripped the chair harder for support. His ears buzzed as though he had been slapped. His breathing momentarily stopped, as did his ability to think or to speak. Bereft of these capacities, he nonetheless knew with immediate and complete understanding that the horrors of the past two years had not, after all, gone away. They had simply ebbed out in order now to sweep back over him. His secret so easily read, so casually announced, he was drowning again.

Meriton looked round for confirmation, dark eyes set in a pale, puffy, lined face. Paul nodded slightly.

'Yes,' said Meriton, straightening up, his derogatory gaze pinning Paul against the corner of the partition, like predator and prey when both know the chase is over. The effect was intensified by Meriton's baldness, the faintest of tidemarks indicating where natural hair-loss met the grade-0 clippers. The paleness of his head was exaggerated by his trademark outfit: ironed black T-shirt, expensive black suit, black belt, black socks, highly polished black shoes. The only note of colour was a large, bronze cowboy buckle on the belt, giving a focal point to the ensemble. Although they were of equal height, Meriton was more stocky. Paul seemed vulnerably thin, almost undernourished. He looked hardly older than the other students who had come straight from school, and the wispy beard and moustache that he had grown for college seemed artificial and exacerbated his air of immaturity. As they stared at each other, the polish of Meriton's bald head amplified the glare in his eyes so that together they could overcome any opposition. But most intimidating of all was Meriton's adamant refusal to be surprised, or shocked, or impressed. In the corner of his mind that was first to recover independent capacity, Paul fleetingly wondered if this withering impassivity was a genuine expression of Meriton's authentic self, or part of a persona that he put on in the morning with the rest of his wardrobe.

'Pretty tame, don't you think?' Meriton said. He pulled a face, as though forced to choose between the unappetising left-overs at a college buffet. 'Visceral, I suppose, in its way. Getting your hands on the stuff of life and all that. Shocking? Well, trying to be, I suppose. But original? Come on!'

A thought seemed to strike him and he glanced sideways at the drawings. 'It is your blood, I suppose?'

Paul nodded again.

'Pity. Painting in someone else's blood might be more interesting. More pagan. Ritualistic. Sadistic even. But, for goodness' sake, people have been drawing in their own blood since before they invented paint.'

There was a pause, which might have been an invitation for Paul to respond, but nothing came.

Meriton glanced quickly along the line of drawings, as if to reassure himself that they were as bad as he thought.

'No,' he declared. 'Come on. This is tame. Tame, tame, tame.' His voice tapered off and he held both hands towards the drawings in a wordless gesture, as if he would scoop them together and twist them up before throwing them in the bin. He seemed to struggle for words that would adequately convey the strength of his feelings, and then his voice rose so that everyone could catch the ones he found. 'What can we say about it? It's derivative. It's lifeless. It's pointless. I mean, what is it trying to say? What's it trying to achieve that hasn't been done a thousand times?'

He returned his gaze to check that Paul had not escaped. Paul was wincing at the thought that everyone in the studio was hearing every word of his humiliation.

'Art must challenge,' Meriton continued to declaim. 'Art must provoke. You must have seen it in Eric's lectures. Art today has to affront people, has to seize them with its boldness. Has to shock them with its content. It has to draw them in and then hit them, hard. You have to compel people to respond. You find their taboos and challenge them.'

Meriton added more quietly, 'You have been attending Eric's lectures, haven't you?'

Paul made an ambiguous noise.

'What taboo are you breaking here?' Meriton demanded. 'Anselm Kiefer was painting in blood before you were born. Sagan used it as the title of a novel. For goodness' sake, people give blood as an act of charity! So you go along to your doctor and persuade him to extract a pint of the stuff, and then you draw a picture with it. What's shocking about that? What, I have to say, is even remotely interesting about it?' Still pinning Paul to the spot with his gaze, he jabbed his finger sideways at the row of drawings. 'Who's going to give that even a second thought? If you want people to take you seriously as an artist, you're going to have to come up with something a lot more profound, and shocking, and original, than pricking your finger and thinking how clever you are.'

Meriton was shaking his head in disbelief as he moved past Paul towards the next student's space. But Paul, as if waking sharply and surprised to find he was upright and fully dressed, was suddenly seized by an awareness of an opportunity passing and by an urge to justify himself.

'I had wondered . . .' he began.

Meriton wheeled round, and there was a slight upward movement where his eyebrows should have been.

'I had wondered,' Paul continued, 'about trying to make a model out of blood. My own blood.'

Meriton's eyes narrowed slightly as he stared, and Paul was momentarily encouraged. At least Meriton was interested.

The idea had come to Paul on returning home late in the evening from the doctor's surgery. His GP, whose own pastoral landscapes decorated his waiting room, had found no insuperable ethical objection to taking blood for the purpose of art, and had even offered to sacrifice to the higher calling of Culture a couple of NHS blood-sample tubes, prepared with an anti-coagulant. He had, however, insisted on performing the deed in his own time, and Paul had attended the surgery once the rest of the staff were out of the way. Later that night, as he had sat turning the tubes end over end, enjoying the depth of unarticulated meaning that accompanied his manipulation of the life force, he had begun to wonder about not just drawing in blood but making three-dimensional models with it. But how would they not simply crumble and decay? Certainly, there was an attractive idea in the fragility of human life encapsulated in an artwork that disintegrated even as the viewer looked at it. But then, when he finally placed the tubes in the fridge, where in the morning they would become the subject of a domestic confrontation when Jan discovered the nature of their contents, he experienced his moment of inspiration.

'I thought, if I could get hold of a refrigeration unit – it's a big "if", I know, but if I could – and a glass cabinet, and link them up, then I thought I could make a model of my own head, out of my own blood. It would be some kind of latex mould, then I'd fill it with the blood and freeze it, and then remove the mould, and then have the model displayed in the cabinet.'

Meriton's head turned fractionally to one side, to view Paul askance. Paul had a sense that Meriton was preparing to pounce, but perhaps he was just listening more attentively. Paul stumbled on, his hands leaving the chair and gesticulating awkwardly, as if advancing a different argument.

'The blood would have to remain frozen, of course, to hold its shape, and it would be sustained by the refrigeration unit. It would only last as long as the unit was switched on. So it would be my own self-portrait in my own blood, in a kind of life-support unit. It would integrate subject and material, and it would play on the sense of identity – we think of ourselves as being who we are in our faces and in our minds inside our heads, but we are also fully physical beings depending on something as basic as blood.'

As he described the project Paul felt his enthusiasm mounting again. In his mind's eye once again he could see the power brokers and judges of the art world agreeing that here was someone ahead of his time. In all their beautiful vulnerability, his life-size portraits in blood would encapsulate the mood of the moment, Cool Britannia bouncing uncontrollably back and forth between confidence and anxiety, fixated on the multiplication of pleasures, frantically postponing the comprehension of death, but now compelled by his works to confront it. These models, shocking and yet compassionate, would capture the attention of the press and establish him as a prophetic voice for the dawning new millennium.

Meriton was staring at Paul with a puzzled frown, as if unable properly to grasp what he was proposing.

'I've done some calculations and I reckon I can draw off one pint of blood each month from now until April, and the volume of blood I'd need for a model of my head would be getting on for the amount of blood in my entire body. So it would have a really neat fit: all my blood supply on view in this one model of my head. And it would have a sense of fragility, because it would depend on an outside source to keep it "alive", so to speak.'

He looked apprehensively at Meriton, who continued to stare in silence for several moments. Behind him, down the aisle, a row of student heads was bent over their work, or determinedly looking away.

Meriton began slowly. 'It sounds a bit *religious*: life depending on outside forces, "the life is in the blood" and all that. And quite what Health and Safety would have to say about all that blood in the studio . . .'

Then he suddenly laughed. It was a strange sound, if only because in all his time at the college Paul had never heard it. He briefly wondered if Meriton had ever heard it either. Was this a unique moment that could itself be the basis for a work of art? There was certainly no laughter in his face.

'The main problem with your idea, however,' Meriton continued, 'assuming that it is your idea and that you really are as ignorant as you appear, and not just playing dumb as a kind of irritating pose: the main problem is that this was all done a long time ago.'

'Really?' said Paul quietly.

'Yes, really!' Meriton snapped. 'What? You think I'd be making it up? Marc Quinn, 1991. Now in the Saatchi Collection. For goodness' sake, you saw it only last year in the Sensation exhibition, and you must have seen it in Eric's lectures.'

'Oh,' said Paul quietly.

'Yes. "Oh" just about sums it up.' Meriton's voice rose again in indignation, and Paul sensed the studied concentration of the rest of the studio as each word registered. 'We are looking for something original here. Something new. Something shockingly new. Not some half-baked child's play in his own blood. Nor another rip-off of other people's ideas.'

Meriton began to back away towards the next student's space, but continued speaking as if addressing everyone, including the textile students downstairs: 'The artist today is the great originator, the pioneer, the boldly-goer, the taboo-breaker. You have already completed two years here without apparently stumbling on a single original idea. Next year you'll be out there in the big, wide, lonely art world, all on your own and needing to make your mark. It's high time now – well past high time – that you started to get your head around some serious work. Once and for all, do something that is seriously original. Find your taboo and break it.'

The next space was empty.

✎ ✎ ✎

For a minute Paul remained frozen, unwilling to look and see if others were watching him, embarrassed to move and draw attention to himself. Then he slumped back into his seat.

How could he have done it again?

In his second year Paul had thrown himself with dedication, enthusiasm and indeed, from a certain point of view, genius, into the delights and demands of conceptualism. During that year he produced a succession of brilliant works, any one of which could have established an artist's reputation. But, sadly, in the course of the year he evinced only one genuine talent: the ability to produce brilliant works of art, each of which had in fact already established an artist's reputation.

The early-warning sign was an arrangement of fluorescent light bulbs, such as might be seen in most of the world's modern-art galleries under the name of Dan Flavin, but this was glossed over as a beginner's error. Not so the bold introduction to the studio of a toilet, which Paul signed with a flourish in indelible marker pen, unaware until that moment that Marcel Duchamp was anything more than a name heard in conversation. Paul's version was received with patronising jeers from even the most fresh-faced of the first-years, and silence from the tutors. His circle of found stones, collected on a country walk, and displayed with sensitively written text and sharp photographs, was greeted, by those who knew the work of Richard Long, with the grimace with which people see minor accidents and pass by quickly.

This series of sparkling failures had at least the merit of helping Paul to clarify the theme of his work. Years earlier, embarking unwillingly at university on his study of English literature, he had begun to reflect on the diminished nature of his protected, suburban childhood, and how much his experience of the world had been at arm's length, kept away from him by anxious, unadventurous parents, or filtered and sanitised through the media. It seemed to Paul that he had been made to float through life, kept from touching the solid earth, as if such an experience would harm or besmirch him. He had a growing conviction that somewhere there must exist a way to engage with reality, raw and unmediated, the substratum for life, where knowing and being were one. The English syllabus itself had made matters worse rather than better, with its devotion to postmodernist gamesmanship that cast everything into a haze of ambiguity and laconic uncertainty. Paul had yearned all the more for a simple, direct experience of things as they are, whatever their nature might be. Now, in Clayforth, these were the works he wanted to make, works that would encompass the absolute, immediate, heavy presence of reality and fill the viewer with the solemnity of existence.

As one invention followed another into the skip behind the printmakers' Portakabin, his desperation and his ambition marched in lock step. But at every halting point it was clear that others had been there first. The principal refused his application to drill a hole in the college grounds and bury a one-kilometre metal rod vertically in it; and Paul's plan to wrap the entire college building in sackcloth was fortunately intercepted before the studio assistant could order and pay for the materials. And when, at the end of the year, he proudly revealed his most outré invention, one which he was sure would establish him as the most scarily inventive student at the college – a sheep (a real sheep) displayed in a vitrine that had been filled with formaldehyde – the entire college was so incapacitated with good humour that the smell of cannabis disappeared from the top-floor corridor for a week and the bursar brought in cake for the staff.

Paul stared again at the row of drawings, willing them to justify themselves. He sensed their merit, the undiscovered meaning of the art-historical references, the continuity with the past and its reinvention in a new material. He resented the fact that his own creations were rendered worthless by what others had done before him, and he hated the fact that his fate lay in the judgement of others.

Paul was officially a 'mature' student. Although part of him knew that his career had yet to begin, another part reasoned that, being so much older than the other students, he should in some way be their leader. A few of them suggested that Paul might be playing a sophisticated bluff, and that one day he would surprise them all. But his earnest enthusiasms, followed by his evident despair, gave his failures a sense of innocence that fuelled the gleeful gossip and shared scorn by which his younger stable-mates bound themselves together and bolstered their own fragile self-confidence.

He had spent the summer months at the end of his second year revolving between anger, resentment, frustration and self-loathing. After two years of visionary ambition and enterprising hard work his portfolio resembled nothing more than a history of plagiarism, albeit without the subtlety with which the more able plagiarist will attempt to conceal their sources. Then the idea of the drawings and models in blood had seemed to offer a triumphant theme for his final year, a pathway to a series of works that would compel recognition and realise success.

A small hand gently squeezed his shoulder. 'Come on. Come and sit for me.' Sheena, who had occupied the space next to Paul in the previous year, was standing behind him. 'You can be one of my portraits.'

Paul obediently stood up and followed her down the room. He felt conspicuous behind her: older, absurdly taller, and yet temperamentally and artistically weaker. He was convinced that several of the students were smiling as they busied themselves in their alcoves. They edged past Andreas, a Greek Orthodox student who, on hands and knees beneath the irresolute gaze of Kurt Cobain, was painstakingly transcribing a Jackson Pollock drip-painting into mosaic. The only place in the studio large enough for his fifteen-foot sand tray was in the walkway that ran along the edge of the studio and formed a link between two of the main buildings. As a result, much of the foot-traffic across the college had to queue and step circumspectly past the kneeling artist, and the whole community had become intimately familiar with the slow, contemplative progress of the work over the previous year. Several had begun to experience sympathetic pains in their knees and had urged him to raise the box up on trestles, so that he could work standing up. But he preferred the worshipful attitude of kneeling in front of the Pollock poster that was stuck to the wall in front of him.

Sheena's new workspace was at the end of the studio alongside the computer suite, a row of ageing Macs, each chained to the workbench. At one of them Martin was shooting alien spacecraft from a starship. The last in the row of screens was obscured by a sellotaped piece of paper with a large hand-written message, 'Out of order'.

'They've let me use this space at the end.' Sheena motioned Paul to a stool by the wall, facing the grimy, cream-coloured computers.

He sat without a word as Sheena got out her camera.

'Turn that down, will you?' she called out sharply, without looking round, as their aisle echoed to the explosion of Martin receiving a fatal hit from an alien craft. Martin pulled a face, mouthing silent words of retort, but obeyed.

The trouble was, Paul thought, there were too many possible connotations in any work he might make, too many references that were beyond his control. He liked the idea of blood, the creative elementalism of it, the suggestion of heartbeats, the transmission of energy and life. But he hadn't reckoned with the direction in which Meriton's mind would veer: tribalism, ritual sacrifice and sadism.

'You could try murder,' said Sheena, as she adjusted some equipment on the workbench. Paul looked up sharply, wondering if he had been thinking aloud.

'You what?'

'Murder. It's not entirely original as an idea, but I don't think anyone's actually done it, as art, I mean. Except in *Seven* of course, and that's just a film. No one's done it for real. And it fits the blood thing, life forces and whatever.'

'Murder?'

'Yes. Some of the old rockers used to talk about it in the seventies. Before our time. Well,' she smiled, 'before mine. But they never actually did it of course, because they'd get arrested and wouldn't be able to trash any more hotel suites. But you could try it and see if you could get away with calling it "art".'

Paul smiled. He had an avuncular affection for her, with her heavily mascara-ed eyes and bright red lipstick, a sharp, calculating face, framed by short, neat hair, and offset by an ever-changing array of charity-shop clothes. Coming straight from school and a Foundation Year at Leeds, she was five years younger than Paul, but her mind was acute and liable to generate caustic opinions, which she freely voiced. After a first year of reading magazines and going to parties, she had suddenly begun producing serious, large-scale, distorted imagery, mostly to the detriment of the male sex.

'You think the police would wear that?' he asked.

'Of course.' Her voice went down two octaves. 'It's all right, officer. I know an 'eadless corpse can look suspicious, but it's just a work of art, honest. So if you could just 'elp me get this 'ere stiff up on the plinth, I'll write the label.'

'Well, it's certainly a taboo.'

'Of course, you'd have to find someone particular to murder.' She peered at him through the viewfinder. 'It would have to be a real murder, a bit mean and grisly. Not just random violence. If it was a complete stranger they'd say you were a delinquent and pack you off to do art therapy.'

'Choosing a victim would be the easy bit. If I murdered anyone, I'd kill Meriton.'

Sheena smiled as she refocused the camera.

'I might have done it just now if I'd had the use of my limbs,' he continued, peering round nervously in case Meriton was within earshot. 'You feel so powerless, the way he looks at you. Talk about life forces. I'm sure, if I was edible, I'd be mingling with his life forces right now.'

'No, you're safe there at least,' she replied, still holding the camera to her eye. 'He's a veggie.'

Paul continued to mull the question over in silence as Sheena adjusted her position and took more photographs.

'Maybe I could claim provocation, or say it was a *crime passionnel.*

I should ask Jan. But wouldn't there be a problem getting my degree if I'd murdered one of the judges?'

'Well, you'd have to manage it correctly,' Sheena smiled again and gestured theatrically with the camera, but then, seeing Meriton moving into the next aisle, dropped her voice. 'Judgement Day dawns for the Final Show. Meriton has been hassling you all term because you haven't got any work for it. Then the judges come round to your space, and you make your great pronouncement: "Professor Meriton, this is my work." And you plunge the dagger into his heart. In fact, if he's really into pagan rituals you might try cutting his heart out – assuming he's got one, of course – and holding it in front of his dying eyes. It would be nice for him to go out with a real work of art in front of him.'

'But I'd have to keep him alive long enough to give me my degree.'

'I suppose that is a problem. And if he popped it, I guess they'd find it hard to recruit a stand-in, given the new risks of the job.'

They fell into silence as Sheena packed away her camera.

'Anyway,' Paul said suddenly, 'killing people is wrong. That's why it's a taboo.'

Sheena looked up from the camera case and affected a drawl. 'Now, let's not go talking crazy talk. You go down the road of moh-rality and you won't even reach Sheet Creek, let alone paddle up it.' She switched to Meriton's measured voice: 'The artist is the great heretic, the transgressor, the offender. The artist questions assumptions, subverts values, challenges taboos.' She resumed her normal voice. 'You let Meriton hear you talking soft-minded stuff about right and wrong and you won't get your degree even if you paint the Sistine Chapel.'

Paul sighed. 'And that's been done as well, hasn't it?' He reflected for a moment. 'It's a problem, isn't it: being taboo-breaking and original at the same time? That's a very small space to work in.'

✎ ✎ ✎

As an income-generating area the cafeteria enjoyed greater investment than the studios. A new stainless-steel servery had been fitted during the summer, aluminium-framed prints were arranged at regular intervals on the cool grey walls, and vertical blinds hung across the windows. Between the slats the students could see the lawn leading to black railings and small grey-brown terraced houses beyond.

The sharp edges of the servers' voices behind the counter cut intermittently through the babble from crowded tables, where odours of three main courses mingled with the cigarette smoke.

Paul was absorbed in pouring coffee in a steady flow from his plastic cup into a second, which had accidentally come with it, while Sheena fished in her bag for a cigarette. At the next table Martin and Gary and members of their gang, all dressed in combat fatigues, were hunched together in quiet conspiracy with Nick, a lanky figure in a large donkey-jacket, sporting a short, neat hairstyle that was unconventional in its own way in an art college. With an ability to veil his intelligence and modulate his accent according to that of his interlocutors, he contrived, on the rare occasions when he appeared in college, to be accepted by most cliques.

He seemed to tire of the conspirators and turned to Sheena.

'The art of war,' he said, with a gesture of his head. 'They're debating the use of force in getting your degree, and whether they would have to use live ammunition to be authentic. What's up with him?' he asked, nodding at Paul.

'I think he's doing a blood transfusion,' she said, still intent on finding the bottom of her bag, 'but Meriton says blood is too passé.'

She described Meriton's studio visit that Nick had, as usual, missed despite the college's three-line whip.

'You've never heard of Marc Quinn?' Nick exclaimed loudly enough for Martin to turn and grin at Paul's discomfort. 'I appreciate that you do have a prize ignorance of the art world in which you aspire to play a role,' Nick continued, his blue eyes, friendly but intense, searching Paul's face for a sign of intelligent life. 'But how can you never have heard of Marc Quinn?'

'I must have missed the lecture,' Paul suggested weakly. With Horton's perversely ascetic practice of lecturing at nine in the morning it was surprising that he had got to any at all. Or perhaps he had been there and had heard about Quinn's work in his sleep. When the lights went down and Horton's voice kicked in, it was hard to be sure whether you were waking or sleeping, and whether the images you saw were the intended accompaniment to the lecture or the unbidden contents of a nightmare.

'Anyway, I'm sure you've got something there with the coffee,' said Nick. 'Blood as blood is indeed passé. But has anyone ever done coffee as blood? After all, you know it's not really your blood that keeps you going. It's the caffeine in the blood that you rely on. So you model your head to look like Quinn's, but behold, it's not frozen blood but frozen coffee. Great swathes of new meaning are added to the work.'

'Meaning?' asked Paul, looking up from his transfusion.

'All right, then,' Nick conceded. 'References. Quotations from the past master – well, Quinn, anyway – pastiche, blood and coffee, coffee as blood. Where is the real life force? Drugs and reality. You could write reams about it.'

Nick looked confidently from Paul to Sheena. 'What did he say about your work?' he asked her.

'Oh, not much,' she said vaguely. 'But, as you mention it, I was wondering if you could help me with my project. I'm doing some portrait heads. I've just done one of Paul; and I want to get Martin and that lot. I wondered if you would sit for me too.'

'Portrait heads?' Nick exclaimed. 'You doing portrait heads? I thought you were supposed to be a one-woman Sabatier-sharp cutting-edge cultural critique.' He shrugged his shoulders and held out his arms, as if protesting the betrayal of ideals. 'Portrait heads are hardly going to undermine the hegemonic forces of patriarchy, are they?'

'That's very supportive of you, thank you,' said Sheena coldly, dropping a cigarette packet on the table and diving again for the lighter.

'Well, no offence, but portrait heads are hardly taboo-breaking either, are they? Why didn't Meriton tear your head off as well, or at least bite an arm?'

'He left me alone, that's all.' She smiled slightly. 'Maybe he's frightened of me.'

Nick's braying laugh and thump on the table made a couple of the serving staff look over at them, and even Paul smiled into his coffee cups.

'Well, he might be,' Sheena insisted, her smile a little wider. 'So, will you help me out or not?'

'Sure. Sorry. Of course. Fine. I've got nothing else to do.'

Paul raised his eyes: 'Yes, your empty space was noted again this morning.'

'Ah well, that's all part of the great masterwork, isn't it?' Nick beamed. 'Not doing anything. It's not that I'm simply being an idle Non-Productionist, lying about in bed all day like a student. I am very deliberately not working. And then, at the end of the year, I shall put up a blue plaque, one of those nice blue plaques you see in London, saying "Borough of Clayforth"' – his hands described the arc of the words – '"Nick Thompson worked here."'

Paul laughed out loud. 'Even I know that's been done before. Gavin Whatsit did it at the Royal College. And,' Paul added emphatically, 'he didn't get his degree, did he?'

'Ah, but your thinking is too constrained,' Nick intoned, stretching out his arms to invade the personal space of the conspirators at the next table. 'Let your mind stretch to the furthest reaches of creative imagination. In other words, think what you can make up to say about it. A conceptual artist is measured by his or her . . .' – a nod to Sheena – '. . . ideas, and ideas are expressed with words. So the heart of the matter, as you must very well know, is not the art-object, which is often of little or no aesthetic or visual interest, but the statement that accompanies it. Ever since the heroic days of Manet and the Impressionists, the artist's manifesto explaining the work has been as indispensable as the work itself, and in many cases a jolly sight more interesting. And the more abstract the work, the more the words multiply.'

Sheena lit her cigarette and blew smoke at Nick, who waved it away without seeming to notice. Paul absently dunked the corner of his serviette in his coffee.

'And the key to success?' Nick continued. 'Ensure your statement contains the two magic words, "problematising" and "transformative". These are the passwords to the academy. Sound off with those two and you're in. You've succeeded. You are beyond contradiction.'

Paul felt jealousy seeping through him like the coffee stain across the serviette. Had he really wasted a whole decade? If he had stood up to his parents, or simply funded himself through art college, he could not, surely, be so shamefully ignorant. He could have been filling his mind with images and knowledge, to be able to spin ideas and navigate the art world with Nick's aristocratic hauteur. Or maybe he should just have worked harder.

'"Transformative" means you take something and make it into something else. Of course, artists have been doing that all the time. But to be properly "transformative" nowadays you take something and you change it into something completely random, totally unrelated. Then the viewer has to try to puzzle out the connection between the two things. And in the process of transforming, you problematise the original.'

Nick glanced round his audience to check they were keeping up.

'"Problematising" means you take something apparently ordinary and straightforward and make out that it's strange and uncanny and alarming. People think that coffee is simple and ordinary: but if we reveal that, while you're pouring it back and forth, you're thinking of someone's blood . . . then, whoa! The scene is not so simple. Hannibal Lecter has joined us in the coffee shop, and is it our own blood that he sees in the coffee? Or take milk. What could be more innocent and obvious than milk? But drop someone in a vat of the stuff and milk is problematised. Especially if they can't swim.'

'So you're just complicating the simple,' said Paul.

'No. It's much more than that. You're implying that nothing is simple. Even what is apparently most simple can be inexplicably mysterious and threatening. We are not at home. Nothing is certain. Nothing makes sense. Everything is a problem.'

'But a bottle of milk isn't threatening,' Sheena objected.

'It is if I smash it over your head,' said Nick with a twitch of his eyebrow.

'But you wouldn't do that,' Paul countered.

'I might.' Nick seemed hurt by the suggestion. 'I'm a very serious artist, innovative and shocking – especially shocking for you when I whack you with a bottle.'

'There does seem to be a lot of violence in this college,' sighed Sheena, clicking her lighter and staring at the flame. 'Martin over there dressed like Desert Storm, shooting aliens in the studio and planning open warfare in the cafeteria. Paul wants to murder Meriton, and now you're threatening to attack me with a glass bottle.'

'But, as I said,' Paul objected with laboured emphasis, 'I wouldn't murder Meriton, because murder is wrong. That's why we have morality: to restrain the violence.'

Nick frowned and looked slowly from Paul to Sheena and back. 'What heresy is this? Who dares to speak the M-word in this cafeteria?'

'I've warned him,' said Sheena with a sigh. 'It's dangerous talk.'

Paul smiled wearily. 'But it's true. We don't murder people because it's wrong. Murder is wrong. Stealing is wrong. Lying is wrong. Not all taboos are bad.'

Nick and Sheena stared at Paul in frank astonishment, as if he had confessed to a secret passion for one of the serving ladies, or membership of the Conservative Party.

'I sink vee hef some verk to do viz zis vun, hey, Professor?' Nick murmured quietly to Sheena. She nodded regretfully.

'Have you been to *any* lectures?' asked Nick. 'In fact, are you entirely new to this college? Have we met before?' Nick slapped the table. 'We are the ones who provoke and attack. We are the shock troops of the culture. We question values and subvert taboos. We undermine and problematise.'

'But what are you "problematising" with your blue plaque?' Paul protested.

'Well,' said Nick, shaking off his jacket and draping it over the back of his chair as he gathered his thoughts. 'First off, the statement on the plaque is demonstrably untrue. I haven't done any work here, nor indeed at home. As a summary of my career so far, the statement is apparently false. But is the falsity falsified by the fact that I have made the plaque? Is it a simple statement of untruth, or does its very existence make it a self-contradiction? It's like the Greeks getting themselves in a twist over whether the statement "This is a lie" could be true or false, until they got overrun by the Romans, who didn't care one way or t'other. So you see, it's a deep and ancient, philosophical and artistic problem. It takes a simple idea, "So-and-so worked here", and problematises it. Or – and this is always another goody – it raises more questions than it answers.'

'It doesn't answer any questions,' Sheena objected.

'Exactly. A postmodern masterpiece, though I say it myself. All questions and no answers.'

'But you've still got the problem that Gavin Whatsit did it first,' said Paul.

'Yes, indeed. His name, by the way, is Gavin Turk. And here we introduce further layers of problematisation. Who says that a work of art should be original? By what authority do they seek to restrict my artistic freedom in this way? If I want to copy another person's work, why shouldn't I?'

'And by questioning that restriction, you would yourself be being original,' said Sheena slowly, picking her way carefully through the minefields of philosophy.

'Isn't it wonderful?' Nick exclaimed. 'But then we go further: am I in fact really guilty of plagiarism? Am I nicking Turk's idea and trying to pass it off as an original idea of my own? Of course not, because we all know Turk did it first. So, I am not copying: I am quoting from the master. I am elevating to the status of old master a work of art that was failed when presented for examination at the Royal College. My work is problematising not just the nature of artistic creation but also the standards by which we judge it. It is a challenge to the conventional values of the college, which, of course, affects to despise conventional values.'

Nick paused and looked brightly from Paul to Sheena, who exchanged a glance of unpersuasion. The problem with living in an age of irony was that you were never sure when someone was being serious.

'Are you really going to do this?' Paul asked eventually.

'Why not? It works,' said Nick. 'It meets the requirements.'

'But it's not *about* anything.'

'What do you mean "not about anything"?' Nick returned to his tone of mock affront. 'It problematises the nature of art and artistic judgement, the key debating point in western art for the past century, and you say it isn't about anything? It's a masterpiece!'

'We always come back to this,' said Paul wearily. 'It's only art about art. It's not about reality.'

'It's much better than that, mate,' said Nick. 'It's art about art about art about art. It stands in the deep spiral of artistic narcissism that is the alternative to looking into the abyss. God is dead. There's nothing there. Crumbs, mate, if we dealt with reality, we'd all top ourselves. Everyone a Rothko. Believe me, art about art is where you want to go, a polite way of avoiding reality and lot less messy, whatever Hannah might say to the contrary.'

There was silence between them and Paul's thoughts again fell into confusion. Hannah and the little group in the Christian Union were an enigma to him. As a child he had been required to accompany his parents to church where, despite God's acclaimed role as Creator of All Things, human creativity was regarded with overt suspicion, and Art was clearly defined as part of the sinful world and therefore bound for destruction. The interior of their chapel was programmatically bare: any kind of imagery would have smelled of high-church idolatry. At home his parents punctuated the walls and surfaces with occasional pictures and objects, but only kitsch images offering sentimental warmth, like the glow of the plastic coal on the gas fire. Above the fireplace a gilt-framed print depicted a snow-capped mountain with a log cabin nestling at its foot among the pine trees, all the windows improbably ablaze with electric lights. On the mantelpiece, a brightly painted ceramic peasant led his burdened ceramic donkey, a relic of a holiday on the Costa Brava. On the opposite wall, above the piano, partially obscured by the standard lamp, hung a series of plates, bought through a special offer in the newspaper, garnished with impressionistic scenes of Paris's more salubrious streets. Images that encouraged viewers into a deeper and potentially more thought-provoking engagement with life were not a possibility that Paul's parents had ever considered.

Set against the drab certainties of his parents' church, part of the original allure of art college had been its offer of a demarcation line at which Paul would turn his back on their way of life. Although attendance at art college was at first denied him, his parents' promotion of English as a 'useful' degree had in fact done the job just as well. As no one at church saw any reason to analyse the culture around them, since it too was doomed for destruction, they had no suspicion of the brutal assault that awaited Paul as he entered the apparently benign domain of the English department. Any lingering attachment to childish assumptions concerning the reality of objective truth and meaning was beaten out of the students with the rubber truncheon of scepticism, enthusiastically and consistently administered in lectures, tutorials and marking schemes. All private convictions were subjected to the shocking thrill of nihilism, and dissidents who insistently clung to fragments of the old faith were regularly placed on public display for denunciation and humiliation.

Paul had at first offered no resistance. He recognised the beguiling promise of reader-response theories: if there was no authority in a text and the reader could make it mean literally anything they wanted, if there was after all no objective basis for truth, Paul felt vindicated in his desire to slough off all traces of his parents' faith.

On arrival at art college in Clayforth, however, Paul had found Hannah and her friends seemingly intent on combining this rejected faith with serious art. They were a paradoxical new species for which he had no category, and he had gone out of his way to avoid them. With their overtly stated beliefs and irritating certainties they invited their own share of scorn from other students and severity from the tutors, but Paul was obliged to concede that the images they showed in the group crits were far from the energy-guzzling log cabins of his youth or the tourist traps of Paris. Hannah came closest with her videos of nature and her infuriating refrain that 'God is the greatest artist.' But Anand was making interesting constructions about consumerism and materialism, while Stuart was performing weird experiments with sound. As his frustrations with the course and its tutors had grown, Paul had begun to sense a degree of sympathy for them as fellow outsiders, although he was reluctant to admit this even to himself.

Martin leaned over and thumped Nick on the shoulder. 'We've got an idea,' he whispered loudly in a rising Welsh cadence. 'You know those charity things you can buy, where they get guns from the Third World and weld them into sculptures? Well, how about us getting hold of some of them and turning them back into guns?'

✎ ✎ ✎

At home, Paul tried to direct water round the washbasin with his hand as the blood clung to the yellow porcelain. It would have been simpler to flush it down the toilet, but it was still his own life-blood, and despite the failure of the project, some aesthetic sense within him required that it be treated with respect. He rinsed out the bottle and, as the remnants of his idea swirled round the plughole, he looked at himself in the mirror. His face was already beginning to acquire a permanent, vertical crease between his eyebrows. It was hard at times to resist the fear that life and its opportunities had already passed him by. But, he thought, as he contorted his eyebrows to try and make the crease disappear, if he had stood up against his parents – and assertiveness had never featured highly in his relationship with them – he would not have met Jan.

Despite the initial thrill of nihilism at university, Paul had not found rest. He devoted adequate time in his first year to developing social skills, such as table-football, pinball and Mortal Kombat, but hedonism proved no more satisfying than nihilism. He was disappointed by the lack of intellectual curiosity among his contemporaries, and their easy contentment with consumerism and clubbing. Meanwhile, in his studies he began to note the incongruity of authors whose argument for the impossibility of understanding an author's meaning was expounded in books which students were expected to read and understand. He started to irritate lecturers by asking why they bothered to turn up to lecture on the incommunicability of meaning. In his final year, at the end of an exposition of the impossibility of certainty about reality beyond one's own mind, he asked a visiting lecturer if she was going to bother going home for tea, since clearly there could be no certainty that her house still existed. She had tried to brush him off with a concession that it was an interesting question. However, when he persisted in asking whether she really believed her house was still there, she ended the session abruptly and left, apparently confident that at least the staffroom and its coffee machine would be where she had last seen them.

Paul's essays provided an opportunity for him to explore his questions, although the department did not encourage answers. But writing was not his medium. He took to hanging round the art department, attending open classes for life-drawing, and doodling through lectures and seminars.

Then, in his second year, his life took an unexpected turn. At a party in the second term he was introduced to Jan, and within weeks was seriously in love. She was a second-year law student, who wore her prettiness like a pair of sensible shoes, poised, demure, but letting the curtain of her shoulder-length hair swing forward round her face as she talked. Amidst the tedium of law cases, she liked his questioning mind and the vulnerability of his uncertainties; and to the astonishment of their friends, and the disappointment of his parents who still harboured the hope that he would marry a Christian girl, they were engaged in their third year and married on graduation.

Paul rubbed hopefully at the crease in his skin, but it could not be erased. It was a trade-off, he thought; something his parents would ascribe to providence. But like all trades, there was a price to pay. He would not want to envisage life without Jan, but life with Jan meant Clayforth and its college – and that cost was significant. For just as it had not occurred to him to examine the details of the college's curriculum before signing up, neither had it occurred to him that famous artists might not be able to teach, or even try to do so; that they might not encourage, or even want to do so. Horton was not so contemptuously scathing as Meriton, but he made clear that if students were not abusing human flesh they were not trying hard enough. As for the other double-act of Barnett and Garnet, who had been on the staff even longer than the caretaker, they offered a critique as minimal and oblique as their own works. Garnet had made her name with gallery-sized, pastel-shaded colour-field paintings which looked like Dulux colour cards for the visually impaired, and she expressed no opinion more forceful than 'Interesting', and no advice beyond 'Keep going.' Barnett specialised in monumental metal assemblages that were widely suspected of signifying nothing more than met the eye, and he deflected all questions that were not directly related to welding.

Paul dried his hands and put the towel neatly back on the rail, as he had been trained by Jan. If he was condemned to study in Clayforth, should he at least have ridden out the opposition and stuck with his painting, instead of risking ending up as that unique conundrum, the conceptual artist with no concepts?

Returning to his studio, otherwise known as the second bedroom, he found Sylvester sitting on his chair. Like all cats he instinctively put himself in the place of maximum inconvenience to others, but he was still young enough to be sociable. He liked to sit on Paul's shoulder like a parrot, or lie on top of the computer screen, pawing at the cursor as it skittered across. Sylvester had spent a brief period as a concrete poet, treading at random on the keyboard, and Paul had incorporated these offerings into one of his works; but the cat had then moved into neo-Dada, striking with precision on the

Break key, and Paul had had to train him to step delicately around the keyboard and not on it.

Paul picked him up, ran his fingers through the long mane of soft fur, and rubbed noses with him. It might be embarrassing to be soppy about a cat, but it was the nearest they would get to having a baby of their own for some years. In any case, there was something very engaging about a cat. He loved its suppleness, as it wound its way like a snake between the bars of the clothes airer. He was amused by its mood swings, at one moment primly self-possessed, then suddenly racing around the house, scrabbling like Tom and Jerry for purchase on the kitchen lino. Most of all, Paul liked the coolness on the back of his fingers as he ran his knuckles down Sylvester's flanks. He admired the generosity of the deep fur, and the genius by which the hairs changed colour at the tips to produce the tabby markings.

He held Sylvester aloft in one hand and swung him gently round in semi-circles. The cat hung limp and unprotesting, but his eyes moved alertly from side to side.

If only I could make something like this, Paul thought. Elegant, tactile, mobile, fun, alive. And it was the mystery and joy of being alive that was beginning to nag at his mind, provoked, almost against his will, by Hannah's nature imagery: the apparently categorical difference between the organic and the inorganic, and yet the fact of birth and death. The trouble was that we took life for granted. If you thought about it, it was too much: too varied, too rich to take in. It was only when you thought you were going to die that you appreciated the reality of life, and the extraordinary and precious fact that it exists at all.

That was what the sheep had been about: a work that brought life and death together, so that you were forced to see the contrast. Something that had once been alive was now dead. Something that was gregarious by nature was isolated in death. You would feel its frisson, and it would make you appreciate the living. You would struggle to grasp both states in your mind at once, becoming conscious only of the apparent impossibility of the transition that this exhibit had undergone.

But Damien Hirst had done that already. Even Paul knew that now.

2

October

In the afternoon sunshine the brown stone of Clayforth's Civic Centre glowed almost golden. Built in an Arts and Crafts style, it radiated warmth across the central piazza to the municipal Museum and Art Gallery, which did not return it. Wide, low and coldly grey, the museum squatted like a toad, unblinking and detached. Designed in a severe classical style, it had been benefacted upon the town by a coal magnate in the 1920s, along with several hundred uplifting Victorian paintings, which now filled the vaults.

Meriton strode heavily up the gallery's stone steps to the portico, which stretched the entire width of the building, and went in through the revolving doors. A poster in the centre of the entrance hall advertised an exhibition of Slovakian metalwork in the basement. A large Perspex collection box reminded visitors that entry to the gallery was free and that, in order to keep it free, they should contribute at least two pounds.

Free entry did not seem to have worked its magic today. A woman was eyeing postcards at the Information Desk, while two attendants, with competing degrees of gloom, discussed Leeds United's prospects for the season, their muffled voices echoing round the hall. Like a railway station in the middle of the day, it seemed that the crowds were elsewhere.

Behind the Information Desk a young woman looked up hopefully as Meriton approached.

'I'm here to see the director,' Meriton announced curtly, staring past her to a poster on the wall.

'And your name, sir?' she asked in a sweet voice.

He looked at her sharply and saw the glimmer of satisfaction as she forced him to make eye contact.

'I am Stephen Meriton,' he snapped, but refrained from adding, 'as you very well know.'

'Just a moment, sir.'

She picked up the phone with the relish of one rarely entrusted with responsibilities. Meriton's gaze returned to the poster. Over a blown-up detail of a man in a rowing boat the text announced a travelling exhibition of graphic work by Dunoyer de Segonzac, opening the following month. But instead of this French mouthful, Meriton imagined his own name. Here he would begin to re-establish his reputation in Britain, a mature artist fêted by his home town, showing the cream of his work, powerful objects touching on the deepest aspects of human experience. And on the poster, instead of de Segonzac's tedious splodges lying about on rivers, would be one of his most striking creations. Something ethereal and pure. Or maybe . . .

It was as if something had sprung up on the periphery of his vision, a movement, a form, shimmering briefly and unnameable, and then appearing just as suddenly fully formed in the front of his mind. Maybe nothing at all.

'Mr Meriton. Excuse me.' The young woman's voice drew him back, and he found that she was waving to him across the desk with her free hand. 'The director's secretary will be down directly.'

'I know my way by now,' he snapped. 'Tell her not to bother.'

He set off up a wide, stone staircase, designed to the scale of the founder's ambitions rather than the gallery's clientele. The upper galleries were vaulted, with doorway arches springing from classical pillars. The first gallery was dominated by three large abstract assemblages.

A lunchtime gallery guide was expounding their merits to half a dozen visitors: 'The linearity of the cross-members is brought into question by the circularity of these forms, which have overtones of wheels without actually being wheel-like. The gallery itself becomes a theatre for the drama of the interaction, suggesting an ambiguous engagement with the culture of technology, while at the same time echoing some of the artist's earlier political engagements and his developing interest in cosmic temporality.'

The group stared stiffly at the work, the joy of enlightenment undawning on their faces.

Meriton passed into the second room, where a young mother was discreetly breastfeeding her baby in front of Guido Reni's *Madonna and child*. An elderly man, with a mackintosh neatly folded over his arm and clutching a dull green trilby in his hand, was leaning forward to read the label beside the seventeenth-century Dutch still-life, a *memento mori* with human skull, time-piece, crystal glass, and fly on the fruit bowl. His wife, her tightly curled hair held under a silk scarf, was stooping to peer at the picture through her half-glasses, returning the sightless gaze of the skull with an interested smile.

Art and life, Meriton thought. Who, he wondered, would be disporting themselves in front of *Bacchus and Ariadne* in the next room? He nodded to the seated attendant as he passed into the next gallery, but it was empty.

Halfway along, between Holman Hunt and Roger Fry, was an elegant, polished wood door marked 'Private', beyond which lay a corridor of similarly dark and heavy office doors. The director's outer office was at the far end. Meriton walked straight in.

Ralph Ellis, the director, was waiting for him, his face already fixed in a smile as if to forestall trouble.

'Stephen,' he exclaimed, striding forward to greet him, silver hair flopping over his forehead. He stooped to offer a cold hand to Meriton.

'Splendid!' Ellis continued. 'Come along in. Coffee?'

'Black,' said Meriton.

Ellis made an indeterminate gesture towards his secretary, and led the way into his office, bending to avoid the lintel. The office seemed almost as large as the galleries outside, decorated in the same heavy traditional style. The deep red walls matched Ellis's handkerchief folded neatly in the breast pocket of his suit.

'How's Pam?' asked Ellis, motioning Meriton to one of the leather sofas in the centre of the room.

'As well as can be expected.'

'Good, good. And the children are OK?'

'As far as I know, when last seen.'

'Right. Good. And the college? How's the college?'

'Same as ever. Budget not big enough. Students not bright enough.'

'Excellent. Yes. Well, well.' Ellis lowered himself gingerly into an armchair. Over the years he had mentally compiled a list of artists whose works most exactly embodied their own personalities, as dogs were supposed to reflect their owners. Meriton, impenetrable and unapproachable, was near the top of the list. If it had not been for the chairman's insistence, he would have happily left Meriton in his state of civic neglect. However, a number of trustees had begun a campaign soon after Meriton's return, arguing that, since he was Clayforth's only famous son, the museum ought to honour him with a retrospective.

Sir George, chairman of trustees, had warmed to the utilitarian aspects of the argument: 'It'll put us on the map as a serious contemporary gallery, and it'll soften up the Arts Council for next time round.'

'But nobody likes his work,' Ellis had objected. 'The early stuff is all wearisome boxes, and rows of paving stones that you could see for free any day in a garden centre, and the recent work is abstruse, idealist twaddle. How many people from this area are going to pay good money to come and see a lot of conceptual works that, as far as they can tell, have no sense, no meaning and no beauty?'

'Doesn't matter,' Sir George had replied. 'He's our artist, and if we don't show him, some other bugger will.'

'And we'll have more tedious letters in the paper complaining about us wasting Council Tax payers' money.'

'All the better. Bit of controversy's what we need. As the Bard said, "There's only one thing worse than being talked about."'

The secretary placed the coffee on the long, low table between them, and Ellis peered across at Meriton. The latter's eyes were roving with distaste over the walls, which Ellis had hung with the museum's less fashionable English landscapes from the 1920s.

'Well,' Ellis began, and then seemed to cast about for something that was not there. He heaved himself out of his chair and frisked through several piles of paper on a wide antique desk in the corner of the room.

'I asked you here today so we can try to . . .' – he found a manilla folder and returned to his armchair – '. . . try to finalise the list of works that will be in the show. Our working list runs to just over two hundred, spanning the whole of your . . .' – he smiled in what he hoped was a convincing manner – '. . . illustrious career.'

'Yes,' Meriton cut across him. 'I've got my own list here.'

He drew a folded sheet of paper from inside his jacket and tossed it across the table towards Ellis. The director opened it and stared at it blankly.

'This is . . . um . . . This is . . . What is this?'

'It's a list of exhibits. I don't want any of the early crap. No one's interested in derivative garbage I dreamed up at college, or looking at hundreds of drawings from years ago.'

Ellis was inclined to agree, but an ingrained sense of professional obligation forced him to protest. 'No, no. I'm sure they'd be fascinated to see the . . . the development of your work. And in any case, there are only . . .' – he ran a finger down the list – '. . . there are only seven works listed here. You can't seriously be . . .'

'Seven's a good number. And it's the right number. It'll be a genuinely minimal show, free from distractions. No boring rooms full of scribbles that no one stops to look at. Just the best works, pure and simple. To be appreciated at leisure, without the pressure of the cattle market.'

There was a moment of silence as each mentally groped in a different direction.

'I want the whole thing to be filled with . . . stillness,' Meriton added.

'Well, yes, stillness, certainly . . . emptiness, perhaps, more like. To be honest, the trustees had envisaged something a little more . . . all-encompassing. A bit more, as it were, about you.'

'Yes, well, I don't want it to be about me. It's not about me; it's about my work. And you're not going to be all-encompassing about me. I'm fifty-three and I've got a long way to go yet. All you need of my life in this show is the best of my work. People can think about the work, not about me.'

It seemed unfair to Ellis that he should be obliged to argue in favour of showing more Meritons than was necessary. But duty must come before aesthetics.

'This is a retrospective,' he began. 'People expect to see the whole of the artist's work: the juvenilia, the student work, the influence of tradition and the previous generation, the first works of the adult career, the experiments, the gradual unfolding of a mature style. All of these add up to a greater understanding of the man and his work.'

'Well, I don't buy this idea that everything an artist does is art. A lot of the work I do is rubbish, and it goes where rubbish goes, in the bin, and not on the walls of a gallery. Frankly, there's a load of stuff I've done in the past that I'd be happy to burn here and now, except I've sold it to someone.'

Ellis shivered at the suggestion of such iconoclasm, even of Meriton's work, and made a mental note to double the guards at the Private View.

'Simplicity and purity, that's what I want. I may be past the sixties minimalism, but I still want that purity of experience,' Meriton insisted. 'Just the best, and stuff the rest.'

A silver lining suddenly caught Ellis's attention.

'Of course, I can see that this concept would be very well suited to our special exhibitions area.'

'It will not!' Meriton was on his feet, walking round the back of his sofa and stabbing his finger at Ellis. 'You're not sticking my stuff down there. I want the five main rooms on this floor. I want space.'

'Five galleries! Oh no, I'm afraid that's . . . that's much too much. It would have to be really out of the question. We have the rest of the collection to display as well, you know. We have to keep the gallery running, as it were.'

'Well, you can stuff the exhibition,' Meriton snapped angrily, grasping the back of the chair and leaving deep finger marks in the leather. He did not like small talk, but he did enjoy negotiation. 'The works on that list need air around them, not being crammed into that foetid glory-hole that's fit only for watercolours and Polish metal-bashing. The *Sounding Bell* alone needs a room to itself, and so does *Strength*.'

Ellis groaned inwardly and shrank further into his chair. *Strength*, a giant spider's web, was well-known among the curating fraternity, having been painstakingly constructed from cobwebs that Meriton had found when he moved into a new studio. It was the work that established his reputation at Venice. There he had dreamed of suspending it across an entire room, but the human reconstruction lacked the inner strength of the spiders' originals, and he had had to settle for fixing it within a wooden frame, fifteen feet square. Despite these anchorings, its extreme fragility tormented curators, conservation officers and art transporters.

'Well, well,' said Ellis, trying to rouse himself from depression. 'I'm sure there's no need to be talking about cancelling the exhibition. We'll be able to find our way around, I'm sure, to some convenient . . . I'll have to speak to Sir George.'

'And while you're at it, you'll need to be putting in new doors for the web.'

'That is certainly something we will need to look at,' Ellis agreed absently.

The American collector who had bought the work at Venice required borrowers to ensure that there were three airtight doors between it and the outside world. This was partly to prevent strong draughts from breaking the filaments, but also to reduce the chances of unfortunate insects entering the room and becoming entangled in them. Whilst Meriton did not object to extra spiders adding to their creation, he insisted that the absence of carrion was an important facet of the work and that it should be maintained.

There was a prolonged pause as Meriton fell into a silent reflection and Ellis mentally scoured his contacts for someone who might be able to persuade the owner to become unwilling to lend the piece.

'Actually,' Meriton said eventually, 'there'll be eight pieces in the exhibition. There'll be another one that will also need careful handling. I haven't made it yet, but it will need special delivery.'

'Oh, really?' Ellis struggled to sound enthusiastic. 'You haven't made it yet? How . . . that is . . . why . . .?'

'It will be a cubic metre of air.'

'Ah. A cubic metre of air.'

Meriton had never seemed the type to make jokes, but Ellis peered at him now, in case he was missing something. Was it worth enquiring after the significance of such a work, or would any possible answer only make him feel worse? At least, surely, it would be easier to handle than some of the other works.

'Well, that should be straightforward enough,' he said. 'I'm sure we can find you a cubic metre of air somewhere here.' He smiled engagingly, gesturing round the room to indicate the multiple candidates standing conveniently to hand.

'No. Wait.' Meriton, thinking aloud as he saw the piece more clearly in his mind, spoke in a slow, emphatic manner, as if on a poor, long-distance phone line. 'It will be a cubic metre of air that I myself breathe into a container. But then the container is removed, and just the shape of it will remain. It's the shape that needs to be carefully handled. I want it brought intact to the museum and placed precisely in a predetermined location. Just the shape.'

'I'm not quite following you here.' Ellis felt suddenly hot, and red patches were beginning to enliven the pale tones of his face. He ran his hand through his floppy hair, the mocking voices of the local press already sounding in his head. He wondered if Sir George would approve pre-emptive expenditure on a PR consultant. 'You want us to transport the shape?'

'Exactly. The shape of a cubic metre. As the shape is moved, the air that I have breathed is mixed with the surrounding air, but the idea of that space is transported in the shape. So the idea is pure, but the reality is mixed. But it will have to be moved perfectly. We'll need skilled people who can hold that shape without losing it. Ballet dancers, maybe, or mime artists.'

Ellis sat up in his chair and blinked nervously. 'Is this not something that might be better assembled on site here?'

'No. Not at all. This isn't site-specific. This is a permanent work. In fact . . .' – a note of warmth appeared in his voice for the first time – '. . . it's indestructible. It can be moved from place to place, always changing and yet eternally the same. The idea of it moving through space is the key to it.'

'But a cubic metre of space?' Ellis's mind struggled to digest the information while his fingers rubbed nervously at his collar. 'There will be nothing to see. Just . . . a space.'

'Exactly,' said Meriton, still more warmly. 'But there will be the shape. The shape as a pure mental idea, but not just an idea, because the shape will be really there. It will have the purity of the idea, but embodied in the real world.'

'I'm not sure that everyone will easily grasp the notion of "embodiment" in what will in effect be empty space.'

'Well, we'll have to encourage them to use their minds, and their imaginations,' Meriton snapped. 'You have to force people to engage with the work. They can't just expect to be spoon-fed.'

Meriton's eyes bore down on the director, who pulled the red handkerchief from his breast pocket and dabbed at his forehead, wondering whether Meriton after all had a dog, and what kind of illegally vicious beast it might be.

'Well, I'm sure, one way or another, we'll be able to manage,' Ellis said without conviction, and decided it was time for a diversion, although the subject of it no longer thrilled him. 'The other reason I asked you here was that there was a call the other day from a TV company.'

He rose stiffly from his chair again and riffled around in the piles on his desk. He retrieved a yellow message.

'Yes,' he nodded, as he returned to his seat. 'They've heard about our plans for your . . .' – the word 'retrospective' no longer seemed appropriate – '. . . for your show. And they are interested in making a documentary about it. About how the exhibition is put together.' He ran his finger down the list of notes. 'Setting up the works in the gallery, of course, but also some film of you in your studio, Private View and all that. What do you think?'

Meriton was sufficiently master of himself not to betray emotions, but it was as though the room had suddenly filled with pure oxygen. He might affect to despise popular opinion, but he respected the power of television. If the documentary could be shifted from the dull mechanics of setting up an exhibition to focus instead on the development of his new work, it could be far more effective than the exhibition, not only reminding older people who he was but reaching a new generation.

'You'll need to get them to go through my dealer,' he said casually, 'but I have no objection in principle.'

'Excellent,' said Ellis, wondering if he could encourage the producer to steer attention away from the exhibition, and focus on Meriton in his studio without mentioning the gallery. 'They'd like to get together to start talking quite soon. Would that be all right?'

'Like I said, you'll need to check with my dealer.'

'Ah, yes. Excellent. Thank you.' Ellis seemed distracted again. 'I wonder . . . just going back to the proposed list of exhibits . . . I wonder . . . the idea of just having seven, or eight, works in it . . .'

'What?' Meriton asked bluntly.

'I mean, I suppose people coming to the exhibition will be a little, shall we say . . .' He was going to say 'disappointed', but, unbidden, the word 'relieved' suddenly jostled with it in his mind. 'Surprised?'

'Yes, well, of course they'll be surprised. That's part of it, isn't it? Surprise, shock. Contradicting assumptions, breaking taboos. That's what everyone's doing these days, isn't it? That's what artists do.'

Ellis sighed. 'Yes, well, as I said, I'll have to talk to the chairman.'

'And handling this new piece?'

'I'll talk to Sir George.'

✎ ✎ ✎

Meriton emerged back into the gallery, his mind too elated to register the elderly couple smiling arm-in-arm in front of *Bacchus and Ariadne*. The complete project for the new piece had coalesced in his mind as he strode among these masters of the past. It seemed such a logical outcome of his career that he wondered that he had not thought of it before. Other artists had made invisible works of art, and works that didn't exist. But his would be different: his would be real. It would be transportable. It would be taken from gallery to gallery round the world, and everywhere it would be genuinely present in all its perfection. And it would start here, in this gallery, exuding a purity and simplicity that would make these older artists look like plodding journeymen floundering in medieval superstition. And yet it would have a complexity of ideas and references that would overwhelm the mind. All preserved for ever on film.

Here he would make reality itself into art.

The guided tour had reached the gallery's Roy Lichtenstein, a large-scale face painstakingly executed in dots to mimic a comic-book illustration.

'Pop Art played a leading role in blurring the boundaries between high art and popular culture,' the guide intoned, 'continuing the tradition of modernism in crossing borders, defying distinctions, making us constantly readdress the most basic question, "What is art?"'

Ellis had fallen back into his armchair. Meriton's coffee, untouched, remained a black presence in front of him. This was not his field. The five main galleries given over to eight incomprehensible works, one of them completely invisible? He recalculated the three years to his retirement. Perhaps if he feigned enthusiasm for the Meriton show he could trade it for Sir George's backing for a final, refreshing display of Victorian narrative paintings from the vaults.

✎ ✎ ✎

Sylvester had settled on a corner of the table under the warmth of the desk lamp. He sat upright, his front paws pressed neatly together, but his eyes drooped and his head tipped gradually to one side, like Paul in one of Horton's lectures. His tail was tucked neatly round his side, the tip flicking occasionally left and right in front of him.

Paul softly ran the back of his forefinger up and down the cat's chest. Sylvester did not stir, although his ears twitched constantly, as if monitoring communications in the ether. Paul reflected that he could happily do this all day, which was just as well since he had achieved little else in the fortnight since his latest humiliation. He had invested hours, alone at home, nursing his bruises from Meriton's fierce contempt, a contempt that, in the warmth of coddled self-pity, seemed all the more personal for it being Paul's own blood that had been rejected. During other hours, sitting dully in the cafeteria or doodling pointlessly in his workspace, he rehearsed the frustration of having to succeed according to other people's criteria. He wondered whether it had been a good idea to try to play the game of shock art at all. Perhaps he had only been driven to it by desperation. His mind, not to mention his blood, had been committed to the project, but maybe not his heart.

Sylvester stood up slowly, slid his front paws forwards then arched his back, unselfconsciously graceful. His long drooping whiskers could have had the absurdity of a cartoon Mexican, but they were saved by the fragile delicacy of the thin mouth and bony chin, and the narrow tongue, which now flicked out as he set to licking the pads of his paws, the rasping noise breaking the silence of the room. Suddenly, as if conscious that he was the object of attention, he sat up erect, looked fractionally from side to side, and then set to scratching himself behind the ear. Moments later, self-consciousness forgotten, he raised one leg heavenward and began to lick his rear end with a degree of concentration bordering on relish.

'Here we are,' Paul thought, propping his elbows on the desk and leaning his chin on his hands as he stared: 'you so beautiful and so stupid; me so clever and so jealous. If I could make anything half as beautiful as you, I'd be world-famous.'

Beauty, of course, was out of fashion. On Tuesday Horton had shown them further works from the Sensation exhibition: life-size plastic mannequins strung up as if they had been brutally executed, their limbs and genitals cut off. And other figures, children with genitals coming out of their faces. Paul regretted the effort he had made to get up so early that morning. Part way through the lecture he had been surprised to find himself agreeing with Horton, who described the images as 'abject'; but then he realised that Horton was using the term as a form of approbation.

Paul felt confused by the spirit behind the work. Surely such painstaking creativity must involve a degree of love of the subject. At college The Incredible James was making a detailed model of Highbury Stadium, with its Art Deco façade, thousands of tiny red seats, and an electronic scoreboard on the front of the upper tier reading 'Arsenal 6 – Spurs 0'. Every detail exuded love, even more so when you saw James at work, his fingers like jumbo sausages and yet working together with tender precision. Meriton had been heard threatening to transfer James to the nearby infant school, but at twenty stone James could not be compelled to go anywhere against his will.

Paul, gazing again into Sylvester's eyes, felt the attraction of such devotion. It spoke of joy and community, a celebration of human warmth, and it was the application of such devotion to images of brutal inhumanity that was so offensive. He remembered Hannah showing her flower images at a group crit the previous week, when he had suddenly become conscious of their air of celebration. It had wafted like a fragrance amidst the fashionable morbidness of the rest of the class. His reluctant sympathy had welled up inside him, and did so again now, a desire to make something that captured joy and hope, something simple and unsophisticated but humane, like himself playing with the cat, rolling over and holding it aloft, something that echoed Hannah's commonsense approach to reality.

Sylvester had started to paw at a pile of slides languishing on the desk. They had lain there for several months, waiting for Paul to label them. The plastic mounts rustled playfully as the pile slid over, and Sylvester prodded tentatively at a slide until it slipped under a sheet of paper. Paul retrieved the slide and replaced the pile. The cat looked at him belligerently and began to chew the perished rubber band that had once held the slides together. Paul picked him up and placed him lightly on top of the computer monitor, watching him nose round the narrow platform. Whatever the dangers of kitsch, there was something powerful about the character of a baby animal, or the shape of a daffodil, the scent of heather on the moors, the colours of a pheasant as it sprang into the air. It was the givenness of the world, its unconditional reality, touched at the same time with one's awareness of its otherness. The philosophers of the English Department had tried to cast doubt on whether it was really there; whether anything existed beyond our minds. Of course, no one in their right mind really doubted its existence, yet there was a caesura in one's experience: we were close to it, but it was closed to us. What kind of art would capture the untamed independence of nature? What would convey our proximity but our alienation?

At the same time, how could one account for the beauty in it all, and that forlorn desire to embrace and possess it, an instinct that seemed to be so congenitally part of human nature but offered no utilitarian benefit or evolutionary advantage? How could one encapsulate the desire for beauty, our love of it and yet our inability to encompass and hold on to it? Wild horses were certainly too kitschy, and Hannah had cornered the market in flowers. Anyway, it needed a human in the scene too, to register the distance between humanity and nature. Birds? A flock of birds taking flight? An image formed in his mind, little by little taking shape. Someone, a woman, releasing birds up into the air, her arms describing the same movement as the birds, a human empathy with their grace and freedom of flight, their tangled ascent a metaphor for her spirit rising up, yearning to experience their freedom yet frustrated by the substance of her figure that bound her to the earth.

Meriton and Horton would certainly hate it. Meriton would sneer and accuse him of sentimentalism. Horton would be happier if the woman were eating the birds, or vice versa. So much the better. If students were required to be shocking, Paul would be shockingly traditional. If beauty was taboo, then surely it must be fair game once again.

The birds would have to be quite small if the woman was releasing them with that upward sweep of her hands, but large enough to be significant. Nothing too twittery. Paul had sometimes sat and drawn the birds flittering around the dovecot in the park. He reached down his sketchbook from a shelf and began to draft the lines of a woman, a simple shift-like dress blowing in the breeze, her arms raised to the sky, a group of birds above her.

It looked like vultures circling a nun as she sent up her last, desperate prayer. Paul smiled as he tore it out and decided to keep it: it might be useful to show in self-defence the next time Meriton had him up against a wall. He started again on a fresh page.

It was all upward motion, through the arcs of her body and the thrust of her arms towards the sky. The birds wouldn't circle; they would continue in an upward flight in an arc between her outstretched hands. It would be simple enough to connect the wings to make the arc stable. It was a timeless image that he would restate in a new, modern form. Something positive, affirming, and joyful.

His pencil skipped back and forth over the image, then rapidly began a second sketch from the three-quarter view. As he did so, he decided to dispense with the dress. It hid the weight of the woman's body and detracted from the lightness of the birds. She would be nude, a generic form, not individualised but not idealised either. He felt his way round the contours of her body, smoothed and simplified, her figure sufficiently full to emphasise that she would never leave the earth to attain the freedom of which she dreamed, and yet also with a hint of joyful fulfilment within her own limitations. He would leave the surface of the figure slightly roughened, imperfect.

The birds in an arc looked posed and unrealistic. He sketched another view, the flock now slightly disjointed as one bird rose above another, taking up the momentum from her movement. Perhaps with linking armatures he could build a structure above the woman with birds rising in a more natural, unchoreographed way, the edges of their wings overlapping, but each bird seeming to be independent in its flight. It could even be a single bird in the various stages of ascent.

He worked through several more pages, experimenting with configurations of wing movements that would capture the progression of a single bird in upward flight, but with points of overlap so that they could be secured into the structure. The direction of release and flight would take the bird directly over the woman's head, so that she seemed to be bending further and further backwards. By implication she would eventually be looking directly up into the sky at the departing figure, glorying in its liberty.

As he drew, words of the accompanying statement began to form in his head.

This work questions the contemporary assumptions we make about the nature of art.

So at least he could argue that it was art about art.

The work transforms the clay of the earth into the spirit of hope. It problematises the current orthodoxy that authentic art has to be about death, destruction and depression. It asserts that life is good, and that freedom and happiness are possible.

Maybe that would be too strong. He rewrote it in his head:

It alludes to the belief that there are positive values in human life, which can be enjoyed, or at least sought after, for their own sake.

✎ ✎ ✎

'What are you doing?'

Nick was peering round the partition into Paul's workspace. Nick had braved the chill morning to confirm his continued enrolment, a necessary part of his work by which he distinguished himself from students who had simply dropped out of the course. His woolly cap was pulled over his ears and his thick jacket hung carelessly from one finger over his shoulder. His programme of non-attendance had prevented him from seeing the progress of Paul's work over the previous week. Now he leaned over Paul, mouth theatrically ajar, staring at the figure.

Fired up by the drawings of the woman and birds, Paul had come into college every day, and had worked diligently on the model. The elderly studio assistant had clearly been pleased by his request for clay and wire for an armature.

'Don't get much demand for that,' he had growled as he led Paul back down to the cellars. 'You lot seem to prefer fag ends and animal turds, and you can get them yourselves.' He produced a discoloured key and led Paul through the same series of windowless dungeons where they had rummaged for paint and canvas in his first year.

After a few minutes of rearranging the stock, he emerged triumphant with an unopened sack of clay. Judging from the design of the supplier's logo, it had been in the college for more than a decade.

The resultant work stood on a piece of white-painted chipboard on Paul's table: a woman caught in mid-step, back foot raised on its toes as she reached upwards, her hands joined by a thin wire curving above her head.

Nick was transfixed with incredulity. 'What is this? *Aging harpy prepares to garrotte her husband? The Spirit of Margaret Thatcher pursues Britain's last miner?* Or is she skipping? Actually, that's rather good. It's de Chirico, the girl with the skipping rope, isn't it? But transformed into three dimensions, in traditional modelling materials. Painting transformed into sculpture. That's better. For a minute you had me worried. Girl transformed into woman. The girl has grown into the woman, but she is still skipping! Must have a lot of puff. It's very good: Surrealism made real. De Chirico's girl decontextualised: out of the airless piazza and into the real world, except for the fact that it's an artwork, so hardly the real world. I think you've really got something here. Except . . .' He slowed as he peered into Paul's face: '. . . except I bet you've never even heard of de Chirico.'

'It's not a skipping rope,' Paul explained wearily. 'It's an armature. She's going to be releasing a flock of birds.'

'You're not serious?' Nick's thin hands seized Paul's shoulders from behind as he stared past him at the guilty woman. 'Oh, tell me it's not so! Please, assure me it's ironic. This is not a serious woman-throwing-doves – I mean, it's got to be doves, hasn't it? – throwing a bunch of doves up in the air? Tell me there's an irony I'm missing. It's not just a . . . well, just a woman-and-doves thing, is it?'

'Yes, it is,' said Paul, suddenly angry at Nick, but more so at his own embarrassment. He nervously began to finger the base, as if Nick might make a grab for it. 'It's a woman-and-doves *thing*. Joy, freedom, life. Celebrating what's good in the world; yearning for something more. And it's original. I mean, no one else here is doing anything like it, are they?'

'There's a reason for that,' Nick whispered confidentially. 'It's because we all want to get our degrees.' He straightened up. 'We haven't all got working wives to support us while we play. Some of us need a degree and a career of our own.'

Paul let this slur pass as doubt once again percolated into his mind. 'But it is innovative,' he insisted, 'and shocking. It's the shock of the beautiful.'

Nick shook his head condescendingly as he looked round for someone to come and share his distress. 'There are different kinds of shock, my friend. Some kinds of shock can be appreciated aesthetically; others just make you want to punch someone.'

Nick called down the aisle: 'Martin, come and look at this.'

Martin, clad as ever in army-surplus fatigues, closed his war comic, swung his boots heavily down from the workbench and ambled over to them.

'Holy Mother of Mildred!' he said quietly as he caught sight of the offending object. Seconds ticked slowly as he looked in silence from woman to artist and back to the woman, seeking the missing clue. Nick finally gave him Paul's rationale.

'It's a suicide note, right?' Martin ventured at last. 'Meriton has finally got to you. You unveil your statue at the Final Show, make a fine speech about the virtues of wholemeal bread and family life, expand briefly on the merits of Omega-3 oil, free-range coffee and unleaded milk, and walk out before you can be failed.' He blinked at Paul. 'He'll murder you. He won't even stop to laugh you out, or pour scorn on your tepid, reactionary, jejune, middle-class, one-eyed conservatism. He'll just tear you open and eat your spleen right there and then in the degree show.'

'He's a vegetarian,' Nick corrected him.

'People make exceptions,' Martin snapped.

'I don't care,' said Paul wearily. 'I'm going to make something I want to make, something I believe in. At least it will be authentically me. Because me, I'm fed up with all this mutilation and "abjection". You can carry on abusing Barbie dolls . . .'

'I do not abuse Barbie dolls,' Martin interrupted forcefully. 'I make artistic interventions in them that compel the viewer to confront the myths of innocence.'

'He problematises childhood,' Nick added helpfully. 'He transforms childhood glamour into real-life horror.'

'But real life isn't all horror, is it?' Paul retorted, feeling his convictions return. 'There is still some innocence in childhood. There is some beauty in the world, isn't there? I want to make something about the rest of life, something that doesn't twist and corrupt things. There are reasons to be cheerful. There are real joys as well as real sorrows. There are dreams as well as nightmares.' He shrugged helplessly. 'And if that shocks and offends you, well, isn't that what we are supposed to be doing anyway?'

There was silence for a moment, as they stared at the half-formed object.

'Anyway, maybe he won't hate it,' Paul offered unconvincingly. 'He has to be consistent. He's always saying that we need to be true to ourselves, and we should be innovative and break taboos. Well, I'm breaking college taboos. I'm breaking the taboo that says, "Thou shalt not be traditional." And "Don't make anything that looks as though you might be happy, or psychologically stable." Just for once, here's a work which is gratuitously positive, and uplifting, and . . .' He struggled for a word.

'Nice.' Meriton's voice was smooth as it slid round them in the workspace. 'I think the word you're looking for is "nice".' They peered round together. It was as if he had stepped through a door from a parallel universe, although, with the studio acting as a thoroughfare, he had presumably only been passing by.

'There are constraints on all our work, and you are right: one of them is certainly authenticity.' Meriton advanced upon them. Nick and Martin backed away uncertainly, but Paul was trapped in his seat.

'We make works to express our values, to act as metaphors for the way we understand reality,' Meriton continued. His gaze was mesmerising and yet, as Paul stared back, he was conscious that Meriton's bald head was reflecting the studio lights, and a thin, bright white aureole surrounded it. 'We conjure up a vision of the world to convey our understanding of what life is about, what makes us human, what are our fundamental commitments. And it is for that reason that so many current artists' work appears recondite, negative and destructive, because that is how they perceive reality to be. They know what the world is like. They know that nature is brutal and violent, that human life is brief and frustrating, that meaning is implied but not apparent, that suffering is widespread, and justice is rarely done.' The creases in Meriton's cheeks and eyebrows were more deeply folded with passion. 'Our works are authentic when they express our vision and our understanding. By all means make a sculpture . . .' – he jerked his thumb contemptuously towards the half-formed clay figure – '. . . that is, as you say, "positive" and "uplifting", but don't you dare do it "gratuitously".' He barked out the word. 'If you are pretending to authenticity, your art needs to be real. You will have to defend your claim that life is full of joy, and I look forward to hearing your justification.' He turned to leave. 'But I warn you,' he added angrily, pointing his finger indiscriminately at all three students, 'this is an art college, not a kitsch factory.'

The three students were still transfixed by Meriton's erect, stalking figure as he paused at the swing doors and added, staring back at Paul: 'And before you go any further with your latest "invention", I suggest you acquaint yourself with the oeuvre of David Wynne. His figure of a woman throwing up a flock of doves – and "throwing up" is probably the appropriate expression – is, if I remember correctly, in the gardens of Sloane Street in London, and sufficiently similar for him to sue for breach of copyright. You probably saw it from a bus one day, but that won't count for much in a court of law – nor in this college.'

He pushed with the tips of his fingers on the swing door. 'Authenticity and originality. Both are required.' He passed silently through the doorway.

Paul swore and angrily swung his fist down on the clay figure, remembering too late the metal armature inside. He yelped and scrabbled in his pocket for a tissue to stem the blood that instantly ran from the side of his hand.

'Now, *that* has got potential.' Nick pointed to the flattened figure. 'Squashed clay female figure smeared with genuine human blood. In fact, you could do it as an installation. Invite everyone to smash a figure and smear it with their own blood. Very therapeutic, or ritualistic, according to taste.'

He looked at Paul and his words died with embarrassment. There were tears in Paul's eyes, and Nick was sure it was not just the pain in his hand.

✎ ✎ ✎

The afternoon was warm for late autumn and they sat out on the grass in the sunshine. Nick and Sheena were idly throwing conkers at each other and catching them in plastic cups from the drinks machine. Paul was morosely holding his tea in his left hand, his right hand wrapped in a bandage from the college office.

'I'm not sure Meriton's right though,' said Nick, rolling backwards to catch a long shot. 'After all, if we now believe in the circularity of time, then the fact that another guy's work is dated before yours doesn't necessarily mean it wasn't your idea first.' He sat up straight and launched a high shot over Paul's head. 'And if he tried taking you to court, you could countersue for proleptic plagiarism. Or malicious anachronism.'

'Or you could just say it's a challenge to the concept of originality,' Sheena suggested, reaching wide for the catch. '"If it was good enough for David Whatever, it's good enough for me."'

'Wynne. David Wynne,' Nick prompted. 'Did trendy portrait sculptures in the sixties: the Beatles, Maharishi Whatsit, Yehudi Menuhin. And lots of animals. Guy the Gorilla's in the park near my uncle and aunty's in Croydon. And flocks of birds. Lots of birds. Like Meriton said, nice work, but a bit too affirmative, a bit obvious for the nineties. You need to problematise them.'

'But I really did think it was mine,' Paul protested glumly. 'I've never been to London, not even as a kid. It was always too far for my parents, or too big and scary. I've no idea where Sloane Street is. I didn't even get to the Sensation exhibition, useless prannock that I am. It's not a challenge to authenticity. It was authentic. It was something I wanted to do.'

He glumly looked at the others, jealous of their youth and their carefree, lazy game on the grass. He felt bereft. For one serenely happy week he had again believed that what had for so long been unformed within his mind and heart was coming to expression. But now he could not make it because David Wynne had made it already. He violently crushed the plastic cup in his hand, forgetting that he had not finished his drink. A perfect circle of tea rose into the air and fell around the group, soaking his bandaged hand, Nick's shoes and Sheena's portfolio.

'My work, you idiot!' she shrieked, grabbing at the handles and dabbing furiously at the tea with her sleeve. 'If you've got it on my drawings, I'll kill you!'

Paul fumbled with his left hand for a packet of tissues and began to help, apologising profusely.

✎ ✎ ✎

When Jan came home Paul had lit a fire and was kneeling on the rug in front of it, watching the flames, his tall frame blocking most of the heat. His tea was undrunk on the hearth. She put down her briefcase in the hallway and peered through the doorway.

'Hello?' she began cautiously. She recognised the warning signs.

'Hi.' It took a few moments for him to pull himself back to consciousness. 'How was your day?'

'Lousy,' she replied, tossing her hair as she untied a silk scarf. She draped her coat over the settee. 'I spent half the day trying to stop Bradley stealing my only interesting divorce case, and the other half trying to get the secretaries to do my typing. They seem to think female lawyers should do their own typing. And Marsden is no support. The sooner you get to be a famous artist – a rich and famous artist – the sooner I can leave these idiots to their own mess.'

Paul did not respond but returned to looking into the fire. She poured herself some tea in the kitchen, and came and joined him on the rug.

'What have you done to your hand?' she exclaimed.

'It's nothing,' he assured her, and fell again to staring silently into the fire. But with some coaxing, he told her about Meriton and about David Wynne. With further coaxing and the promise of dinner, she persuaded him to show her his drawings, spreading them out on the carpet in front of them. As he did so, he remembered that the figure, although simplified, was still recognisable. The fall of her straight, fine hair as she tilted back her head in the drawings echoed its forward sweep now as she leaned forward over them. He smiled at her awkwardly.

She gazed at her nude figure, arching up unashamedly into the open air, her arms upraised, her breasts lifted, confident, natural, joyful. She stared silently at herself, the dourness of the office forgotten. It was a dream, an imagination, a hope.

'They're lovely,' she said quietly after a while. She carefully piled them up to one side before drawing him towards her. 'And so are you.'

3

November

Meriton slouched rudely in his armchair. His body was almost horizontal, elbows splayed out to the sides, but his head was upright against the chair-back, eyes fixed with horror on the baby-faced monster that had been sent to represent NorthEast TV. It talked too much, smiled too much; its curly hair was too profuse; its shirt was too bright, and its tie too large and too loose. It exuded ignorance and condescension in equal measure, the journalistic disdain that came from treating everyone as a subject. Meriton, never noted for his hospitality, wondered how this abomination had got into the house.

'So what's it going to be like, then, this exhibition of yours?' The boy leaned back on the sofa with an air of comfortable worldly wisdom.

Meriton did not speak immediately. The depth of his loathing was intensified by frustration as he recognised the power that this creature held to progress the project or not. Only the minimalist clock, sporting two hands but no numbers, could be heard ticking from the wooden beam above Meriton's head.

The boy hardly noticed Meriton's lack of response. ''Cos a lot of your stuff is pretty wacky, isn't it? I mean, I was looking through the cuttings, and it's all bits of metal and string. Is that the kind of thing you're going to be showing?'

Meriton grimaced as he hauled himself up more vertically, trying to gain some height in order to talk down to the loathsome infant.

'I use a variety of materials,' he replied stiffly. 'I select whatever is appropriate to the idea I have in mind. I have certainly used metals and string in some work.'

'It's really abstract, don't you think? Kind of hard to get hold of.'

'I am interested in essences, and some of my work certainly tends towards minimalism as far as its form is concerned. And, no, I do not engage in narrative or moralising, if that's what you're suggesting.'

'So it'll be a roomful of these . . . what do you call them?' The boy motioned round the wide space of the living room, where a number of Meriton's smaller constructions intermingled with works of other artists that he had gathered over the years. The house had been converted from a barn and its rough wooden frame set off the starkly stream-lined metal forms and polished stone carvings of the collection. There were deep carpets and heavy curtains with which Pam tried vainly to stem the heat-loss from the room. Meriton, however, hardly felt the cold, and was glad he had not bothered to light a fire for this excrescence.

'Constructions.'

'Constructions, right. Roomfuls of constructions, and you're sure that the world and his wife are going to pack the place to see them?'

'Art finds its own audience, Mr . . .'

'Fairbright. Just call me Charles.'

'And it will not be, as you put it, roomfuls. It will be a small selection of objects representing the best of my work.'

'OK. And these objects now: where are they at the moment? Do you keep them here, or are they stored somewhere?' It clearly did not occur to Charles that anyone might have paid money for the privilege of taking such things off the artist's hands.

Meriton pondered. 'One is coming from New York, one from Buenos Aires. Two are in Germany, one in Italy. Two are with my dealer in London. And one I am in the process of working on.'

Charles took the bait and leaned forward eagerly. 'You haven't done it yet?' he exclaimed.

'Is that a problem?'

'I thought retrospectives were for, like, a whole life's work, stuff that has "stood the test of time".' His fingers clicked out the inverted commas in the air, while his tone implied that he doubted whether much of Meriton's work would meet such a criterion.

'Retrospectives certainly cover a career and, as my career is still continuing, I see no difficulty in including a new work.' As icy as he tried to make them, Meriton's words melted on the boy's insolence.

'And what is this great new work you're making? What's it going to look like?'

'I'm hoping it will be about the fundamentals of life – breath, space, continuity.'

'So no more death and destruction then?' Charles asked cheerfully, leaning back and looking accusingly over his intertwined fingers. 'No chopped up body parts or smashed crockery?'

'I think you are confusing my work with that of someone else,' Meriton replied as evenly as he could manage. 'Destruction has never been a feature of my work; and death, whilst always in the back of our minds, is something we seek to transcend.'

'So what's it going to look like, then?'

'Well, you might like to come and see for yourself,' Meriton said with forced geniality. 'If it were of interest, you might like to bring your cameras and do some filming in the studio.' He winced inwardly at the very thought of such an intrusion, but needs must. 'After all, I don't think the rather boring mechanics of putting on an exhibition will make hugely gripping entertainment for your viewers. They might be more interested in seeing how a work of art comes into being.'

It was like feeding a baby. Open wide, and in it goes.

'Brilliant,' Charles exclaimed, oblivious to the air of distaste with which Meriton was peering at him. 'That would be great. Really great. I'll get the lads and we'll come over and size the place up.'

Meriton attempted a smile, hoping that the costs of this undertaking, which even now he could feel beginning to mount up, would be worth the benefits.

✎ ✎ ✎

Meriton made a cup of tea and took it up to Pam. She had been installed, for the period of her recuperation, in a separate bedroom at the far end of the long wooden gallery. She was sitting up in bed, propped against several pillows, reading a novel.

'Have they gone?' she asked, putting the tea on the bedside table.

'There was only one of them. Charles something-or-other, hardly older than the students, and just as irritating.'

She smiled at him. 'We're getting old, my dear.'

She shifted with difficulty in the bed to make space for him to sit and talk, but he retreated towards the door. She continued lightly: 'If you're due a retrospective, you must be old.'

He did not smile back. Turning forty had sobered him up; but turning fifty had proved traumatic. He felt newly vulnerable: the finishing line seemed suddenly within sight, and the range of his remaining possibilities had shrunk to what appeared to be a very narrow and short path marked out ahead of him.

'I've suggested he come down to the studio and do some filming of me working,' Meriton said uncertainly, propping a hand against the door jamb.

'That will be good.'

'Will it? Why?'

'To see you at work. Your work is so . . .' She hesitated. Getting the right word could affect the rest of the evening. 'You know people find it hard to get hold of. I'm sure it would help if they could see the process that leads up to the finished article.'

Meriton drummed his fingers on the door frame and thought. The work reflected the artist: he knew that. Unwillingly, he knew it. All his life he had resisted autobiography in his art, and yet his work was hermetic because he was hermetic, dry because he was dry. Perhaps it wasn't such a good idea after all. He wanted people to understand the work, but not to think that thereby they understood him.

'They could just look for themselves; sort out their own experiences.'

'But people need some direction. I know you hate being interrupted in your studio, but we do want your work to be better known again. We've said before that people need some help to know how to approach it.'

'You've said it before. I don't remember agreeing with you.'

'But you could afford to give a little.'

'What does that mean?'

'Well, open up a bit. Talk. Explain.'

'Doesn't sound like me, does it?'

'No,' she smiled again. 'But it might be nice for people to see another side of you. You don't have to be dark and fierce all the time.'

'Hmmph.' Meriton's public persona had been assiduously cultivated, and he was not about to sacrifice it for an arrogant nobody like Charles whatever-his-name-was.

The phone began to ring downstairs. Glancing at his watch, he turned to go. 'I'll start on dinner,' he said. 'The nurse will be here in an hour.'

She blew him a kiss and manoeuvred herself to reach for her tea. Four months on, she was still surprised by this willing dedication to her care in her stricken state. In twenty-seven years of marriage she had by turns been awed, irritated and amused by the severity with which he faced the world. Now he had taken up the unexpected burden of domesticity with what might, in other people, have been described as good grace.

Downstairs Meriton answered the phone with a grunt that indicated that he was listening.

'Stephen! Excellent. It's Ralph.'

Meriton waited in silence.

'I just wanted to let you know, following our conversation, that I've been talking to Sir George, and I'm pleased to say that he is open to the possibility of accommodating your new piece. In fact, he wanted me to ask you about the possibility of us maybe actually installing it in the gallery ahead of the other works. A kind of pre-publicity.'

Ellis's nervous laughter told Meriton that there was a significant degree of misrepresentation in what he was being told, and he left a pause for Ellis to squirm a little longer.

Ellis had in fact done nothing about Meriton's proposal until Sir George had called in for their monthly meeting at the end of October. Then, in a rehearsed tone of apology, helpless in the face of overwhelming reality, he had mentioned Meriton's proposal for a non-existent work. But Sir George had become regrettably animated: 'Blimey, that's a good one. Gerrit in here early. We'll have it as a teaser.'

Meriton was not immune to the praise of others, no matter how lowly. He broke the silence: 'That is very gratifying. As it happens I am intending to start preparations for it tomorrow. It could be ready as early as the new year.'

In the kitchen Meriton set to work. Like Pam, he had been surprised at the pleasure he had found in domestic tasks. Cooking, in particular, had turned out to be a welcome counterpoint to the art world. Creativity and happy accidents had their place, but Meriton enjoyed the simplicity and structure of following instructions, practising skills, and working to a relatively objective basis for good taste.

Through the window behind the sink he looked across the lawn that was again covered with leaves. The early nights had crept in, but in the gloaming he could make out Pam's print studio, a low, white-painted, brick-built outhouse. She had been excited by the move north, being able to spread out into her own workspace, although following the accident it was not clear when she would be able to return to it. Their sons had not been so thrilled and had both gravitated back to London at the earliest opportunity. For Meriton, however, the move still seemed like a retreat. In theory he knew the process by which one generation supplants its predecessor, but he still resented the disrespectful movement that had eclipsed him. He missed the excitement of being at the centre; showing in New York; being invited to Kassel or São Paulo; waving the flag in Venice. Now, instead of requests for press interviews, he was more likely to be approached by students wanting to make him the subject of their master's theses. One student had revealed inadvertently that she was approaching him because her first-choice subjects had already been exhausted by previous researchers. He could almost hear the soil being heaped on his coffin.

Meriton continued to receive commissions, mostly from abroad where he retained a dedicated following, particularly in Germany and the United States. These were works exploring pattern and texture, attempting to induce or force the viewer into a moment of clear, existential awareness; to enjoy, if that were an appropriate word, a visceral grasp of their physical and psychic reality in that moment of experience. But the more pure and direct that experience, the more opaque the works seemed to become. It was hard to steer the viewer without detracting from the immediacy of the result.

Perhaps Pam was right, he reflected, as he chopped the onions. He had always wanted his works to stand alone, without explanation and without confusion with his own life story. But perhaps, if they followed the creation of the new work, they would understand some of the wonder and mystery that he sensed in it. He crushed the garlic and scraped it into the wok. Perhaps he would let them in that far.

✎ ✎ ✎

The next morning Meriton set off early for his studio. As he queued for the traffic-lights on the hill down towards Clayforth, he looked over the rooftops to the canal frontage winding through the town. With the upswing of the economy in the new mood of Blairite optimism the derelict Victorian warehouses were being renovated into smart shops and offices in a spirit of off-the-shelf postmodernism: warm brown brick façades crowned with new and improbable cornices, linked by atria that glittered in the cold sunlight. Work was underway nearby on a pair of blackened four-storey mills to create space for more craft shops, upmarket cafés and gift shops for the industrial-heritage tourists.

Meriton's studio, however, was safely tucked away further across town at the far end of a cobbled cul-de-sac. One side of his street was occupied by two factories built in the 1930s, separated only by a small side-turning: they were two-storey, brick buildings with rusting, flush-set metal windows. The one at the far end had been a shirt factory until the business succumbed to competition from the Far East in the 1980s, and it had remained vacant until Meriton took over the ground floor. Facing them were the arches that carried the railway line across the valley. Each archway had been bricked up to form a small workshop. A minicab firm at the end of the road sat next to an unnamed unit where a changing selection of eastern Europeans produced cheap T-shirts overprinted with the names of bands that Meriton had never heard of. Further along, opposite Meriton's studio, was a noisy gang of panel beaters and paint sprayers, who never failed to break off from their labours and admire as Meriton arrived outside his studio, preceded by the throb of his six-litre engine.

His two-door Corvette was incongruous in the street, longer than any of the other cars, and so low that from inside his studio it could scarcely be seen above the windowsill. Its brightly polished black paint sat uneasily next to the rough, darkened brickwork. Meriton had already been stopped twice by the police on the assumption that anyone in such a car was likely to be a drug dealer. On the edge of the noisy motorway he had twice had to shout the unlikely explanation that he had funded the car with the proceeds from an exhibition in New York the previous year. The centre piece had been *Progress*, a one-metre cube of ice, which Meriton had arranged to be cut from a location within the Arctic Circle and flown down in a freezer unit. For the opening few days of the exhibition it had sat on a plinth in the centre of the gallery, the melting water funnelled into a container below. When the block had finally gone, Meriton transferred the water to small, numbered containers, which he offered for sale at $10,000 each. The talismanic effect of a small phial of certified Arctic meltwater embodying the reality of global warming – an effect intensified by the word-of-mouth sensation that the gallery's well-connected directors and enthusiastic press officer succeeded in generating – meant that the entire edition was sold out within six hours. In an excess of entrepreneurial zeal, the gallery had pressed Meriton to order another block of ice, and he had had to explain that further depredations of the ice cap would be against the spirit of the work, and would open them to accusations of exploitation.

Nonetheless, the success of the exhibition burned in his pocket as he had stood one day in the gallery window and seen the new Corvette C5 moving gracefully among the traffic with the self-conscious majesty of restrained power. It set the emotions of his youth ringing again like tubular bells in his head. The open top, the soft leather seats, the absurdly detailed instrumentation, and the front grilles like snarling teeth embodied the myths of freedom and self-realisation in the wide American landscape that had drawn him as a student to Abstract Expressionism. At the same time the understated lines of the Corvette's bodywork echoed the austere gravity of the Minimalists that had later won him over. Fifteen feet long and obviously capable of 0–60 before you were out of the driveway, it had touched Meriton at a vulnerable spot. No longer constrained by parenthood to own a tediously practical vehicle, his young man's dreams returned with unexpected vitality.

'You're only trying to postpone your mid-life crisis,' Pam had told him on the phone from England, but not in order to dissuade him.

'The whole of my mid-life has been a crisis,' he had retorted.

Thus flush with the proceeds of melting ice, he defied the truth that all Corvettes are red, ordered a black one and had it shipped back to England.

The panel beaters straightened themselves and stared as Meriton parked under his studio windows. One or two nodded approvingly; another slowly shook his head in admiration. Meriton unlocked the studio and pushed the door open over the free newspapers and junk mail. He turned off the alarm and flicked on the lights. Even on the brightest days the studio remained in shadow. Once painters had sought studio space on the top floors to catch maximum light, but Meriton preferred the seclusion of gloom.

The studio was still much as the last shirt-maker had left it, an open-plan work floor, an office behind a glass partition, and a short corridor to kitchen and toilet. Meriton had kept the old sewing benches, which punctuated the space. Some were cluttered with tools, some with drawings. On others were projects in various stages of completion: a deconstructed camera; a pure white construction of intersecting circles; and a companion piece with the five Olympic rings interwoven in three dimensions. A set of Japanese fans and paper petals was beginning to accumulate dust, part of an unresolved plan around the idea of the sound of one hand clapping. There were piles of ironed and folded sheets and thick, soft blankets: Meriton had become interested in evoking the peaceful oblivion of deep sleep, of which increasing age was robbing him, but he could not see that a bed on its own would be very interesting.

He made coffee in the kitchen and then returned to the centre of the studio. He stood silently in front of one of the tables, then impulsively picked up the heap of drawings and dropped them on a neighbouring table, and used the length of his arm to sweep the remaining paraphernalia of marker pens, pencils, rulers and glue sticks into a cardboard box. He spat on the bench and rubbed vigorously with his fingers at a group of felt-tip pen marks, then stood contemplating the empty surface.

The purity of nothing. How do you capture that? The question had churned in his mind over the month since his visit to the art gallery. He had seen Anish Kapoor's beautiful, shimmering constructions with their ambiguity as to what was solid or space. But these still required the tangibility of the object to evoke the intangible, the physical to imply and shape the nothingness. In Kassel he had admired Walter de Maria's *Vertical Earth Kilometer*, a one-kilometre brass rod inserted straight down into the ground. The viewer could see only the end of the pole: the rest you knew was real, but had to be imagined and believed. It invoked the sublime, as the mind groped for the ungraspable, but still the end was there to be seen, the visible trigger to generate the transition to the discarnate.

Meriton stood silently, hands warming round his coffee. He wanted something that was non-physical, but real. It would not be nothing. It would be really there, but with the sparkling purity of the idea alone, charged with the connotations of life and reality. A part of the real world, but invisible and intangible.

He began to visualise the work in front of him, defining it with his hands. It needed to be a rational shape, a cubic metre like the ice, something that could be conceived perfectly in the mind. He would begin by defining its boundaries. He rootled in a pile of debris and returned with lengths of dowelling. Within an hour he had produced a framework for a cube, simple but precisely measured and cut. It would do for now. Later on he would want to replace the wood with something lighter, like transparent plastic rods. There was a roll of clear plastic sheeting by the window. He roughly cut a shape and encased the frame. He needed to figure a way to breathe into the cube and allow the air inside to be pushed out.

He stood in silence, arms folded, and looked at the model in all its objective imperfection, as if willing it to be pure.

There was a bang on the window swiftly followed by three more. Meriton cursed and turned round. Charles's face was pressed against the glass, squinting through a space in the filth that he had wiped with his fingers. Behind him a couple of figures were idly looking up at the first floor.

Meriton stamped across the studio and opened the door.

'Hiiii,' Charles greeted him, the syllable extended in proportion to his cheerful insincerity. He peered into the studio and then slid his way past Meriton without waiting to be invited. His henchmen followed without a word.

'This is my crew,' Charles explained as he twirled around the room, eyes flitting from surface to surface. 'Dave and Shunt. Camera and sound.'

Dave, a heavy, middle-aged figure with stubbly hair and a trim, salt-and-pepper beard, managed a nod and a 'Morning'. Shunt, in his twenties and dressed in combat trousers and a baggy jumper, was short and eager like his spiky hair. He could only muster a nervous nod. They followed their leader, looking with interest in all directions at the same time, like visitors to a stately home.

'Bit dingy,' Dave muttered to no one in particular. 'We'll need extra lights.'

'We were in the area,' Charles called across the room, 'scouting locations. Your gallery said you might be in your lair.' He picked up a Japanese fan and waved it vaguely.

Meriton, aghast at this intrusion, croaked out: 'Please, do not touch anything.'

'The plan is,' Charles continued, replacing the fan and running a finger through the bowl of petals, 'we shoot some footage down here; you know, you in creative flow, doing what you do and all that. Maybe talk a bit about your plans for this mighty new work, see you working at it. Cut in a few examples of your drawings of whatever you do, along the way. Then, I thought, track it being packed up and transported to the show – all that back-room stuff, you know? – to its final glory before the admiring hordes. So viewers get the complete idea, initial concept to final work, studio to gallery. So, from here, a picturesque shot of the van disappearing up the cobbled street. There's a rather nice car outside. We'll have to get whoever's that is to shift it. Spoils the effect of the lonely artist struggling away in his garret.'

'The new piece is already underway,' Meriton said.

'Oh, no worries.' Charles pressed down idly on the pile of bedding. 'We can fiddle with the early stages. Cut in some general shots of you drawing or whatever, make out these are prelims for the major opus. Now, which bit of this place do you work in?'

Meriton felt the need to try to regain some authority. 'And the car outside, by the way, is mine.'

Charles, Dave and Shunt all turned and stared.

'No way!' exclaimed Charles. 'How d'you manage that? It must have cost a bomb.'

Meriton forbore to reveal that it was only a quarter of the cost of a Ferrari, a discovery that had warmed his Yorkshire heart.

'I had an exhibition last year in New York,' he said casually. 'The proceeds were more than enough.'

Charles struggled to keep the admiration from his voice. 'So what does your stuff sell for?'

'Usually between £20,000 and £200,000, depending on what it is.'

'I think I'm in the wrong job,' said Dave genially, settling his backside on a bench.

'Not necessarily,' Meriton snapped and moved across the studio to stand in front of Charles and prevent him from touching the Olympic rings.

'Still,' said Charles, wandering further, 'maybe you could leave it round the corner when we do the shooting. Can't go portraying the lonely artist struggling away in the heat of creative ferment, and then have you driving home to the missus in a swanky Cadillac. That's too much to explain to the viewers.'

'Perhaps, on the contrary, you might consider taking the opportunity to challenge your viewers' stereotypes, rather than pandering to them. As you see . . .' – Meriton gestured round the studio – '. . . I am not a Romantic Parisian dying of consumption in a neglected garret. I find the industrial environment is much more conducive to artistic production. Not all creative artists are lonely or starving, just as not all American cars are Cadillacs. And there are still enough people worldwide convinced of the value of my work to put food on my table.'

'And fuel in your tank,' Shunt offered shyly, but Meriton refused to be distracted.

'So which bit of this place do you work in?' Charles repeated, gesturing vaguely at the multiplicity of surfaces and works. 'Where are the creative juices flowing for the new great work?'

Meriton motioned to the cube on the workbench in front of them.

'Is this it?' asked Charles in surprise. He stared. 'I mean . . .' He searched for another way to phrase the question. 'I mean . . . is this it?'

'It is a working model at this stage,' Meriton explained.

Dave walked round the bench to stand opposite Meriton, stroking his beard in an attempt to suppress a smile.

'What you see here is a trial for delimiting the boundaries of the work. The work itself will consist simply of a cubic metre of air, or, more specifically, air that I will have breathed. I will fill the cube with my breath, then remove the covering.'

'So you're just left with this wooden thing, and the air in it and around it?' asked Charles in disbelief. 'And this is what they're going to pay you two hundred grand for?'

'No,' said Meriton. 'The frame will be removed as well. You will be left with the air.'

'You're kidding!' Charles stared at Meriton, uncomprehending.

Meriton again felt resentment rising up against this round-faced youth and his curly-haired lack of respect.

'We're going to film a cubic metre of air?' Charles thrust his arms forwards, hands extended towards the work. 'There will be nothing to see. The viewer's going to be looking at . . .' – he leaned forward, spreading his arms out to the sides and gawping unintelligently – '. . . literally nothing. Nothing's going on. What kind of TV is that?'

'You are the televisual expert,' said Meriton as coldly as he could manage. 'I might have thought that, as a professional communicator, you would welcome the challenge to communicate to your viewers the significance of the reality that you are filming.'

They stared at one another again in silence.

And then a voice: 'Bloody brilliant.'

It was Shunt. He had been admiring the drawings on the neighbouring bench but listening to Meriton's explanation. He sidled up to the plastic construction now and spoke with a quiet, awestruck voice: 'It's brilliant. It's kind of nebulous, there but not there, nothing but something. It's really there but you can't see it. Like the sublime. Yeah, that's really good.'

'I'm relieved that it meets with someone's approval,' Meriton replied drily.

'But . . .' Charles found his voice again. 'But there are some practical problems here. I mean, how do you know where the work is if you can't see it? How do you pick it up and transport it? How do you stop it blowing away when you're outside? I mean, this is the great new work for the museum thing . . .'

'Retrospective,' Shunt prompted.

'Retrospective. And how are you going to get it there? How will you know it's arrived safely if you can't see it?'

Meriton was pleased by Charles's discomfort. 'We know exactly where the work is,' he explained. 'It is where the defining plastic cube is. Remove the cube and it will still be there. When the time comes to move it, we pick up the cube shape and carry it carefully out. You see, Mr Fairbright, there are different kinds of truth. Some things are real, even though you can't see them.'

'But . . .' Charles paused in confusion.

'And yes, when the shape is picked up, the air it contains will be left behind. Well, that's true, although some may be drawn along. No one can tell how much. But ambiguity is one of the prerequisites of art. So it leaves your mind free to play over the sense of continuity of life and reality, and how our own lives dissolve into time. Meanwhile and much more significant, the pure idea of it will travel, completely and perfectly; the precise shape conveyed from place to place, exactly as originally conceived and made.'

'Are you seriously going to exhibit some empty space?' Charles asked. 'I mean, there'll be nothing there! Talk about the frigging emperor's new clothes.'

'Oh, get with it, Charles,' Shunt intervened. 'This is conceptual art. Of course there'll be something there. The emperor didn't have any clothes, full stop. But this is a work of art. It doesn't need an art-object. The work is in the idea. It starts here in the studio, and it carries on wherever it goes, with or without the object. It doesn't matter that there'll be nothing to see. The idea will be there.'

'Thank you,' said Meriton, more warmly than usual. 'At least somebody on the team seems to have an appreciation.'

Shunt grinned sheepishly. 'I've always liked your stuff, sir, Mr Meriton. It has a kind of stillness to it.'

Meriton inclined his head to acknowledge the compliment.

Charles, fearing that he was losing his standing in the conversation, had begun to pace round the workbench. He looked at Dave: 'How do you film something that isn't there?'

'It is there,' Shunt insisted.

Charles waved a hand to shut him up. 'Something that has no

visible presence. No physical reality. Something you can't flipping well see. How does that make interesting TV?'

And how, he thought, do we make sure that the person who ends up looking like a prannock is the artist and not the film-maker?

'Perhaps you'll see something of it – or at least where it should be – when it's being carried,' Dave offered hopefully.

'Yes,' said Meriton. 'It's my intention to find two experienced mime artists who will be able to preserve the shape as they move it from here to the gallery, and then on again at the end of the exhibition.'

'What if it's blowing a gale outside?' Charles was beginning to raise his voice. 'Or raining? Won't it get blown away, or washed away?'

'No,' Meriton replied coolly. 'The air will mix that much more vigorously, but the essential idea will remain the same. You cannot blow away an idea.'

'But what if they fall over?' Charles persisted. 'Or one of them sneezes or has a fit? What happens to it then?'

'The transportation of a work of art is always attended by a certain amount of risk,' Meriton agreed.

'But are people really going to come and look at this . . . thing? Or non-thing? To stand around and stare at this . . . this absence, this lack of anything, this space? Why would they do it? What's it about?'

'As I said, it is about reality, about being,' Meriton explained. 'It's also about the sheer wonder of being alive. About ephemerality and continuity. Above all it is about the beauty of true purity, which can be achieved in the realm of ideas even if not in the messy reality of the physical world. It is about what we call the sublime.'

'It's the stuff you breathe, mixing with the world around you,'

Shunt added helpfully. 'It's obvious really, er, no offence, Steve, Mr Meriton, sir. I mean, it's obvious in its simplicity. But simplicity can be very profound, very complex.'

'It can also be very simple,' Dave muttered. He added more loudly: 'If it's just a matter of filming an empty bench, I could do it now. Would you like me to haul in my kit and start shooting?'

'That would be inauthentic,' said Meriton testily. 'It would be untrue. Art is about reality and truth. The whole point of the work is that it will be there, even though you can't see it.'

'It's beginning to sound a bit religious to me,' Charles snorted.

Meriton's eyebrow line flickered. 'I prefer to think of it in Platonic terms, rather than religious. It speaks of the numinous, without getting into metaphysical claptrap.'

Charles laughed and slapped his hands together as if to end the discussion: 'Well, if you're trying to get people to part with two hundred big ones for a work of art that isn't even there, I'd be cautious about bringing up the idea of "metaphysical claptrap". And by the way, if we're talking about purity here, how are you going to be sure that the cube contains all your breath and nothing else. How will you tell when all the original air has been pushed out, and that what's in it is all your own breath?'

'That is what I am working on at the moment,' Meriton conceded quietly.

'Of course,' Charles continued cheerfully, 'it doesn't really matter. I mean, no one will know. You just breathe into the box and tell everyone it's your breath. They'll be none the wiser.'

'Of course it matters,' Meriton snapped. 'I will know. It matters to me.'

Charles recoiled slightly. 'Right. Yes. Got you. Got to be authentic, yeah? Got to be honest and true and all that?'

Meriton did not reply. He stared at the cube, trying to resolve the problem. He could fill it with coloured smoke, and blow into it until all the smoke had cleared.

Charles smirked and added glibly: 'You could do it as a vacuum pack. You know, suck all the air out, then you puff it all back in again.'

Meriton's stomach contracted with momentary panic. It was the obvious answer. Why hadn't he thought of it?

4

Later in November

The young blonde reclined gracefully across the front of the open-top Rolls Royce. One hand gripped the winged mascot; the other was propped against the windscreen, holding a glass of champagne. Her short blue satin dress clung to her slim body. It matched the colour of the stilettos strapped to her tiny feet, which hung over the side of the car. Her eyes were wide open, soft and appealing, and her long hair stroked the surface of the car. The only discordant note was the axe that separated her head from her body, its blade embedded deep in the bonnet. In the driving seat an equally beautifully groomed young man stared nonchalantly ahead, a cocktail glass in one hand while the other, holding a pistol, rested on the steering wheel. A cigarette was glued to his lips. Across the back seat a gleaming black grenade launcher lay next to a sniper-rifle.

'It's a challenge to romantic escapism,' Martin explained, moving round the side of the table. 'Barbie and Ken represent the myth of eternal youth and happiness amidst the reality of fading beauty and the empty pleasures of life.' Martin had been made to attend chapel in his youth, and the voice of the preacher was still in his head. 'But now they have become Beauty and the Beast and there is no happy ending. Beauty gets her throat cut, and the Beast gets away with it by sheer force.'

'Nietzsche,' Gary murmured in reverential antiphony.

Horton inclined his head to indicate that this was moving in the right direction. He looked round the group. 'Any comments?'

The students avoided his gaze and stared dutifully at the pink plastic car. Its glistening, smooth perfection was abrasively at odds with the dilapidation of the seminar room. Behind the table was a free-standing whiteboard on wheels, rendered unusable by generations of indelible marks left by tutors using the wrong pens. It had been roughly pulled alongside a torn projector screen to mask off the end of the room where heaps of ragged card and paper, the cast-off work of previous generations, lay across all available surfaces, punctuated by tins of spray adhesive, jars of dried-up felt-tips, and sliding piles of glossy magazines.

Horton mildly raised an eyebrow as he looked round for a response. But it was his penchant for violent imagery that had made him famous, and students found it difficult to articulate a path between rebellion and sycophancy. Many were awed into silence by the knowledge that, at their age, Horton had already achieved international notoriety thanks to the assemblages that he had exhibited at his degree show, works purporting to be made of deformed human foetuses. He had thoughtfully sent photographs in advance to the London papers, news agencies and TV stations.

The resultant publicity had guaranteed that, after graduation, his star had continued to rise with shows of new work in London and New York. The campaign of outrage in the tabloid press, assisted by politicians calling for the exhibitions to be closed, inflated the galleries' attendance figures. Horton began to appear on the invitation list for the more up-market parties, and his name and photograph migrated from the arts pages to the gossip columns.

'Are you working on anything else?' Horton asked to fill the void.

The attic room, with its roof lights closed against the autumn rain, was getting stuffy.

'Yeah, I've been working on this.' Martin delicately moved the Rolls Royce to safety, and replaced it with a disposable barbecue. The plastic wrapping had been removed, but the coal had not been lit. Arranged on the grill, like kebabs, were six Barbie dolls, as naked as the day they were manufactured, their feet bound together, and their hands tied behind their backs.

'I was thinking of calling it *Barbie-Q*,' Martin explained with an ingratiating smile.

'Creep!' someone shouted from among the students, and others laughed. For, after the foetuses, Horton had achieved further success, in equal quantities of coverage and protest, with *Food of the gods*, a series of barbecues on which were arranged lovingly re-enacted tableaux of the last moments of Saints Lawrence (slowly turning on a spit), Bartholomew (skinned and marinated) and Sebastian (perforated by an array of wooden skewers, each decorated with slices of onion and green pepper).

Horton did not enter into the hilarity at this small tribute. For the hubris that followed this *succès de scandale* had led him to exhibit a collection of manipulated images of the Holocaust, at which point he found himself to have unwittingly crossed an unmarked boundary. Media critics, who had only recently been honoured to refill his champagne flute, dismissed the work as childish and derivative. He was condemned as exploitative by Jewish leaders, as blasphemous by Catholic clerics who were still deliberating on his previous exhibition, and as anti-choice by women's groups who had belatedly woken up to the foetus imagery. Gallery invitations dried up overnight, and Horton, making a calculated guess that defiance would still be a more lucrative long-term strategy than apology, had spent two years in the wilderness before being rescued by Curridge's invitation to Clayforth.

'Excellent,' said Horton. 'A work with a good pedigree, I think,' he added, earning another laugh from nervous students. 'Anything else?'

'We've been thinking,' Martin said, 'Gary and me and some of the others, about other ways of challenging middle-class fantasies of the neat and perfect life. Maybe a neo-Nazi rally in the town, or perhaps a bank robbery.'

Horton smiled indulgently. 'Interesting idea,' he said. 'Just a shame about the prison sentence after graduation.' More laughter. 'You'll need a pretty good artist's statement to persuade the judge not to lock you up in the Scrubs.'

Martin smiled ruefully at Horton, exchanged glances with Gary, but said nothing.

'Well then,' said Horton as brightly as he could muster. 'Who's next? Hannah. What have you got? Are we still tiptoeing through the tulips?'

Hannah's pink cheeks got a bit pinker as she swept her fluffy hair back off her forehead. 'Well, as you know, my work is about God being the greatest artist.'

There was a groan from the corner and an uncomfortable stir round the room as the students prepared themselves for another endurance test. Hannah affected not to hear and pushed a video into the player.

'The western fine art tradition traces its roots back to the Byzantine icon makers. Icons were a representation of who people worshipped; and all art expresses some sort of worship, a sense of what we believe is most sacred or valuable, or, if you don't believe in God, a belief at least about what is real. As you know, I believe that God has created everything that exists, and I'm trying to find ways to capture that sense of awe at what God has done, a sense of worship for God as the great designer.'

The screen lit up with a wide shot of a field of daffodils, thousands of bright yellow heads, motionless in the sunshine, interspersed in the foreground with patches of green, but blending into a solid yellow stripe towards the horizon. The field was closed off by a row of poplar trees.

There was another groan. Gary yawned loudly, his legs buckled, and he slid by degrees down the wall until he was sitting on the floor, knees bent and head thrown backwards. His mouth hung open, as if straining to hold on to life.

'I took this in Holland earlier this year,' Hannah explained as the others watched. 'I liked the strength of the form of the daffodil head.'

The camera sank downwards until it was looking at a shallow angle over the blurred sweep of intense colour, set against the smooth blue sky punctuated with delicate strands of white clouds. Then in the foreground a small group of flowers, standing slightly distinct from the mass, came into focus. The lens heightened the particularity of each flower. There was more obviously now a range of tones created by the sharp sunlight: some petals seemed densely yellow, while others were translucent with traces of pale green. Dark spaces appeared between the flowers, allowing vistas into the jungle of stems. Most of the flowers in the group were facing to the left, like spectators fixed on the main event. But the central flower looked directly into the camera, as if it had turned to face the approaching viewer. As the camera moved forward to meet it, the flower acquired a character of its own. Its demeanour was no longer frail: it seemed instead to stand aloof and impassive, as if the viewer were venturing onto alien ground. Its petals no longer seemed formulaic, but each, with fibres as strong as parchment, was folded and kinked with an individual character and its own role to play. The flower-head filled the screen, and the students, against their expectations, were silently drawn in by the immediacy of the encounter. The tips of the uppermost petals were almost white in the sunshine. Inside the central bell, across the top, was a clear lemon yellow, while the shadowed area at the bottom gained a touch of tan. As if viewer and flower were sizing each other up, the camera paused and stared. Then it continued forward until the image on the screen was enclosed inside the bell.

Suddenly there was a change in scale. They seemed to be looking up into the domed ceiling of a prodigious arena. But instead of concrete beams supporting the roof, there was only the integral strength of its undulating surface. The strong yellow of the sunlit upper part melted into a green towards the end of the dome, where the six-legged form of the pistil stood tall like a radio mast. That first impression of gentle fragility was forgotten in this strange, proud cavern.

'Well, that's very pretty,' said Horton as the film came to an end. 'But what does it mean? Do we have to read meaning and purpose into any particular form? After all, everything that exists has to have some kind of form. Couldn't it just be contingent? Do we have to find design in everything just because it happens to have ended up one way rather than another?'

'Well, of course that could be the case,' Hannah agreed primly, brushing the hair out of her face again as she swapped in a new video. 'But it always seemed to me that, if the universe was just random and meaningless, then you would expect the things in it to be random and meaningless as well.'

The screen showed a snail crawling across a pineapple, its grey antennae waving back and forth as its body glided forward.

'I've been doing some research into Fibonacci numbers and the Golden Ratio,' she continued, 'and it seems there are lots more connections and patterns in the world than you would expect in a universe that was just purely random and where everything happened by chance. The Golden Ratio, as you may know, is a number with amazing properties. It's fascinated artists and mathematicians for centuries, and it turns up all over nature: in the number of swirls on the shell of a snail, the number of lines on a pineapple, the spirals of seeds in a sunflower head, the petals on a daisy, and even the way the pips are arranged in an apple core.'

The camera was closing in on the pineapple, at the base of its green shoots. Then it slid down, steeply to the right, following the parallel rows of the six-sided spines. At the bottom of the fruit, the camera continued right but sharply upwards, following the contrary alignment, drawing ever closer in. Then it abruptly turned again to follow the third spiral line, rising in a shallower pitch. Each spine was enclosed within a dark green contour, and then grew lighter towards the centre, where dried, brown leaves of its flower were wilting away. Each seemed uniquely fashioned, and yet was meshed with the others in the interlocking pattern of spiralling lines.

'There are always five spirals moving round the fruit in one direction,' Hannah explained, 'and eight and thirteen in the other two, or sometimes eight, thirteen and twenty-one. All Fibonacci numbers.'

The camera rediscovered the snail, which had made good progress round the circumference. It moved in on the scrolling shell, tightly coiled in the centre, and then the spiral growing broader as it unfurled, each segment glistening with a black smudge at the base, with pale brown stripes radiating outwards.

'Like many creatures that live in shells,' Hannah explained, 'the shell grows like a logarithmic spiral, so that, even though the radius of the shell is increasing, the outside curve of the shell is always the same. And there are well proven connections between the logarithmic spirals, Fibonacci numbers and the Golden Ratio.' Hannah unfurled a roll of paper, which volunteers, their earlier impatience forgotten, held for her against the whiteboard. It showed a logarithmic spiral neatly fitted within a series of diminishing rectangles, each related to the other by the Golden Ratio.

'And if we as artists create works with meaning and order,' she concluded, 'and then we see meaning and order in the world around us, it certainly looks like evidence that there is a greater artist at work there too.' Gary wailed loudly, but Hannah persisted. 'I think it's also interesting that we recognise beauty in the way the numbers themselves work, and not just the way they are expressed within these natural forms. Our appreciation of beauty would be very hard to explain in a universe that was entirely without meaning, or purpose or design. Beauty implies a recognition of something "other" behind the numbers.'

Martin slid down the wall beside Gary, whose head was now hanging between his knees. But the other students entered into an enthusiastic discussion that circled around the themes of number, order and meaning, and then spun more rapidly through numerology and cabbalism to science and Scientology, until, like all good theological arguments, it was sucked inexorably down the double helix of freewill and determinism.

Horton, whose mind was beginning to turn towards coffee, brought them back to order. 'Thank you, Hannah. I'm sure we all respect your beliefs, even if we don't share them.'

'Amen!' Gary called from the floor.

'However, it's one thing to hold traditional beliefs if you must, but that doesn't excuse you as an artist from finding contemporary ways to express them. Like it or not, you're an artist in this generation, not seventeenth-century Holland. You need to come up with something a lot more raw and punchy, and just more twentieth-century, than fields of daffodils, and a lot more challenging than pictures of pineapples.' Hannah blushed, as Horton continued. 'That's the nut, if you'll excuse the expression . . .' – Martin laughed appreciatively – '. . . that you've yet to crack. Now,' he looked round hopefully, 'Sheena. Have you got anything for us?'

Sheena, wrapped in a bright orange woolly cardigan that did not match any of the colours in her tartan skirt, glumly set out on the table a row of portrait heads. Her movements were restricted by a long, knitted scarf, which was wound several times round her neck and still dangled to the floor at both ends. The drawings, all in pencil, were mounted on card, which she propped up against the defaced whiteboard. The students edged round to inspect them.

Paul was able to recognise himself second from the left, next to Bridget, with her mid-length black hair and a dark complexion from her West Indian father. Then came one of the textile lecturers and the principal himself. To Paul's astonishment further along the row was Meriton. Much as he wanted to like her work, he could see little merit in the drawings. They were angular and heavily stylised, but neither shocking nor innovative, a mere clunking attempt at a standard of realism that was evidently beyond her technical ability. He cringed at the critical whipping Sheena was about to receive.

Horton, however, merely asked pleasantly, 'So how's the project going?'

'It's fine,' Sheena replied firmly, the heavy mascara giving her eyes an air of vulnerability behind defiance. She added, as if an afterthought: 'These are just experiments. Just . . . trying to capture appearances.'

'Right. Good. Well, that's excellent. Keep going. I'm really looking forward to the results. Any comments?'

But if students were in awe of Horton's reputation, they were also afraid of Sheena's temper, and forbore to speak.

Paul frowned as he looked from Sheena to Horton and back again, puzzled at the politeness of this exchange. He wondered if there was something between them that he was missing. However, he did not have time to ponder it, as he heard his name called.

'Now, maybe time for one more before coffee,' Horton was saying. 'Paul. Have you got anything new for us?' Several of the students picked up the nuance on the word 'new' and smiled at each other knowingly.

Paul awkwardly produced some small photographs, and put them in a pile on the table, his movements hampered by the sling round his right arm.

✎ ✎ ✎

On inspecting the injury to Paul's hand, Jan had insisted that he take it to the hospital. Here he had waited in A&E for three hours before a sympathetic nurse cleaned it with what she said was iodine, although he thought it looked suspiciously like soy sauce. She then wrapped it in a bandage and tied it up with a sling. He had discarded the bandage after two weeks, but retained the sling for sympathy.

The experience of parting with his blood in other than the controlled circumstances of a doctor's surgery had surprised him. Waiting at the hospital, frustrated and anxious about when he had had his last tetanus booster, he had begun to recognise flaws in his earlier project. His blood seemed now quite urgently precious, not something to be toyed with, or poured carelessly from bottle to bottle, or used as paint when paint itself was so easily available.

The wait at the hospital had also shaken his conviction, one that was foundational to every art student, that art was the fulcrum of civilisation: not the caviar and champagne of high society but the bread and water of human experience.

Paul's upbringing had shielded him from encounters with social deprivation. Even as a student he had instinctively known which parts of town did not belong to him. The experience of an A&E waiting room was new to him, and its degradation shocked him. Abandoned food wrappings and paper cups littered the unwashed floor, along with crumpled newspapers and plastic bags. It was like waste ground for which no one, not even the hospital staff, accepted responsibility. As the hours ground by, he watched with fascinated horror the succession of his fellow sufferers. A drunk in a scruffy jumper and dirty jeans, bleeding from a head-wound, was pacing round the waiting room swearing to himself, oblivious to the security officers who were trying to coax him towards a seat, and a nurse threatening to have him thrown out. An elderly woman, with grey permed hair and a cheap raincoat, was bruised from her eye to her mouth. A group of teenagers, talking more loudly than they needed, half-carried a friend through the automatic doors and stopped, looking around helplessly, unsure of who to speak to. Paul tried not to stare, but he need not have bothered as no one returned his gaze. This procession of miserable helplessness filled him with dismay. Had the grey-haired woman fallen in the street, or been struck by her husband? And why was she alone? If the drunk could not control himself and was thrown out, where would he find help? Like the teenagers, startled by the disjunction between a convivial night's drinking and the cold bureaucracy of the medical system, he felt the gulf between his own experience and what he assumed to be the poverty that attended these unexamined lives, the limitations of their horizons, the illiteracy in meaning and beauty. Did art ever impinge on their lives, he wondered? Was there any way his art could speak to them, to bless them with aesthetic enrichment, to help them towards deeper self-reflection or awareness of the reality they inhabited? He was suddenly aware of how much there might be of which he knew nothing.

Days later, back at home and lying on the couch in the living room, he looked at one of his drawings of the bird-woman, which Jan had had framed and hung on the wall. You wouldn't find her down the casualty department, he thought. With the artist's controlling will to beauty, there would be nothing wrong with her. In fact, with the simplification of her form, there was not much that could go wrong. The trouble with real people was that they were always there in every detail, with everything, large or small, that can go wrong, from the disproportionate pain of a toothache to the ghastliness of an open wound that Horton would so lovingly recreate. And, in all this relentless specificity, people lived in a wider world that was ungraspably complex. How could one capture reality when it existed in such a super-profusion of detail?

The answer was obvious: photography. The camera would record every smallest detail, even the ones that the photographer had not noticed, all registered faithfully and uncritically. As he lay in comfortable self-pity, tugging at the frayed edges of his sling, a project began to form in his mind: a series of photographs, in the right setting, conveying this sense of the multiplicity of details in appearance. Unidealised. Just the facts. He could select some down-market scenes suggested by his visit to A&E: a drunk man sprawling across a sofa in a dishevelled living room; his untidy, overweight wife in the background watching the telly; their unkempt and probably unruly children disengaged at various points in the scene. But they would be non-judgemental images, even loving, affirming the humanity of the figures that was undiminished by the indignity of their physical condition and environment, free of any prejudice against their distance from classical images of beauty. An appeal to reality, unadorned and unmediated, should actually meet with Meriton's approval, he thought, although Horton would probably prefer the figures to be dead and decomposing.

He began to wonder how he could construct such photographs. He knew no one in that stratum of society. He had no access to their homes. Even if he had, would the occupants consent to be part of such images? Such practical difficulties, however, would never need to be resolved.

✎ ✎ ✎

Paul nervously began to tape sheets of newspaper over the whiteboard. There was a murmur round the room, and Horton called out, 'I hope this isn't it.'

'No, this is just a background,' Paul explained. 'I only just managed to take these photos, and I haven't had a chance to mount them properly.' Individual frames, he explained, would be incongruous to such subjects; black card would be too arty; white card too stark. So he had decided on sheets of newspaper, black and white.

He began to stick the photographs on the newspaper backing. They were small prints, and the class shuffled together to peer more closely. Paul had taken them in a hurry the previous day and had had to pay a premium to get them developed quickly in town. They showed a few of his fellow students whom he had asked to lie among piles of debris in the student common room, apparently drunk. It was not a challenging role, and he had emerged with a dozen usable images of limp bodies and unfocused eyes, set among the detritus of everyday life. The images were not, he explained, as sharp as the final ones would be. Even so, the camera seemed to exaggerate the bathos of the second-rate logo on the lager can, the abstract form of the crumpled cigarette packet, the jumble of the ashtray, the ripped end of the sofa.

'What is this?' asked Horton. 'A student party?'

There were a few laughs and supportive cheers for the idea.

'They're just trial images. The final ones will be working-class families, focusing on the details of their environment, not judgementally, just factually, bringing out the humanness amid what we think of . . . what might be thought of as . . . as degrading, degraded circumstances.'

There was another stir round the class, but this time no laughter and no cheers. Paul felt more secure. At last, he thought, they are taking me seriously. Horton, having looked at the photographs, was staring at Paul.

'I wanted the pictures to emphasise the detail of reality. How everything is so minutely *there*, so . . . so real. And it's about how you can see beauty in the unbeautiful, in drunks or drug addicts and whatever.'

'But how can your pictures be "not judgemental",' Martin interrupted, 'when you talk about the people being "degraded" and "unbeautiful"?'

Paul blushed. 'I'm just trying to feel my way into the subject.'

'Well, I'd go and feel up somebody else, if I was you,' Martin snapped. His friends laughed.

'Well,' said Horton slowly and loudly to quell the noise, 'I think there is something to commend here. You might see it as a kind of anti-minimalism, a sort of counterpoint to Mondrian. He tried to get to reality by stripping away the details and leaving just the abstract structure that he felt underlay reality. This . . .' – he gestured to the photographs – '. . . is trying to grasp reality by going the other way, trying to embrace every detail. I like the gritty, urban feel.' Horton paused, savouring the moment. 'But I wonder,' he continued smoothly, 'whether you have come across the work of Richard Billingham.'

There was an inarticulate jeer from the centre of the group, and a movement as everyone simultaneously nudged someone else. And in that instant Paul realised that the stir he had felt in the class was not enthralment but embarrassment.

His silence answered Horton's question.

'Well, I suggest you do, in case he's feeling litigious.' Another laugh from some of the students. 'I think you will find that his photographs are an alarmingly close match to the images you have just described, and they are already in the public domain, where you have presumably seen them, if not remembered them. And, if I may say so, I think his works carry a degree of authenticity which yours, frankly, would not, as he himself comes from the milieu that he is photographing.'

There was a loud grunt of agreement from Gary: 'Quite right. Arrogant tosser. You should have stopped with the newspaper. That was going somewhere.'

Another laugh.

Horton cleared this throat loudly. 'Well, why don't we break for coffee there, and I'll see you back here in forty-five minutes.'

Paul stood red-faced, staring at his photographs. Around him the group drifted away, talking and laughing loudly. Sheena paused for a moment, taking in Paul's body language, and decided he was best left alone.

She turned to Nick: 'How about that portrait you were promising me?'

Horton busied himself while the class departed, then spoke across the room as he piled papers into his bag.

'You know, this has got to stop. You obviously have an uncanny ability to think great men's thoughts after them, or at least to submerge them in your unconscious. But, sadly, that isn't going to get you anywhere in the uncharitable world of art where originality is the hallmark of the authentic artist. That's not to say there isn't always a market for pastiche. But if you're going to go down that route, you'd be better off copying the Impressionists rather than the conceptualists. People can't get enough of Monet or Dufy. You could maybe ask for a grant to hop over to Paris and do some café scenes. People pay serious money for them. But if you want to succeed here,' he tapped his finger on the table and ground his foot into the grubby carpet, 'you need to find your own voice.'

He left the room, whistling to himself.

Paul still did not move. Once more, his face was hot, his ears buzzing, and the floor giving way beneath his feet. It was so hard to assess your own work. Images that had looked excitingly provocative could in a moment seem garish, shallow and patronising. He was sure he had never heard of Billingham, and had no memory of seeing his work. His intentions had been personal and genuine and, as far as he knew, original. And yet Gary's sneer, and the echoes of the laughter, had stung him. The photographs, still stuck to the board, suddenly looked soiled and superficial. He had been grasping after what seemed like reality, but maybe this was something beyond his grasp. And yet how could he be original if he only stayed within his own narrow circle of experience? He had wanted an art that dealt with reality, that said something significant, that touched the lives of other people, including those outside the art world. Now, as he roughly pulled the photographs off the sheets of newspaper, he wasn't sure that he could reach anyone at all.

✎ ✎ ✎

Paul did not have the courage to reappear for the second half of the group crit. He slipped out of college and wandered idly round the town before catching the bus home for tea. To his surprise Jan was already there. She was lying on the sofa with Sylvester, absently watching a game show. Her eyes were red, but it seemed unlikely to Paul that it was the intensity of the competition that was upsetting her.

'Hi,' he said, kneeling down beside her. 'Are you all right?'

'Well, it depends what you mean by "all right",' she said sharply, as if it were an accusation. 'There's nothing wrong with me except that I'm pregnant.'

Paul was silent. He stared at her, and then down at Sylvester, as if he were the responsible party.

'Well . . .' he finally managed. 'Well, that's great. That's really great. I mean, when did you find out?'

'This morning. I've been sick a few mornings. I don't suppose you were awake enough to notice. So I went in for a test on the way to work.'

'Were they all right about it at work?'

'Are you kidding?' she exclaimed angrily. 'They want to get rid of me.'

Paul looked surprised. 'They can't do that, can they?'

'Not legally, not outright. But they have enough ways to make you want to choose to leave. Mary handles all the personnel stuff, and she's in cahoots with the partners. I went to ask her about maternity leave and by the time I got back to my desk Marsden was on the phone wanting to know if I was serious about my career, because generally he found that mothers with small babies did not manage well in the law.'

'You mean Mary just told him straight out that you had asked about maternity rights? They can't do that.'

'Maybe not, but they did.'

'What did you tell him?'

'That I am serious about a career in the firm.'

'Just that? You didn't tell him to stick his face in the paper-shredder?'

'It's about relationships, Paul. I need to keep my job. We need me to keep my job. How are we going to manage with a baby, if you're trying to be an artist and I haven't got an income?'

Paul resented the implications of this question, but let it pass.

She took a tissue and blew her nose.

'We'll be all right,' said Paul as warmly as he could manage, squeezing onto the couch with her. 'It's not all bad. We do want a baby. Babies are good. It'll be fun. We'll manage.'

'That's all very well. But how? Are you going to stay at home and look after it? Because that's what it looks like.'

Paul paused and thought. Looking after a baby couldn't be all that hard. They slept most of the time, and he could get on with his work then.

'Well, if necessary, yes, that's what we'll do,' he said.

She looked at him in surprise. 'Do you mean that?'

'Sure,' he said with unfelt conviction.

'Anyway, no, I didn't tell him to shove his nose in the paper-shredder, or anywhere else. I just thanked him for his advice and then typed up a verbatim account of the conversation, in case it goes to a tribunal. For an intelligent lawyer, he really is an idiot.'

An hour later, as Paul was making the dinner, Jan called him urgently back into the living room where she was watching the news. As he came through the door he saw Meriton's face on the television. Paul felt instantly diminished in stature and confidence. His stomach contracted, and muscles throughout his body began to ache. He looked at the clock and calculated that the national news had finished and this was the regional roundup.

Meriton's face shrank to a small inset portrait, while in the main picture an earnest young reporter, her dark hair blowing in the chilly wind that swept through the civic square, was speaking to the camera from the steps of Clayforth's Museum and Art Gallery.

'Yorkshire boy Stephen Meriton has built up an international reputation as one of our leading artists,' she said, 'although critics have been known to label his work as "bizarre" and "unreadable". One even described him as having "removed the minimal from Minimalism". Meriton's work has rather gone out of fashion in recent years, but all that may be about to change. Here in Meriton's home town of Clayforth, the municipal art gallery will next year be hosting Meriton's first retrospective. And it seems that Meriton's taste for controversy has not weakened. A spokesman for the gallery today announced that, for his exhibition, he will be making a special new work, and that work will be . . . wait for it . . . non-existent. I've got with me Charles Fairbright, a film-maker currently working with Meriton on a documentary about the show.'

The camera drew back to show Charles, wrapped in a smart overcoat and a plain scarf, offsetting his untidy hair. Behind wire-framed glasses he was frowning thoughtfully at the reporter.

'Mr Fairbright: tell us about this new work.'

'Well, Stephen tells me that the work involves a cubic metre of the artist's breath. It is going to be breathed into a container of that dimension, and then the container is removed, and the "shape" of it will be transported to the museum.' He gave a slightly knowing smile: 'But on the way, of course, the breath will get mixed up with the rest of the atmosphere.'

'So by the time it gets here to the museum it won't be there any more? It will have disappeared . . . into thin air, so to speak.'

'Yes, although you have to remember that, according to the artist, the idea will still be there.'

'The idea?'

'Yes.'

'What idea?'

'The idea of the work,' said Charles, with just enough nuance to indicate that he was not persuaded either. 'The shape of it.'

The reporter raised her eyebrows: 'Just the shape of it?'

'Just that.' Charles smiled slightly. 'That's the . . . er . . . work.'

The reporter turned back to the camera: 'We tried to speak to the artist, but he was not available for comment. However, earlier today I did manage to get a few words with the gallery director Ralph Ellis.'

The picture switched to Ellis on the leather sofa in his office, sitting stiffly as though trying to restrain a nervous tic.

'Stephen is one of this country's best-known artists, and we are delighted to be able to host this exhibition, his first retrospective anywhere in the world, right here in his home town.' His face seemed to twitch slightly, but it might only have been a glitch in the editing. 'The work in question has, as I understand it, not yet been made, and it would be quite inappropriate, as I'm sure you will agree, to comment on it before anyone has had a chance to see it.'

'But there won't be anything to see, will there?' asked the reporter.

'Ah, well that, I think . . . I don't think . . . I think it would . . . We will have to wait and see. Stephen is a very serious artist and it would be best not to jump to conclusions before we have . . . before we have the . . . the work in front of us.'

'But people are bound to say, aren't they, that this is more taxpayers' money being spent on elitist art that ordinary people can't understand and now can't even see. How would you answer such a question?'

Ellis attempted a reassuring smile, although it looked more like the effects of stomach cramp. 'Well, as I say, I think we will just have to wait and see. It is, we are told these days, the job of the artist to surprise, and even shock, the audience, and Stephen is certainly no stranger to controversy. Different art appeals to different kinds of people, and I'm delighted to say that later next year we will be having a wonderful exhibition of beautiful Victorian painting, based around our own extensive collection, and this will be part of a rich and varied programme throughout the year.'

The reporter was back on the steps of the museum. 'Well, as the director said there, we will just have to wait and see. But whether there will be anything to see when the exhibition opens remains to be seen.'

As the programme reverted to the studio, Jan laughed contemptuously, but Paul stood motionless in the doorway, unheeding of tomorrow's local weather. A non-existent work of art. Why hadn't he thought of that? While he had been on a fool's errand to try to capture reality through all the microscopic detail of everyday life, there was Meriton with the genius of simplicity: the power of the image of life, symbolised in the artist's breath, drifting out into the atmosphere; the reality of the idea remaining present, on show, really there; and yet with the purity that only an idea could have.

Paul was impressed. He was jealous. And he was inspired.

5

December

Through the tall windows of the cafeteria, in the half-light of the short winter days, a raw wind could be seen pulling at the trees along the perimeter of the college grounds. Inside, the grey blinds were linked by paper festoons, bunches of balloons made the most of their brief existence ahead of the college Christmas lunch, and the air was thick with the smell of institutional meat and vegetables.

In the centre of the room, however, the mood was serious and intense. Hannah was flushed with anger, as if someone had blasphemed, and Anand was talking loudly about solipsism and the end of hope. Forsaking their usual cliques, the students had come en masse from the lecture theatre, bound together by an electric thrill of uncertainty. Had the speaker just confessed to a crime and, if so, should he be denounced? Or was he guilty of no more than ill manners, like belching in public, which might amuse as many as it offended? Had he blurted out a family secret, or had he bravely named the elephant in the room? United by an unspoken need to explore what they had witnessed, they pulled several tables together as their forum for discussion.

For the previous hour and a half they had been listening to Jason Presteigne, one of Horton's London contemporaries. Horton had scheduled the lecture as a light, end-of-term treat, in which the aspiring novices could learn at first hand about the life of a successful, practising artist.

Presteigne, in check shirt and torn jeans, lank brown hair falling around his gaunt face, had given an illustrated account of his short life's work. He talked quietly in a faraway tone, his narrative addressed to the floor except when he turned to face the screen. Like many artists of his generation, his quest for certainty had found no anchorage outside the narrow circle of his own experience, and by a spiralling reductionism he concluded that the locus of reality must lie somewhere within the compass of the human frame. But where other artists used their own bodies as sculptural material, or swallowed endoscopic cameras for the contemplation of the inner self, he had wanted to capture the sense of the human organism as a whole. He had experimented fruitlessly for several months with images based on spare ribs, and then dabbled in cremation. A work entitled *Seven ages of man* ended with an urn containing what were rumoured to be real human ashes, although for legal reasons this was denied. He had contemplated joining the school of artists who mutilated their own bodies, but, as he explained to the class, his wife had objected that she could not stop the children biting their nails if their father was cutting off his own fingers. He found solace therefore in disfiguring the bodies of others, and producing constructions made of, or at least purporting to be made of, various of their bodily fluids and other by-products. The students, seated in half darkness, gaped in silence at the vile and sometimes violent slides. They could almost smell the foulness, while the intertwining themes of grim horror and artistic acclaim seeped through the theatre like poison gas.

When it was time for questions, it was the Christians who led the charge.

'I am still not clear,' Anand began, seizing the initial silence, 'what you are hoping to achieve with all these mutilated and befouled bodies. What is it that you are trying to say?'

'All my art,' Presteigne declared vaguely to the parquet, 'points towards the question, "Who am I?" But as that isn't a question that anyone can really answer, it pushes you off into other directions, like "Is that really a dead body?" and "How much do you think this stuff is worth?" So, one way or another, it deals with the ultimate questions of life.'

'Are those really the ultimate questions?' Anand persisted.

'Sure. "What's it made of?" and "What's it worth?" – that's what most people ask these days.'

Anand shook his head as he tried to formulate a response. Stuart took advantage of the hiatus, calling out: 'But do you think this kind of in-your-face material is really going to last the test of time?'

'It's for today,' Presteigne replied matter-of-factly. 'So long as people buy it now, or stick it in their galleries, I'm not bothered. The future's not my concern. The judgement of history is all a matter of perspective, anyway, innit? The difference between fact and fiction is a personal thing. And values depend on your standpoint, so who's to say what's good or bad?'

Hannah was flushed deeper red than normal as she waved her hand. 'You seem to be deliberately choosing to work in provocative and apparently intentionally distressing materials. Is this really necessary? Isn't it possible to explore the same ideas by more normal means?'

Presteigne's answer had been so astonishingly frank that it had even broken into Paul's trance-like mood as he grieved over his latest work, which was buried in his bag, which in turn was hidden under his folded coat beneath his seat. His whole body jerked as Presteigne replied: 'It's a big, bad world out there and you gotta get yourself noticed.'

Horton, sitting to the side of the podium, grinned broadly and nodded, but the students collectively straightened themselves in surprise, as if Presteigne had gratuitously insulted their mothers.

Hannah, like the others, was taken aback for a moment, but stumbled on: 'But surely . . . it can't just be careerism? There must be some kind of allusion in your choice of materials, some artistic meaning in why you choose one rather than another?'

Presteigne was of sufficient stature in the art world not to be subject to no-smoking signs, and lit another. He slowly put the lighter back into his shirt pocket and shrugged slightly as if he did not properly understand the question: 'Don't knock careerism. Gotta eat like everyone else.' He reflected for a moment, pulling on his cigarette, then added pleasantly, 'And, hey, it worked.'

There was a silence. He looked round the room, for the first time making eye contact with the students, sensing that he had not fully carried them with the force of his argument. He added, more loudly, as though English were their second language: 'You gotta make your mark. Gotta get yourself known. No point poncing about doing "art" . . .' – his index fingers shaped the inverted commas – '. . . if nobody knows who you are. Who are the guys making the money now? Who? Is it the ones doing "art" and maybe getting into a mixed show once a year down the back alleys in Cork Street, or the ones who are making a splash, making a noise, getting themselves noticed, getting talked about? You guys don't like it, you need to get straightened out. You want to make it as artists, you gotta think about how you make it as artists. "Art" is OK, but marketing is everything.'

'Warhol,' Gary affirmed sagely to no one in particular, nodding his head at his boots, which were resting on the back of the chair in front.

In the cafeteria, Hannah was asserting loudly that art was a gift and should be valued as such. 'Art is one of the defining elements of civilisation. It separates us from mere animals. Art is one of the things that bind society together. It's a way of creating communities of understanding. Artists are there to serve other people. It shouldn't be mocked, or exploited so cynically like that.'

'Trouble is,' said Nick quietly, 'much as you may hate the guy, he is right. He's succeeded. He's got himself known. Everyone takes him seriously. So now he's one of the people who define the art world and says what's art and what's not; what's in or out. I mean, like he says, there's no point producing great works of art if no one is going to know about them or look at them. And how do you get yourself known these days?'

'But what is the point of producing works of art at all if they mean nothing?' asked Anand, his spiky quiff trembling with suppressed anger. 'The whole thing is so sterile.'

'Actually, I'm not sure those bodies were sterile,' said Nick with a smile.

'You know what I mean. It is more art about itself, about the artist, and it just ends up being ugly and offensive.'

'Maybe that's how he understands reality,' Martin suggested.

'But in that case, he has to check his line of reasoning, and if necessary, his starting point,' Anand replied. 'As human beings we have a concept of beauty. But you can only have a concept of beauty if you know a reality outside yourself. If you have no confidence in a reality outside yourself, you have no grounds for recognising beauty. It's all just yourself. It is what it is. You have no grounds for wonder, and no grounds for hope. You end up with nihilistic ugliness and, as you saw, cynicism of the most naked kind.'

'And the reality is,' added Hannah, not averse to stating the obvious, 'that we do have a sense of beauty, and a sense of morality.'

'But what are you objecting to?' Paul asked quietly. 'The art, or the ideas?'

Various heads turned in surprise to find him among them. He was sitting towards the back of the group, hunched forward, chin in his hands, elbows planted firmly on top of his bag which lay across his knees, covered once more by his coat. 'Presteigne thinks reality is just physical, and his only way of getting at it is through his own body and what he experiences. But I guess the problem for him is that it's hard to make a positive, attractive image from the human body that isn't either pornography or kitsch. So pain is the easier way to go.' He paused before adding: 'That's what's so interesting about Meriton's new thing: it seems to be all about a kind of pure, sort of spiritual reality, but he can only do that without the human body; just the human mind.'

There was a brief moment of confusion. The cafeteria had never witnessed such a positive reference to Meriton or his work.

'Stone me!' said Martin. 'Are you a fan of Meriton, now?'

Paul smiled slightly. 'Not a fan. But I liked the idea of his latest piece. It sounds very pure. And very real.'

'Beurgh,' said Martin. 'Meriton comes breathing over me, I'll punch his lights out.'

'No, no, no!' Nick called across the group with mock sternness. 'You can't attack Meriton. That's Paul's idea.'

Martin looked surprised but was always willing to accept a challenge: 'Well, we'll see who gets there first.'

Paul smiled again and shook his head.

Nick continued: 'Anyway, I'm not sure they are that different. It's like I said: it's all just avoiding looking into the abyss. Presteigne gets you hooked on his gruesome materials to deflect you from asking embarrassing questions about the fact that it doesn't mean anything. Meanwhile, Meriton floats off into the purity of the ether for exactly the same reasons – he's hoping to find some meaning up there because he doesn't think there is any down here among all the inconveniences of daily life.'

'Like getting a degree,' Martin suggested, 'and getting a job.'

'And keeping some sense of moral integrity,' snapped Hannah.

✎ ✎ ✎

Paul trudged down the path from college, through the iron gateway, and towards the bus-stop. The wet pavements glistened in the light of the street lamps. By going at a steady, slow pace he hoped to continue to avoid drawing attention to the painfully heavy weight in his shoulder bag. Inside was the most beautiful object he had ever made, but he could not show it to anyone.

Inspired by the news of Meriton's planned work, he had swung back again to the idea of seizing reality in its essence rather than its detail. The bird-woman had been intended to combine a simplification of form with a celebration of life. Perhaps he could go further, paring down a natural form to such a pure elegance that it would retain nothing more than a hint of the living reality of the original subject, transcending the particularities of daily existence to convey an experience of beauty that was almost spiritual in its elementalism.

Sticking with the idea of birds, for the simplicity of their form and their freedom in flight, he had fashioned a tall, gracefully curving, upright form, carved for now in soft stone, although ideally it would be cast in bronze and polished to the highest possible sheen. It was reduced to an almost completely abstract design, tapering in above the base to a point so narrow it was hard to believe that it could support the upper section and keep its balance. For above it, the form filled out as it moved slenderly upwards, before tapering again and shooting, with one huge beat of its wings, vertically into the air.

Then, leafing idly through a history of modern sculpture in the library before Presteigne's lecture, he had found his work, in all the pristine beauty of its polished bronze incarnation, attributed to one Constantin Brancusi, and made some sixty years previously. Paul had never heard of Brancusi and, as he stared at the photograph and felt the wave of disappointment crashing once more within his head, he had no desire to learn more. He closed the book slowly and solemnly, as though it were a book of remembrance, and replaced it, clutching the shelf for a moment to let the dizziness pass. When he recovered, he opened his bag discreetly and wrapped his scarf around his sculpture and then covered it with his jumper, so no straying eye might know the depths of his ignorance, nor the heights of his ability.

He safely negotiated the distance to the bus-stop without meeting anyone, but was surprised to find Sheena waiting there.

'Hello,' he said. 'You're going the wrong way.'

'I know,' she said simply. Wrapped in a man's overcoat that reached almost to the floor, and swathed in a large woolly hat and her long scarf, she seemed even smaller than usual, and more withdrawn.

'You off anywhere exciting?'

She paused, and the silence hung so heavily that it was plain that she was unwilling to trust Paul with an explanation. She looked at him edgily and then seemed to muster a degree of defiance as she declared: 'I've joined an evening class.'

'Oh really? What are you studying?'

Another pause.

'Life drawing.'

Paul looked at her vulnerable form, and felt a trickle of compassion as understanding dawned on him.

'You saw my stuff at the crit,' she said weakly. 'It was pathetic. It's all right for you: you're good at it. But no one's ever taught me. I'm never going to learn to draw here, so I found an Adult Education class and I'm going to learn there.'

'Good for you,' said Paul simply.

They returned to an awkward silence. Sheena was too embarrassed even to ask Paul to keep her secret. Paul could not think of any further encouragement to offer that would not also give away his opinion of her drawings. Sheena stepped into the road between the parked cars and peered out for a sign of her bus. Paul took the opportunity to rest his bag on the floor between his feet, and rotate his aching shoulder. He thought about the statue's beautifully formed, long, slow curves, the contrast between the small base curving up and in to the narrow hip, and the large upper section opening out from it, soaring up in exaltation, slightly concave on one face, before ending in the sharpest point he could fashion. He was suddenly tempted to show it to Sheena, as a gesture of solidarity amidst the humiliation of her self-revelation, and perhaps so that at least one person in the world could admire it dispassionately before it was thrown away. However, her bus arrived and she bade him a subdued farewell.

As the bus turned the corner, Hannah came rushing along the road.

'Was that the 67?' she panted.

''Fraid so.'

'Bother.' She blew clouds of warm breath as she recovered from the exertion of running. Paul stamped his feet to encourage circulation, and looked up idly at Hannah's flushed cheeks and mass of hair bursting out from under a beret. He had never warmed to her bossy certainty, but she had a confidence in her self that at least made him feel safe.

'So you weren't that impressed with Presteigne, then?' he asked.

'I thought it was awful,' she said briskly, as if surprised that there might be an alternative opinion. She added apologetically: 'That level of cynicism just makes me cross.'

'I don't disagree with you.'

They both gazed in the direction of the buses, but none was in sight. Paul wondered if he had the courage to open the conversation that was nagging at him. He took the plunge.

'My parents are Christians.'

'Really?' She looked surprised and pleased. 'What kind of church do they go to?'

'Oh, Baptist. Old-fashioned, simple kind of church. Pews, preacher, hymns. Nothing remotely arty.'

'It didn't persuade you.'

'No,' he said simply. 'Never seemed relevant, not to the things I was interested in.'

'That's a shame.' She paused, in recognition of Paul's diffidence. 'My church was always strong on relevance, thinking, using your mind, being in touch with the culture and all that. And very strong on the arts.'

'So what do they think of you going off to art college?'

'Fine. They're very supportive,' she said. 'It was never an issue. Creativity and art – they're not intrinsically sinful or anything, so we enjoy them. And – I'm afraid it can sound a bit pompous – we try to redeem them for God.' She smiled apologetically.

Paul returned her smile. 'We need a lot of redemption here.'

He remembered Horton's snide joke about nuts that needed to be cracked.

'Don't you ever just want to hit back?' he asked.

'I'm sorry?'

'Don't you ever want to hit back? You want to redeem art, but it's not in your control. They control it. They decide what's "in" or not. What's OK. Don't you ever just want to fight back against Horton and Meriton, not to mention Martin and Gary and the others?'

'Oh, they're all right,' Hannah said. 'They're irritating at times, of course, and condescending. And yes, that hurts when it happens. But we're probably all like that from time to time. And anyway, unfortunately they're not always wrong, are they? It's not easy for me to admit, but I decided in the end that Horton was right. I like my videos, but they do need something extra. Something to give them a bit of . . . zing.'

Paul smiled again and fell silent, idly prodding at his bag with his foot.

'Do you mind if I ask you something?' Hannah said.

'No. What?'

'What's in your bag?'

Paul looked up sharply at her.

'It's obviously very heavy, from the way you've been carrying it all day,' she continued. 'And you seem very protective of it. I don't suppose it's gold bars, and it's unlikely it's just a lump of concrete. I just wondered . . . I'm sorry. I'm being nosey, but there you are. I was just wondering.'

Paul agonised for a minute. He wanted to close the episode as quietly as he had closed the library book and put it away as though it had never been opened. He had been momentarily tempted to show the work to Sheena out of pity, but nothing in him really wanted to reveal what he had done. But neither did he feel Hannah deserved to be treated rudely.

'It's another disaster,' he said quietly. 'Another great work of profound genius that turns out to be worthless.'

'What is it?' She seemed genuinely interested.

'I'd rather not . . .'

'OK.' There was a pause. 'It's just that you do such varied things. I never really get away from plants and flowers – except for the odd snail. I was just interested. And from the weight of it, it's obviously quite something.'

Paul slowly bent down, unzipped the bag, peeled back the jumper and scarf, and stood the piece up on end.

'Brancusi!' Hannah gasped. She clapped her gloved hands and hopped from foot to foot, held her hands to her mouth, then clapped them again. It seemed for a moment as if she might embrace Paul, but then thought better of it.

'That was the name I found in the book this morning,' Paul said.

In the half-light of the street lamps Hannah walked all the way round the sculpture, admiring its dramatic curves, its minimal articulation, its refined balance in its zestful, upward sweep, full of confident hope.

'It's amazing!' Hannah exclaimed. 'You did that? And you didn't even know about Brancusi? You created that all on your own? That's incredible!'

Paul gave a reluctant gesture of acknowledgement that was lost in the darkness.

'What are you going to do with it?' she asked breathlessly, as she came to rest.

'Drop it in the bin with the other things.'

'You can't do that! It's wonderful. It's great. It's beautiful.'

'It's embarrassing. That's what it is. It's just a copy.'

'That doesn't matter. It's one of the most beautiful things ever made.'

'But it's not authentic. It's not mine.'

'But it's still beautiful.' Hannah returned to staring at it, while Paul turned hurriedly to check if a bus was in sight.

'Could I have it?' Hannah asked quietly. 'I mean . . . if you're really going to throw it away.' She turned even pinker. 'I mean . . . I would buy it off you, but I haven't got much money to give you.'

'You don't really want it.'

'I do. I love Brancusi. I've always loved that piece. Although,' she added with rare humour, 'I'd rather have the polished bronze version, if you want to do that as well.'

Paul smiled.

'And I'm never going to own one myself, am I?' she continued. 'It's beautiful. Oh, please don't throw it away. If you really don't want it . . .' Her voice almost cracked with tears. 'I would love to have it.'

Paul looked at it, and then looked at Hannah. It was the first time they had ever really made eye contact.

'You can have it,' he said.

6

January

Meriton had retreated to the kitchen. It felt as though barbarian hordes had invaded the temple and driven him out. In the studio Dave and Shunt were setting up extra lights. Meriton flinched every time he heard a bench being moved. Meanwhile, the van sent by the museum was outside in the road, its impatience vibrating through the floor and up Meriton's legs. Meriton had conceded to the economics of television that, as the crew were at the studio to film the creation of the work, they might as well film its transportation on the same day. But the driver, clearly moonlighting from his more regular job as an underworld enforcer, had been sent too early, and was registering his dissatisfaction by leaving the engine running.

Somewhere outside also was the pair of clowns that Ellis's secretary had dredged up from Sheffield. Due to a lack of precision in the booking, Mime OK You're OK had arrived in full Pierrot costume with whitened faces, and Meriton, in a paroxysm of fury, had sent them away to find alternative clothing.

Meriton leaned against the cooker and tried to clear his head for the task ahead. From one perspective it was no more complex than blowing up the paddling pool when the children were small. But from the perspective of his career as an artist this was a landmark work, and he wanted to savour all the richness of transforming the ordinary into the ineffable and absolute. The sound of Charles's voice, offering unnecessary advice to his crew, kept cutting through his attempts at calm, and instead brought to mind rancorous memories of the snide tone in which Charles had discussed the project on television. Meriton resented the fact that no one at the museum had consulted him before making the announcement to the press; but he took particular exception to the mocking slant that the reporters had put upon it. He had received no support from Ellis or from Charles's boss. Ellis, under orders from Sir George, had argued that Meriton should be glad of the advance publicity. The television company had refused to accept Meriton's complaints about snideness of tone: all their reporters spoke like that.

'All right, Steve?' Charles's bumptious voice called down the hallway.

Meriton grudgingly emerged and threaded his way amongst the work benches. After phone calls to several manufacturers of air beds and beach balls, he had found one that made inflatable toy dice and was prepared to undertake a one-off commission for an inflatable cube with straight edges precisely one metre long. The result lay now on a table, top and bottom vacuum-flat, two sides folded in and two squashed outwards as triangles, spot-lit from three angles like a Rembrandt crib. Around and above it stood a metal framework marking off the eight corners of the one-metre cubic shape.

Meriton looked with distaste at Charles whose knitted tank top made him seem particularly immature today.

'OK. All set?' Charles commanded, hoisting himself up on a bench, legs dangling. 'Camera rolling. You just go ahead when you're ready, Steve. On with the magnum opus.'

Meriton sat down at the table, suddenly overwhelmed by the smell of hot dust from the lights. He looked round in distaste and was surprised to catch the eye of Shunt, locked inside his headphones, who gave him a thumbs-up and mouthed 'Good luck', as if Meriton were sitting an exam.

Meriton closed his eyes and tried to block out thoughts of the crew, the van driver, the mime artists. He opened the mouthpiece to breathe into it.

'Actually,' said Charles, leaning back lazily, one leg now crossed over the other and hands clasped round the knee, 'I'll just get you to talk about this a bit before you start. You just talk back to me. I'm out of shot, so the viewer will be seeing you. OK?'

Meriton sat back and sighed.

'OK. Well, can you just tell us, before you start . . .' – the wheedling sneer had returned to his voice – '. . . what this work is all about?'

Meriton looked at the camera, but Dave signalled with this thumb for him to look at Charles, which he reluctantly did. 'This is a cube, one metre each side, made of clear plastic. I'm going to be breathing into it until it is fully inflated. The corner locations of the shape are already identified.' He indicated the metal gantry. 'Then I shall slowly cut along the edges of the plastic and remove the sides, one panel at a time. This will leave a perfect cubic metre of my breath in the space that is precisely defined by this construction.'

Meriton paused, and Charles leaned forward, releasing his knee and indicating with an impatient circling of his hands for Meriton to say more.

'We will then be moving the work to the gallery for the exhibition.'

He paused again.

'How will you be moving it?' Charles prompted.

'The gallery has engaged two mime artists who, as specialists in this sort of work, will carry the shape very carefully out of the studio, into a van, and then in the van to the gallery.'

'Right,' said Charles. 'Don't worry about the pauses. We can edit them out later. But my question was really, "What is this work of art all about?" You've told us how you're going to make it, and transport it, et cetera. But . . . er . . . well, why? What's with a work of art you can't see? What are people supposed to take away from this?'

Meriton eyed Charles levelly. 'There are many ways to approach a work of art. We all bring our personal baggage to a work of art; we see in it all sorts of things; we take from it what we want. I don't think it is for me to tell other people what the work will mean to them.'

'Oh, come on,' Charles burst out. 'You can't expect viewers to buy that. You must have some idea what the work is about.' He leaned further forward and spread out his hands to indicate a smorgasbord of meanings that lay before them. 'You must be able to give them some clue what to make of it!'

Meriton glowered at him. 'If the question is, "What does this work mean for me?",' he began, 'it raises for me, in a new way, the age-old issues of life, of reality, being here and breathing, being alive and yet passing away. It is about individuality and continuity, being separate, with your own identity, and yet knowing you are part of the world around you.' His mind was beginning to work. Putting aside the irritation of Charles, and the unblinking stare of the camera, he began to feel again the potential of the idea behind the work. 'It's also about the possibility of purity, the simplicity of the essence that is provided by an idea, in counterpoint to the messy and often disappointing complexity of daily life; the reality of that idea despite the fact that you can't see it; the beauty of its simplicity and its eternity. And to me it's about the glory of the power of the human spirit, the human mind, to imagine and to reflect and to know – all supported by such a simple and basic thing, which is our life-breath.'

Charles was rocking back on his bench, clasping his knee again and fixing Meriton with a quizzical look. 'All that in . . . this?' he asked, nodding his head towards the folded plastic on the table.

'Yes,' Meriton snapped. 'All that . . . in there.' He stared angrily into Charles's round, childish face with its arrogant, mocking smile, and whatever self-control he had been exercising gave way suddenly as he added: 'And frankly, if you, as the director of this programme, haven't got the wit or imagination to see it, or the intellect to understand it, then perhaps you should be back on *Blue Peter*, and not pretending to make a documentary for grown-ups on art that you clearly cannot appreciate.'

Charles's rocking came to a temporary halt. He wagged his

head slightly from side to side in the manner of one conceding that Meriton might have a point, while he calculated how this brief tirade could be worked into the programme. Meriton turned suddenly to stare into the camera, and Dave recoiled as though caught by the evil eye. Shunt seemed to be dancing to music on the headphones as he hopped from foot to foot in delight, convinced that Charles had received a verbal blow to the chin.

'Now, if we can begin?' Meriton said sharply.

He bent forward to the mouthpiece and halted to compose himself. Then he began to breathe into it. He closed his eyes to shut Charles out of his peripheral vision. He breathed slowly, and the cube moved fractionally, as though disturbed in its sleep. He breathed again, and again. Ten, twenty, thirty breaths. He opened his eyes, expecting to see it taking shape, but there was little to show for his efforts. The cube was made of heavy-duty plastic, so that it would not collapse later during deconstruction. In addition, Meriton realised that he had not calculated how many lungfuls would be required for one cubic metre. He was clearly going to be there for a while. The studio was silent apart from the sound of breathing, the creaking of the plastic as it began to unfold, and the van's engine grumbling outside in the road. Dave focused on the video image; Shunt, awestruck at the privilege of being witness to such a moment, gripped the sound-boom with unconscious ferocity. Charles returned to rocking gently backwards and forwards. Like Meriton, he was only now realising the prospective length of this operation. He fell to wondering how few seconds of airtime they could get away with before they cut to something more telegenic.

Every few minutes Meriton paused to clear his head of dizziness.

After twenty minutes the cube was soft and spongy, and Meriton's mind was becoming suffused with the meaning of the piece. As he returned to blowing, he felt uplifted with thoughts of the elemental quality of breath, the magic of life itself, the beauty of purity. After half an hour the cube was noticeably swelling towards its full shape. Meriton, now slightly light-headed, closed his eyes again and continued in his transcendental state, the simplicity of the action of breathing contrasting with the multiplicity of reality. A confusion of images came to mind: a younger Pam, moving lightly and charmingly through the throng at the opening of her first solo exhibition; the children, innocently young, playing in the garden; the children, now grown up, home for Christmas just past, but disappearing back to London for the new year; Ellis's floppy silver hair and cold handshake; the grey corridors of the college, punctuated by half-baked examples of students' work; the sorry hopelessness of the student who kept coming up with other people's ideas; the van outside and the two mime artists in idiot's clothing.

'I don't want to interrupt here, Steve,' Charles's voice cut in.

But it was too late. Meriton had forgotten to stop. The plastic cube was taut, pressed up into the gantry and beginning to bulge through the gaps on all sides. And a metal arm had found an unsuspected weakness in one of the seams. As Meriton opened his eyes, his mouth still over the mouthpiece, there was a long, long, long, rasping, high-pitched elemental expression of flatulence as the cube depressurised. Time seemed suspended as it squealed and wheezed and groaned.

Charles shrieked with laughter and thumped the table several times. Dave and Shunt smiled patiently but, in the absence of contrary instructions, continued to capture the scene. Meriton at first tried to stem the flow with his finger, but gave up and watched the shape collapse clumsily, the rude exhalation eventually giving way to a low squeak and then a long sigh of relief before finally coming to rest.

'The authentic voice of modern art, eh, Steve?' Charles boomed joyfully, as if justice, long denied, had finally been granted to him. 'We'll put that one in the Christmas outtakes!'

Meriton looked at him bleakly, said nothing, and walked past him across the studio. He returned with some duct tape and repaired the leak. It looked like a bandage on a wound. The cube had lost its perfection. But perhaps, Meriton thought, it worked out just as well. The plastic itself would be discarded, symbolic of the imperfect, material earthiness that would be removed to leave the purity of the intangible idea.

Still without a word to the crew, Meriton set to re-inflating the cube, his eyes open this time. It quickly began to resume its shape, the top plane angling up and the sides gradually straightening. As it neared completion there was a ruck in one of the corners. Meriton blew harder to shift it, but it would not come straight. He puffed harder still, feeling the strain in the glands under his ears. He grew slightly red in the face and began to feel light-headed again. He broke off for a moment, then recommenced his attack. Three, four, five more breaths and then, with a slight creak, it straightened. The seams were neat, the corners crisp, and they met the arms of the gantry with a precision that was beautiful in itself. It was perfect: a metaphor for the ideal, and yet composed of the breath of human life.

But there was a higher perfection to come. Without ceremony, Meriton stood up, took a Stanley knife from his pocket and sliced along the front top seam, then along the sides and across the far edge. As the top panel came loose he held it firmly with his free hand to prevent it falling into the space of the cube, then removed it, up and away, laying it on a bench behind him. The other faces held their shape. He repeated the procedure with the side panels, supporting them so they did not fall forward into the sacred space within. Finally, he slid out the base, cautiously, so as not to disturb the air above.

He laid the base panel with the others and took a step back to gaze at his handiwork. 'And there,' he said reverentially, 'you have it.'

The four of them stood and contemplated the space in a silence broken only by the van continuing to throb outside.

'Or not,' said Charles, hoping to provoke another tirade. 'Are you sure it's still there?'

'Of course it's still there. The breath is there; the shape is there. Just because you can't see it, doesn't mean it does not exist.'

'It does sound religious,' Charles sneered.

'We just have to use our minds to think, and our imagination, if we have one, to wonder at the poetry of it,' said Meriton. 'Now, let's see if the mummers have returned.'

Mime OK You're OK were sitting contentedly on the steps outside the studio, sharing a cigarette and nodding laconically to the driver's list of complaints, which was extensive. They had driven up from Sheffield early in the morning to avoid the rush-hour traffic on the motorway, and had taken the opportunity, when sent off to find a change of clothes, to find breakfast as well. Despite their initial bruising encounter with Meriton, they were feeling relaxed and at peace, glad of a commission that broke from the normal round of infant-school parties. They were especially pleased to be earning an extra fee for appearing on television. Their unappreciated costumes were in a suitcase, and, taking their cue from the irate Meriton, they had obtained matching black jeans and black roll-neck jumpers. However, the command to remove their face paint had seemed like an insult against their profession. So they had attempted a compromise, wiping off the worst of it, but retaining a pallor appropriate to their comic solemnity.

They left their suitcase inside the front door, and Meriton led them to *Breath*. They bowed silently to Charles, Dave and Shunt, whom Meriton cursorily introduced, and nodded sagely as Meriton explained the task. In traditional fashion one of the mimers was tall, thin and sombre; the other short, round and comic. Meriton turned to dismantling the gantry, leaving just four small right angles of masking tape on the table, which had been placed in advance to mark the bottom corners of the work. Meanwhile, the taller of the two mimers went through some limbering-up exercises while the other, unable to resist the presence of the camera, pretended to pick something up, juggle with it precariously, and catch it within inches of it crashing to the floor.

The mime artists took their positions opposite each other across the bench. Meriton was ready with a metre rule, but they did not need it. They put their hands flat on the faces of the cube, felt round its corners and then, satisfied that they had identified all three dimensions, each slid the back of his left hand along the workbench to get underneath the work, and grasped the right vertical with his other hand. They looked each other in the eye, nodded one-two-three, and slowly raised the work, inching sideways to be free of the bench. Meriton and Charles opened the double doors, while Dave panned round and followed the procession, Shunt obediently at his heels. He held the sound boom over Dave's head, although there was nothing to record other than the shuffling of feet. As he edged towards the door, Shunt looked back and made a mental note of which bench the work had been on, determining to return later to try to cadge it from Meriton. To the artist it was probably no different from the other benches in the studio. But to Shunt it was like an altar of transubstantiation. In the living room of his flat, just the brush of his fingers on it would connect him to a transcendent realm.

'OK, hold it there,' Charles shouted as they emerged into the street. The mimers halted, their heads turning in surprise, but their hands in perfect stillness.

'What's the matter?' demanded Meriton.

'Nothing,' said Charles. 'Just need to check. OK, Dave?'

'Yeah, think so.'

'Right, well, if you two can just pop back inside for a mo, we'll get another shot of you from outside as you come through the door,' said Charles breezily.

'Are you mad?' said Meriton.

'Just need another angle. For editing,' Charles explained. 'Insurance. Won't take long.'

The air was tinged with the smell of chemicals from the paint sprayers who, across the street, were nudging each other and pointing at the new entertainment. Dave and Shunt stepped outside and the mimers backed indoors again. A minute later they re-emerged, feeling with their feet to negotiate the steps. Safely on the pavement, they stopped to rearrange their hands, moving their right hands to the bottom corners, and the lefts to the upright. The short one paused in mid-manoeuvre, supporting the work with his knee while he exaggeratedly wiped perspiration from his brow and winked a solemn, dark eye at the camera. Dave backed ahead of them as they checked left and right before stepping off the pavement and walking round to the back of the van, Dave and Shunt going backwards up the ramp towards the interior of the van.

'That's great,' Charles announced. 'Thanks, everyone. Now we need to get Dave out, and shoot the move from out here as you get into the van. A single moving shot from the doorway right round into the van. So if you two could just move back to the doorway . . .'

The mimers, at the bottom of the ramp, raised their eyebrows and wagged their heads in mock exasperation. The short one for a moment disengaged his right hand, leaned his shoulder against the vertical face of the work and drummed his fingers in irritation on the plane of the air. An angry shout from Meriton, however, brought him abruptly back to attention, and he and his partner manoeuvred back to the building again.

The paint sprayers had been joined by a small crowd of T-shirt printers and local passers-by as, in a single, seamless, stately progression, like Duccio's *Maestà* carried in triumph through the streets of Siena, the mimers carried *Breath* out of the building once more, back to the van, and up the ramp. They shifted their hands to grasp the bottom four corners before stooping and entering the van, where they perched gingerly on the built-in benches that covered the wheel-arches, leaning slightly forward to preserve their distance.

The driver, rising to the occasion, slammed the doors with as much force as he could muster, and turned the handle to secure them.

'Cut!' shouted Charles. 'OK,' he said to the driver, 'we're going to get a shot of you driving off from here. Then, when you get past that side road, I want you to stop and reverse up again, and we'll shoot from the other end of the street, coming up to the end and turning out. OK?'

'No, it's not OK. I've been sitting on my backside for hours here. I need to get home.'

'Actually, you're right. We should have done this earlier with the van empty. But just do it, will you, and then it's done, all right?'

The driver stamped round to the cab, mentally adding to his list of complaints as he climbed in. He rammed the vehicle into gear and moved off. In the back, the mimers swayed slightly, but held their shape as their entire bodies responded to the jerky driving. Three minutes later the van was back where it started, and Charles, Dave and Shunt were moving themselves to the other end of the street, Dave and Shunt umbilically linked by the sound boom and the camera.

When they were settled, Charles gestured the all-clear and the driver, whose curses now encompassed his onlookers, employers, and ex-wife, advanced purposefully, changing rapidly up to third gear as knocking-off time beckoned. He was therefore obliged to make a smart emergency stop as one of the panel beaters, returning from a test drive, came out of the side road with the carelessness of one accustomed to the quiet life of a cul-de-sac, and confronted him bonnet-to-bonnet. In the back of the van the mimers, their hands still a precise metre apart in the air, were powerless to resist the laws of momentum. They instinctively turned in the air to protect their cargo, but landed inelegantly, one atop the other, sliding forward until their heads collided with the partition to the driver's cab.

There were ironic cheers from the watching mechanics, whilst Meriton cried out in disbelief. He ran up to the van and threw open the rear doors. Mime OK You're OK were lying where they had fallen, their hands still vainly attempting to hold their shape, but facing upwards instead of towards one another, and clearly no longer a metre apart.

Meriton gaped speechlessly, and they, keeping their torsos perfectly still, raised their heads to stare back as, with pounding feet, the camera crew arrived. Dave, the hint of a smile around his mouth, needed no bidding to keep filming, lingering over the pathetically hopeful smile on the faces of the mimers, before pulling back to take in Meriton.

'That's a bit unfortunate,' said Charles. 'Which of them has got it, do you think?'

Meriton bit his lip, and then suddenly lashed a fist against the van door. With a kick at the bumper he turned on his heel and strode back into the studio, slamming the doors behind him. Dave's camera followed him and lingered soulfully on the closed studio while the sound of the van driver's remonstrations against the panel beater drifted over the top of the van.

'OK,' said Charles to the mimers. 'I think that's probably the sign for you to get up now.'

They were reluctant to let go of their shape. Extricating

themselves carefully from the heap, each in turn rolled lightly to his feet and they resumed a seated position opposite each other. They looked at Charles with eyebrows raised expectantly.

'I don't think so,' he said. 'I think you lost it somewhere in there. But thanks for trying.'

Still wanting to salvage what they could, they each gravely set down their now separated burdens on the two benches before stepping out of the van.

A moment later one of the doors to Meriton's studio opened, their suitcase spun through the air onto the pavement, and the door slammed again.

Charles was already on the phone.

✎ ✎ ✎

Meriton spent the next morning in frustration. Having seen himself and his work mocked on the ten o'clock news, he had spent the end of the evening kicking and thumping furniture that had already been thoroughly kicked and thumped when he got home, and threatening Charles with an evisceration worthy of Eric Horton. Now he wanted to shout at someone, but Charles's mobile was not answering, and the programme director at NorthEast was said to be in meetings all day. The only targets offering themselves up to his fury this morning would be the students on his studio visit.

Pam had remained quiet, if amused, while the furniture was punished the previous night, but over breakfast together in her bedroom she had broached the possibility of his making a replacement work.

'It's not that simple,' he grumbled, making a conscious effort not to vent his anger on her. 'It never is. Everyone knows it's a replacement. It's not the real thing.' He chewed noisily on his muesli, as he sat across the small table from her.

'Rodin did multiple versions of some of his sculptures. I do editions of my prints. It doesn't mean people can't enjoy each copy individually.'

'But they're meant for multiple editions,' he said, stabbing the butt of his spoon down into his knee. 'If someone sees one, they know there are others like it, and it doesn't affect the way they look at it. But if something is a one-off, it always has that uniqueness – the moment of creation, the hand of the artist on it. If it's destroyed, you can't just make a copy and pretend it's the same thing. It isn't. Everybody knows it isn't. People don't engage with it like the original. They see it as part of a story about what happened to the first one. So the whole thing becomes about something else, a distraction. They focus on telling the story, and not on what the original was about.'

At college Meriton forced himself to go through the routines of collecting the post, making coffee and sitting at his desk, before gripping the phone. But Charles was still not answering, and the boss at NorthEast continued apparently unavailable. Denied cathartic release, he strode along the corridor to the studios to unleash some thunder on the students, a mood already perfectly expressed in the black suit that today was offset by a pristinely smart black shirt and black tie.

He had clung to a vague hope that the students might have been in the pub the previous evening and missed the news. But the giggles followed by an instant hush in the studio told Meriton otherwise. Gary, marooned at home by acute shortage of funds, had been playing on the computer in his room with the TV on in the background. He had been alerted by the tag line at the start of the news:

> *And later in the programme: the case of the disappearing artwork. Internationally renowned artist Stephen Meriton's latest work seems to have disappeared into thin air!*

Gary had thoughtfully slipped a video into the recorder and captured the rest of the programme. First thing in the morning, his colleagues with access to the editing suite had isolated the relevant section and, in the interests of both education and recreation, made it available on a continuous loop in the student common room.

In the studio they braced their mental and emotional faculties for an onslaught in which neither Giotto nor Pollock, nor any master in between, would have been likely to escape censure. Downstairs, Paul was glad to find the atrium deserted as he struggled through the main doors, a large, shapeless burden strapped to his back.

✎ ✎ ✎

For the first week of the Christmas holidays Paul had borne an outward resemblance to Rodin's *Thinker*, albeit without the heroic musculature and graced with a small tuft of beard, which he continued to stroke thoughtfully, as if such outward reflective behaviour would produce inner revelations. Scarcely bothering to dress, he sat, head bowed in endless, hopeless reflection. Confusion possessed him once again, about his work, about his purpose, about the value of anything he did. Self-loathing was interspersed with resentment towards Meriton; and the resentment was aggravated by jealous admiration for Meriton's work. The elemental engagement with reality in Meriton's work, the seen and the unseen, the material and the spiritual, haunted Paul's brooding. Meanwhile, Meriton was also bravely breaking boundaries of what counts as art: that a work of art need no longer be an object that you could see and touch and trade. It was a challenge to collectors to put their money on trust in the artist.

But Paul had no idea what to do to emulate Meriton's example. In brief moments when the torpor of depression abated, it was replaced by paralysis driven by panic as he remembered his glib promise to Jan that he could stay at home and look after the child. She had begun to shop for baby paraphernalia, and the implications of their situation and the weight of potential responsibility had begun to take form in his mind. He had, in effect, until Easter to come up with his big idea, if he was to have any chance of turning it into a worthwhile exhibit for the final show. Otherwise, he would soon thereafter find his prospects as an artist squeezed into the uncertain spaces between bottle-feeding and nappy-changing.

Given his inability to think for himself, he decided at the end of the week to spend the rest of the holidays reading in the public library and at home. At least that way he would fill some of the more egregious gaps in his knowledge of the masters of modern art, seeking some germ of inspiration in their work while at the same time hoping to avoid a recurrence of the horror of finding his most beautiful and uplifting creation already existing, illustrated and attributed to someone else. Over Christmas he ploughed through the Post-Impressionists and Fauves. As the new year dawned, he began on Cubism, and an idea coalesced in his mind.

Sitting on the sofa at home he was looking at a photograph of Picasso's sculpture of an absinthe glass. The commentary in the book was excited about the use of mixed media, that Picasso had used a genuine silver absinthe spoon, which lay across the top of the glass, supporting a model of a sugar-lump. However, it was the glass itself that caught Paul's attention. Part of it was represented by the solid material of painted bronze to show its outer contours, but part of this outside skin had been cut away so that the hole conveyed the glass's translucence. Through this hole was visible a solid circle representing the surface of the liquid inside the glass. But Picasso could, Paul reasoned as he swirled an inch of cold coffee in a mug and pictured himself as a poverty-stricken genius in Montmartre, have represented the whole liquid by a solid, showing it all from the outside, through the hole, although it might then have been unclear where the drink finished and the glass started.

But what was that shape of the liquid? In a glass you could see it because of the transparency of the container. But in many containers you could never experience the whole of the shape within, because the density of the material prevented you seeing in. You could never see the shape of the coffee in the mug, because the mug itself was solid. You knew the shape was there, and you could imagine what it must look like, but you could never experience it directly. What if, instead of casting the outer appearance of an object, you cast the inside, the shape it contained, making solid and visible what was normally immaterial and unnoticed?

He felt suddenly energised, and determined to develop the possibilities of this idea now at home, so he would have something to show when term started. Two days later he took delivery of a sack of plaster from a builder's merchant, and began casting the inside of a mug. From this he learned two lessons. First, plaster bonded well, and the only way to extricate the work of art was to smash the mug. He put the pieces in a plastic bag and hid them at the bottom of the dustbin, to avoid awkward explanations when Jan got home from work. As he looked at the liberated lump of plaster, he realised that there would be a tinge of nostalgia in this line of work: the cast represented the object by its absence. The original was broken and thrown away. Only the cast remained to give it a ghostly presence, evoking the reality of the physical and the invisible; existence and time passing; life and death; presence and memory. Secondly, however, he discovered that once the model was free of the mug, it was impossible to tell what it was. A neutral observer might guess it was a model of a tin can, or just a surplus blob of plaster. Clearly, he would need to choose objects and containers that had sufficiently interesting and distinctive internal shapes and surfaces to allow them to be recognisable from the castings.

From the local charity shops he accumulated a variety of cast-off domestic items, including a teapot, a milk jug and a flowerpot. Then he had found, abandoned on a street, a chest of drawers, from which he retrieved one of the drawers. For this last he graduated to working with concrete. It caught a pleasing effect of the wood-graining and the head of the screw that held the handle, but it was difficult to lift. He envisaged the possibility of casting the whole of the inside of a cupboard, but that would have to wait until he had registered success with a smaller idea, and could persuade someone to lend him a fork-lift truck.

He hunted round the house for interesting ignored spaces: under the stairs, under the table in the hallway where the phone sat, the inside of a computer monitor, the space around the books on the shelves in the living room. He stopped at the last of these. He could take a bookshelf, load it with books, and pour concrete into the space that was left behind and above them. Removing the shelf and the books, there would be not just a model of the space – an objectification of something real but unseen – but an evocation of books that were no longer there. The references were endless: lost books, unwritten books, books never returned to the library, censored books, banned books, books as lives, lives that were cut short, lives that were never lived.

He set to work sketching out some ideas, drawing freehand the spaces that he envisaged. It was surprisingly difficult to visualise space without the objects that defined it. But that, he supposed, was the point.

In a rush of creative excitement he secured a battered, chipboard bookcase from a second-hand furniture shop, and a job lot of paperbacks from a charity shop. Laying the bookcase on the floor in the garage, he stacked the books onto one of the shelves, and encased them in concrete. He spent a restless night, excited and anxious to bring this work to birth, a creation he knew was going to be worthy of a degree: an unseen reality brought into three-dimensional form. Literally, the concretisation of the invisible.

In the morning, after Jan had gone to work, he took a hammer and cold chisel to the bookcase, which offered little resistance. Within minutes the cast was free of its casing. He heaved the block over so that the books were exposed. They were firmly held by the concrete, which had seeped into the pages. Roughly he began to rip them out, throwing the pages and covers onto the floor around him. It was laborious and physically demanding. The concrete had bonded well with the tops and spines of the books, and the pages could only be torn out a few at a time. He worked steadily, not noticing the time passing. When the pages had gone he began to pick minutely at the remaining scraps that were embedded in the concrete, taking pains not to damage the detailing of the shapes of the spines.

When Jan came home at the end of the afternoon she found Paul seated on an upturned bucket in the centre of the garage, surrounded by a mass of paper and fragments of chipboard and melamine, as though he had been trying to exorcise a literary neurosis. But in his eyes was a bright gleam she had not seen for a while.

'Come and look,' he said, and she picked her way down the three steps into the garage, and applied her lawyer's mind to the detritus on the floor.

She looked doubtful. 'Well, it's to do with books and bookcases. And concrete.'

She inspected the block of concrete on the floor more closely.

'Is this it?' she asked, trying to sound as matter-of-fact as she could.

He nodded and beamed inarticulately.

'Hmmm. It's the cast of some books. No?'

He shook his head.

'No. Wrong shape,' she conceded. She looked again at the block, flat on most faces and irregular and jutting out on one. 'I'm sorry,' she said. 'I'm a bit tired. You'll have to help me.'

'It's the space *around* the books,' he explained excitedly, and took her step by step through the process.

At various points she remarked 'Oh', in the sense of 'Why would you do that?' but Paul was not listening.

'Interesting,' she said after a while. 'And certainly original.'

✎ ✎ ✎

With difficulty Paul carried the work into college, wrapped in a blanket and tied to his back with a harness cut from an old backpack. He chose a later bus in the hope of getting a double seat for himself and his package. Arriving in the studio, he found Meriton already advancing down his row. He was equally surprised to find Nick next door in his workspace. Nick seemed buoyant. As Paul manoeuvred his burden onto his work table, Nick explained that he had come in to college partly to enjoy the fallout from the previous evening's news. But also, in the centre of his space, he had installed his blue plaque: 'Nick Thompson worked here 1996–99'.

'I thought I'd test it out,' he told Paul, gesturing with his head towards Meriton. Paul went round to Nick's space, leaned up close and ran his finger lightly over the plaque. It seemed to have been cast in resin and painted. It had a pleasing authority: the circular form was simple, rational and complete; the lettering understated.

He returned to his own space, unwrapped the concrete block and shifted it slightly from side to side, to see if it offered a particularly engaging angle. For the final show he would mount it at eye-level, so that the viewer would see it as from within the wall on which the shelf had ostensibly hung.

Meriton was sneering at Martin's comic-book drawings of commandos that were pinned to his workspace. The words 'juvenile' and 'dishonest' resounded before he moved along the line.

He came to Nick's plaque. He looked at it and then at the artist, who rose politely from his chair.

Meriton demanded: 'Is this a joke?'

'Not at all,' Nick replied pleasantly.

'Well, what is this garbage? This plagiarism? This nonsense?'

'Really, I must ask you to moderate your language, Mr Meriton,' Nick said in an even voice. 'Plagiarism is a very serious charge.'

'You know very well this is not an original idea.'

'Indeed, so. And that is why it cannot be plagiarism. This is a new work *in the style of* Gavin Turk. Just as Raphael painted in the style of Perugino, and Van Dyck in the style of Rubens . . . no one, alas, worked in the style of El Greco, but I am working in the style of The Turk. After all, it does have my name on it, not his.'

'Rubbish. Just juvenile play-acting. Turk failed his degree with this . . .' – he gestured at the plaque – '. . . and so will you.'

'Absolutely,' Nick answered enthusiastically. 'Which is what makes my work so interesting. Gavin Turk was scorned by his judges but is now an acclaimed artist. So my work addresses this college directly: will you make such a gross error of judgement again, or are you open to learn from history?'

Meriton's fury, already stoked by Martin, was so intensified by Nick's insolent pleasantness that he could find no response beyond an exasperated explosion of air. His eyes narrowed, he turned and bore down on Paul. 'And what new thing do you have to regale us with?'

'I've been working on this,' Paul said with unaccustomed confidence, placing his hand on the concrete block with paternal pride. Meriton stopped suddenly, his eyes widened as he stared at the work, then he frowned, bent down and examined it closely.

He's not saying anything, Paul thought with relief. He's definitely interested.

He watched Meriton peering at the work. His mind buzzed with the profundity of his creation. He also felt a reluctant warmth towards Meriton. He remembered Jan laughing the previous evening at the footage of Meriton's accident, and his own contrasting sense of wonder at the sight of the mime artists emerging with the shape between them, the almost religious ceremonial formality of the occasion, and the grandeur of the conception in all its simplicity.

'It's an attempt to capture empty space,' Paul explained. 'To make the invisible visible. It's the cast of the space round a bookshelf. It takes an ordinary everyday space that we often overlook and displays it as an object in itself.'

In the next workspace Nick, sitting at his table, flung his head back and covered his face with his hands. Meriton straightened up sharply.

'Is this also a joke?' he demanded.

'No,' Paul replied earnestly. 'It's entirely serious. It's an attempt to catch an intense sense of reality. It makes the viewer more aware of their surroundings, gets them to see the forgotten spaces of everyday life, and to think about them from a new perspective. To see them in a new way. At the same time, I thought it also has something about it of absence, something of loss.'

'I mean,' Meriton said heavily, 'does the name Rachel Whiteread not mean anything to you?'

'No,' Paul said hesitantly.

Meriton raised his hands in despair, paced up the aisle, spun round and returned. 'How can you claim to be a serious artist and not know the name of Rachel Whiteread?' he exploded. 'As your colleague says . . .' – he gestured to Nick, who was now audibly banging his head on his work surface – '. . . plagiarism is a serious offence. But so too . . .' – he flung out an accusing finger at Paul and raised his voice to near shouting – '. . . is pig-ignorance. If you cannot come up with a single original idea of your own, you should at least do us the courtesy of informing yourself sufficiently about the art of your own day so that you don't bring ridicule on us by trying to pass off, as your own, ideas that are already world-famous!'

Paul went through what was now becoming a familiar routine. He felt his heart stop and then just as suddenly restart, pounding violently. He felt hot. He wanted to swallow, but his mouth was dry. He clutched the back of the chair for support. He was aware of everyone in the studio determinedly looking away, but he felt as though they were crowding in upon him, with blank, zombie-like stares, sensing his vulnerability and pressing in to suck out all remaining hope and to draw him in to join the living dead.

He blinked back tears to look again on his creation. It was so rich in associations. It spoke so poignantly of absence and loss. It was almost transcendent in making the numinous tangible. Between the tears he noticed tiny, multicoloured fragments of paper still caught in the concrete, final vestiges of books destroyed, lives unlived. Like watching a child teetering on the edge of danger, he wanted to reach out, call out, throw himself forward, do something to save it.

'I wanted to capture the reality of reality,' Paul explained distantly, 'to show how everything is so concretely . . .' – he paused apologetically at the pun – '. . . there. So real. Even empty space. I thought it was, in some way, a kind of counterpart to your own work.'

Meriton seemed to swell to twice his size.

'My work?' he shouted. 'You're comparing this travesty to my work?'

'Well, yes,' Paul continued faintly. 'I'm really sorry about the accident, by the way. I saw it on television last night. I could see it – your work – was about a kind of unseen reality, about getting behind the details of everyday existence towards a kind of purer reality, like a kind of spiritual realm. Mine, I thought, is similar but different, about concretising something that is real though you don't see it, but in this world.'

Meriton was beside himself. 'There is nothing remotely similar between my work and your tepid pastiches,' he bellowed. 'How dare you even mention them in the same breath?'

He paced up the aisle again, once more temporarily bereft of the power of speech, this time by the effrontery of a youth who pretended to understand his work and presumed to offer him sympathy. He was also stung by the repeated suggestion that his work was religious. With all the morning's frustration pouring forth, he spun again and returned to face Paul. 'Do not imagine for one moment that, because you and I find ourselves temporarily inhabiting the same time and place in this college, that there is any connection, *any* connection, between my art and whatever word we use to describe what you do. You have produced nothing but tawdry and simplistic imitations of the work of people who are far greater than you. You have so far evinced nothing of your own. You have expressed nothing original, from which I can only assume that there is nothing original within you for you to express. Are you really so ignorant of anything and everything that surrounds you? Or are you genuinely just trying to hijack other people's creativity for your own cynical amusement and profit?'

Meriton seemed to tire suddenly. His voice fell. 'Your work has as much originality as a plate of cold chips – and you have the hope of a cat in hell. Frankly, if the college didn't need the fees, I'd have them throw you out here and now.' He leaned in closer and dropped his voice still further for the conclusion. 'Can I make myself any plainer?'

Tears welled up in Paul, stinging his eyes. He pushed past Meriton and ran out of the studio, barging open the swing doors without regard for who might be beyond them. Students on the stairs looked on curiously and Phyllis Garnet, clutching an armful of essays, obligingly pressed back against the banisters as he stumbled down and through the foyer. He careered along the driveway and out of the college grounds. Halfway along the street he suddenly stopped and screamed, a long, wordless howl of torment, of loneliness and failure and despair. He grabbed hold of a tree and kicked it as hard as he could, pummelling it with his fists. Two women at the bus-stop peered round at him but, living close to an art college, they were inured to such behaviour and resumed their conversation. Paul walked on, kicking every tree and lashing out at road signs with his fists. He turned left and right at random along the terraced streets, heedless of his direction. Some of the houses were dilapidated, others newly renovated with plastic window-frames and colourful stone cladding. Over the previous couple of years Paul had been inside a number of them that were rented by students, but today he registered nothing through his tears.

He walked round the quiet streets in a frenzy, trying to evade the pursuing army of demons who would consume him if he stopped, and continuing to lash out sideways with his fists at any solid object. In occasional lucid moments he looked back and recognised faces among the demons, and cursed them furiously. He cursed Meriton for his cruelty and contempt; for his refusal to be impressed, or surprised, or sympathetic; for his refusal to recognise the obvious connections between their work; and for his vicious willingness to humiliate Paul in front of the whole group. He cursed the college, for its layers of deceit hiding behind the bland grey walls. He cursed its students, who laughed and conspired and betrayed. He cursed his parents for the smallness of his upbringing and their blinkered church; the insincerity of his English teachers; the lack of ambition of his contemporaries. And skulking at the rear of the malign horde he saw his own demon. He cursed himself: his laziness and ignorance; his failure to discipline himself, to work harder, to read and to study. He cursed his confusion and his lack of answers. He cursed his insecurity, his yearning for recognition, and his dependence on others.

He finally came to a halt by a featureless brick wall, screamed again and beat it with his fists. He raged against himself for a wasted life: to have nothing to show for ten years of education but a worthless degree in a subject he did not care about; to have finally achieved the dream of going to art college and then to leave with nothing; to be twenty-seven years old and find that life had passed him by. If he could start again, he would go about it so differently. But he had missed it.

He paused for breath, turning and leaning back against the wall, banging his head against it rhythmically. His anger against the college reminded him of Hannah standing at the bus-stop, flushed and angry at Jason Presteigne. And yet her anger didn't make her despair. She somehow absorbed Horton's mockery. Paul felt jealous of her too: jealous of her self-confidence, of her ability to distinguish criticism of her work from criticism of herself, of her certainty where Paul had only questions.

Paul had rejected God without a second thought when he rejected church and the shrunken horizons of his parents. But now, to his surprise, he found himself seeing a different kind of logic, as though the wretchedness of pain and injustice made God more likely rather than less. He stumbled on to the end of the road where he leaned his back against the window of a corner shop, clasped his hands behind his head, forcing himself to bow, and he prayed inarticulately to a God he doubted. With images rather than words, he called out for justice, for inspiration, for salvation from despair, for help. He made no promises: he had nothing to offer. But he asked.

He looked round into the shop window, seeing not the symmetrical piles of fizzy-drink cans and cheap biscuits, but his own reflection. He scowled at himself, suddenly aggressively critical. He was embarrassed by his pathetic beard, a symbol of the sham he had been playing. It typified his childish ignorance and play-acting.

It stank of weakness. It invited humiliation and bullying. He determined to shave it off as soon as he got home. And with that moment of determination came a greater, if ill-defined, resolve. He could do nothing about Meriton, or the college, or his fellow students, or his past history. But he could take himself in hand. Looking past the beard, he resolved to refuse any further humiliation. From now on he would stand up for himself. He would justify himself. There must be some originality in him somewhere. And there must be some way of fighting back. There must be some creative use of their weapons, some way to play their game and still win.

He stared harder into the shop window, fixing his reflection in the eye. He forced himself to remember Meriton's shouting, his own tears, Nick's head banging on the work surface. He made himself feel again the shame as all the other students looked away and, at the same time, seemed to press in on him with their cold, dead faces. But never again. He had no idea what he might do but he felt the stirrings of obstinacy once again, a hint of returning strength that was unexpected but real. Taking stock at last of his whereabouts, he turned back towards the college.

✎ ✎ ✎

Nick and Bridget, coming down from the studio, saw Paul on his own in the cafeteria and decided to take pity on him. Bridget commiserated quietly with Paul, who barely responded, so she resumed what was evidently a lengthy explanation to Nick of her experiments with digitally manipulated photographs.

They were interrupted by Martin and Gary, who, without

invitation, sat themselves at their table. Martin looked suspiciously at Paul, and then leaned very close to Nick and Bridget.

'We've got it,' he whispered.

'Syphilis?' asked Nick innocently.

'No. Well, at least I haven't.' He looked round at Gary, but Gary's eyes were already in the middle distance, and his mind somewhere beyond that.

'We've got it. The answer. The ultimate taboo.' He leaned even closer, until his nose was nearly in Nick's stubble. 'You saw that thing outside Meriton's studio? The accident.'

Nick and Bridget nodded.

'Well, we do the same thing. Chances are, he's going to make a replacement, or have something else taken up from his studio. We find out when it's being transported, and we intercept it. Stage an accident; take the van.'

Bridget blinked in disbelief. 'You're going to steal one of Meriton's works?'

'Exactly.' Martin's eyes were wide with excitement.

Gary, who had moved his focus to the ketchup bottle in the centre of the table, nodded slowly.

'And serve him right for slagging off my drawings,' Martin added. 'Carefully crafted cartoons of wounds and entrails, oozing with irony, and he says they're juvenile.'

'Just unpack this for me a bit,' said Bridget. 'Setting aside the practical issues, like the involvement of the police, and the fact that Meriton will be assessing the work for your degree: how is this a work of art?'

'It's taboo-breaking, innit? It pushes the boundaries: theft as a work of art. Finely crafted, deeply moving, thought-provoking. And if the police get really sticky, we can always hand it back at the end: it's only theft if you mean to keep it. And anyway, we're only doing what we've been taught to do.'

Martin looked scathingly at Paul, who was sitting opposite them practising origami with his serviette, and apparently unmoved by the brilliance of the proposed undertaking.

'Well, it's novel, I'll give you that,' said Nick. 'And it will certainly problematise the relationship between artists. If you're expecting Meriton to stand above the fray and judge this performance dispassionately as a work of art, well, I think you'll need to arrange him a personality transplant first.'

'Yeah, well it's Horton as well as Meriton doing the judging. And you heard Horton a while ago – well, maybe you didn't, if you weren't there. But I suggested we might pull a bank robbery, and he was quite up for the idea.'

Bridget and Nick both looked unconvinced as Paul blew into the rear end of his creation and it expanded into the shape of a frog.

'Very impressive,' Martin sneered, then turned back to Nick. 'We need to get hold of this guy who's making the documentary on Meriton, and cosy up to him. See if we can get him to tell us what he's up to. Meriton's bound to be working on something else in place of this pile of nothing he's just lost. He's not one to just sit round and feel sorry for himself. And they're bound to want to film it being moved like the other one, in case anything else happens. So we just need to pick a place on the route – can't really use that same street, as they're going to be on the lookout down there. But if we stage some roadworks round the corner, and then jump 'em with some guns . . .'

Nick and Bridget looked alarmed.

'Well, you know, replicas. But convincing.'

'Does that count?' asked Paul, who was concentrating on trying to make the frog jump across the table by flicking down on its rear end, but the paper of the serviette was too thin.

Martin looked round, surprised to find that he had been listening. 'Does what count?'

Paul's gaze continued to concentrate on his frog. 'Does it really count if it's not serious? If you're not really going to steal it? Or if you're not using real guns?'

'We are artists,' Gary suddenly volunteered, ponderously shifting his gaze from the ketchup to engage Paul. 'We are not constrained by rules. If it's beautiful, it's good.'

''Sright,' said Martin.

'Flaubert,' Gary added.

'But surely, if it is going to be a real work of art, it's got to be serious,' Paul continued, still looking at his frog, and speaking as though teasing out a philosophical conundrum. 'It's got to be real. If you're going to steal it, you've got to really steal it. Really, for real. It's got to be authentic. Otherwise, it's just mucking about.'

'Well, mucking about has its place,' Nick objected mildly. 'It's better than going to prison.'

'And you,' exclaimed Martin, pointing his finger in Paul's face, 'the maker of "tepid pastiches", are not the one to lecture us on what it takes to be authentic.'

'Leave him alone,' Bridget snapped at Martin.

Paul shrugged, unwilling to continue to contest the point. He looked up at Martin and his voice trembled with the emotion of the morning: 'I just feel we're being corrupted. We're losing touch.'

Bridget leaned across and had a go at making the frog jump. Nick and Martin merely raised their eyebrows at each other and fell to discussing whether Horton might have contacts in the East End to help them get hold of replica guns.

7

February

Paul lay on the sofa watching children's television. Around him was a muddle of books from the college library: *Art in the twentieth century*, *The twentieth century in art*, *The history of modern art*, *The story of contemporary art*, *Art of the modern era*, *The key to modern art*, *Bluff your way in modern art*, *The idiot's guide to modern art* and *The only book you'll ever need to read about modern art*.

Stung by Meriton's taunts, and without any other source of inspiration, he had continued to plough through the history of art, looking at the photographs, noting the captions. Some looked familiar from Horton's lectures; others must have passed Paul by in his sleep. But the cumulative effect of these myriad paintings and sculptures, movements and manifestos, worldviews and stylistic arguments, was to further congeal his mental faculties into a homogeneous swamp of self-pity, no breath of wind above it, no bubble of oxygen within, no miracle of evolution to persuade its constituents to spring into spontaneous life. His most creative act had been to shave off his beard. The subsequent daily act of shaving, requiring him to look in the mirror, had proved a useful vehicle to remind him of his resolve to fight back. For whatever resolution he might accrue seemed to dissipate by the evening. He had become, as he had feared, a conceptualist without concepts; an idealist without ideas; an artist who produced no art.

Perhaps, like Nick, he could brazen it out by exhibiting nothing at all: not even a plaque, just an empty space as a poignant representation of his mind and the breadth of his achievement at art college. Whereas Meriton's empty cube had been full of hope in the perfect satisfaction of Platonic reality, his would be an equally complete embodiment of existential hopelessness.

He had heaved his concrete cast into the skip behind the printmakers' Portakabin, and returned home to find Jan in a bristly mood. After a dispute with the senior partner over maternity pay she had little energy to deal with Paul's mood. As he dragged himself in and sagged into the couch, she had peered out of the kitchen door and asked sharply what the problem was. Paul gave her an outline account that cast him sympathetically as a hapless, wounded victim, but his self-indulgent tone had irritated her.

'For goodness' sake,' she exclaimed, gesticulating with a peeling knife, 'you've got to stand up to him. He's supposed to be your tutor. He's supposed to be there to tutor you, to help you. It's your fees that are paying his wages.'

Paul was silent, staring at the carpet.

'Don't you think that's maybe what he wants?' she continued. 'A bit of opposition? Can't you fight back a bit? Sounds to me like he thrives on conflict.'

Paul pulled a face. Meriton might thrive on the bodies of his enemies, he thought, but that did not mean that he respected his opponents before he finished them off. But Paul was also recalling enviously the image of Nick, a picture of self-confident politeness, arguing Meriton into angry silence.

'Well, you've got to do something,' she persisted, raising her voice as she returned to the kitchen. 'You can't pay for three years at art college and have nothing to show for it!'

That, Paul thought, looks exactly like something I can do.

They spent the evening in silence, one angry and the other hurt, slept fitfully, and awoke the next morning feeling little better. The prospective stresses of the day at work did not improve Jan's mood, and the sight of Paul's depressed figure drooping over his mug of tea impelled her back to the attack.

'Surely you can just play their game. Put your principles to one side for a few weeks to get through this, get your degree, and then carry on with the work you want to do.'

Paul did not mention that, at that moment, there was no work that he wanted to do.

'But you have to be strong,' Jan persisted. 'Stand up for yourself, and come up with something you believe in.'

How long Jan continued, with passion and persuasive eloquence, Paul did not know. For he had registered the primary message: he was on his own. He remembered Martin's finger pointing in his face, telling him not to lecture others on authenticity. He heard Gary calling him an arrogant tosser. The figure of Meriton loomed over him, black eyes glinting, bald head shining in the fluorescent lights, telling him that the college should finish with him there and then; he remembered the insulting whistling of Horton as he walked away after suggesting Paul should turn to full-time pastiche. Out of the corner of his mind's eye he saw Nick alternately burying his face in his hands and banging his head on the table. He had noticed Sheena keeping a distance on the pretext of being busy with her portraits, but he had caught her looking at him furtively, as if making a judgement about him. Now even Jan had lost patience.

So he lay on the couch, surrounded by multiple copies of the world's most famous artworks – images that he knew he could not use because they belonged to other people – and confused by endlessly repetitive commentaries which gave the history of a work, a list of its constituent materials, a description of its appearance, but never the heart of what it meant. After reading four accounts of Warhol's cardboard boxes, which he had sedulously hand-painted with the Brillo design, accounts that agreed only in their failure to explain why he bothered, Paul had briefly lost consciousness. When he awoke, the cartoon on television had been replaced by a programme showing children how to draw a portrait. The simplicity of the technique and directness of the task roused in him a faint memory of innocent youth, which felt now as if it had been lived by someone else.

The early evening news came on, and Paul stirred himself to begin thinking about making tea. He moved listlessly around the kitchen, taking in more of the news now that he could only hear the soundtrack. It was followed by the local news: an accident on the motorway, police appeals for help to find a missing child, and the name of Meriton.

Paul returned to his position in the kitchen doorway, and could not now suppress a sense of pleasure as the television began to rerun its footage of the loss of Meriton's work.

Over the long shot down Farlane Street, the newsreader continued: 'According to Sir George Eldwick, chairman of the museum's trustees, preparations are nearly complete for a show which, he said, will put Clayforth on the art map of Europe. Of course, one of the works that won't be in the exhibition is the now infamous work called *Breath*, the so-called "invisible work" that was lost in a traffic accident.'

Viewers were treated again to the choicest moments of Mime OK You're OK emerging from the studio and climbing into the van, the confrontation of van and car, and the sight of the helpless pair piled up in the back.

The newsreader re-appeared on the screen. 'However, it is not all lost, as Sir George explained earlier.'

The chairman's red face appeared, blowing small clouds of mist in the cold wind. The classical façade of the museum appeared behind him to give context.

'It's all good stuff,' he said to the unseen reporter. 'We've arranged to include the van in the show as well, because, according to some people, the work is still in there, you know. And also, I'm pleased to say that Stephen is proposing to make another work, along similar lines to *Breath*. Not a replacement, of course, as such, because, you know, you can't replace a unique work of art like that. But I'm told it will be similar, but also this time something encased in glass. So obviously it will be saying something a bit different . . .'

What the difference was, Paul did not hear. He was standing up straight, his mouth once again hanging open as he stared unseeing at the television, not registering either sight or sound. His final show had suddenly appeared in his mind, fully formed, in a single Gestalt: the shape was clear to him, the form, the meaning, the impact; its unity, and complexity; its intensification of perception, and its multiplication of thought-provoking references. He could not see all the details yet, but he knew that they were there to be found, as surely as the Pig and Whistle was to be found in all its particularity just by walking to the end of the road and looking. Suddenly, he knew exactly what he was going to do. He went to the phone and dialled.

'Nick?' he said. 'I've got an idea.'

8

March

Meriton leaned against a table in his studio and surveyed the glass cube in front of him. It looked to be of light construction, but the metal edges covered heavy sealed joints between the glass panes to withstand the force of the vacuum that had been created within. Next to it was another of the flat-packed plastic cubes into which he would breathe. He would then allow the breath to be sucked into the glass cube through a valve in a bottom corner. This plastic cube was slightly larger than the previous one, to ensure there was sufficient air to completely fill the vacuum.

His decision to make the new work – he refused to acknowledge it as a replacement – was due to pressure from Sir George who had paid him a personal visit a few days after the accident. Anxious not to lose the public relations momentum that the news coverage had gifted them, Sir George had suggested that Meriton should include the museum's van in his exhibition. Meriton had refused absolutely.

Sir George argued that the work was still there in the van, and it would be fun to ask people to look for it. Meriton was in no mood for fun and was easily riled by a suggestion that seemed to add insult to embarrassment. Making no effort to conceal his fury, he denied that there could be any possible aesthetic interest in the van, and reiterated his refusal.

His first objective thus successfully attained, Sir George had played with equal skill on Meriton's resentment in order to persuade him to make a replacement work. He listened with all appearance of sympathy to the artist's complaints about sneering and treacherous reporters, intrusive cameramen and back-stabbing television companies, although through some deeply buried vein of tenderness Meriton made no derogatory comments about sound recordists. Sir George nodded in agreement with Meriton's insistence that every work was unique, and a so-called 'replacement' would be no better than a copy. Then he gradually worked Meriton round to recalling the pleasures of taking the offensive: to answer the laughing hordes with a new work, not a replacement but a parallel one. It would divert attention from what had been lost, and focus visitors' minds on the important issues of life and being, creativity and as many other buzzwords as Sir George could recall.

Sir George left in high spirits after an hour. He had neglected to mention his consultation earlier that morning with the museum's lawyers. According to their advice, Meriton had now renounced any possible claims upon any putative contents of the van, and the museum could do with it as they chose. Meanwhile, Meriton had agreed to make a new work for the exhibition which, whether he liked it or not, would seem to the press like a replacement, and would keep public interest alive ahead of the show's opening. From his office Sir George phoned Ellis to advise him, in a way that was not to be denied, that he should keep the van in quarantine. When the exhibition opened, it was to be placed prominently in the foyer, where it would attract far more publicity than anything upstairs.

Meriton continued to stare at the cube. He was glad he had agreed to do it. It had taken him some weeks to think around the possibilities and settle finally on a title, *Breath of life*, which related to the lost work but suggested something new and vibrant. He had then needed another month to arrange for the construction of the cube. Now he would reluctantly have to negotiate with Charles's diary to see when the work could be made and transported. For in a surfeit of emollient diplomacy, Sir George had also convinced Meriton, quoting the Bard once again, that the best way to overcome the sticks and stones of outrageous fortune was not through violence against Charles, comforting though that fantasy might be, but through high-minded perseverance with the film that would promote his work and ideas.

At the thought of Charles, Meriton glanced at his watch and swore. He had agreed to meet the crew at college, to be filmed in his role as teacher and inspirer of the younger generation. He hoped, without conviction, that the students would at last have produced something worthy of his approval.

He took a last look at the cube. It still carried the idea of the perfect form, but now it would have a different set of connotations: it would be completely filled with the artist's breath, symbolising life and playfully engaging with the idea of inspiration. It would also celebrate the power of humanity to create and communicate in works that were simplified and purified down to only the essential components.

✎ ✎ ✎

Charles strode confidently toward the college reception and asked for Meriton. In the driveway Dave and Shunt were unloading metal boxes of gear. Miss Grimm, receiving no response from the staff-room, phoned the principal's office. Within two minutes Julian Curridge, drawn to the power of television like a child to the sound of an ice-cream van, was in the foyer, greeting Charles warmly. He walked him upstairs towards the staffroom, gladly sweeping up Phyllis Garnet in the corridor to help smooth the conversation.

Garnet, now in her sixties, or perhaps her eighties, fell briskly into step and began to tell Charles the story of when her own painting had featured on television. An arts programme had asked to include her most recent work in a discussion about the significance of size in art. Unfortunately, they had also focused on a Land Artist who was reshaping part of the desert in Nevada. The comparison still irked her, since anyone working with a fleet of earth-moving vehicles must automatically appear at an advantage over one using only a paint-roller.

As the staffroom played no part in the public face of the college Curridge had never felt the need to invest in it, and it spoke convincingly of malaise. Above the picture rail, the grim magnolia paintwork was coming away in large, ragged patches. Below the picture rail, the state of one long wall was mostly masked by a row of filing cabinets of various faded hues, on which were heaped piles of seminar handouts, old prospectuses, health and safety leaflets from the union, and superseded drafts of the curriculum development plan. The chairs, worn and dispirited by years of hard use, faced pointedly away from one another. In the corner was a sink unit, with a kettle that produced hot water tasting as though it had been burned. Most of the staff had brought in their own coffee machines to keep in their offices.

Horton was sitting in a corner when they came in, and did not get up. His previous experience had rendered him adept at handling the press. He gave Charles a restrained wave as they were introduced, and Charles gave him a wary nod in return.

'So where is the great master?' asked Charles, looking round the room as if Meriton might be playfully hiding behind a chair.

'We're trying to track him down,' Curridge explained. 'Can I offer you some coffee while we wait?'

Charles accepted, and after a few moments of Curridge looking hopeless, Garnet sat down and Horton wearily rose to his feet to undertake the task.

'I'm so glad he's doing a replacement piece,' Garnet said brightly.

'It's not a replacement,' Horton called out. 'Don't let him hear you call it that.'

'All the same, I'm glad he's thinking positively again. He's had a hard enough time these last few years.'

'And you like his work?' asked Charles, perching himself on the back of a chair, and inflecting his tone with enough of a note of surprise to suggest that Garnet's own reputation was also now on the line.

'Well, it's interesting work, certainly,' she answered defensively. 'And he brings a lot of gravitas and respect to the college.'

'You don't think he's brought it a fair share of ridicule?' Charles persisted, leaning back and splaying his hands before him as if the case was obvious.

'Certainly not.' Garnet's tone became suddenly heated. 'If you're referring to the tragic loss of his recent piece . . .' Charles raised his eyebrows, as if inviting her to hang herself with her words. 'There is a good long tradition to non-substantial works of art. I'm proud to be associated with him, just as I was proud to be friends with the Non-Productionists.'

'Oh, please, Phyllis,' Curridge exclaimed. 'I thought we had agreed that you would not talk about them. We really do have to steer the students away from that line of thinking.'

'But surely they learn about them in their history of art overview?'

'I think you'll find,' said Curridge, with a sidelong look at Horton for confirmation, 'that we manage to skate over them. It's bad enough trying to keep our funding with what the students actually produce, without half of them giving up making anything at all and still expecting a degree.'

Charles, scenting another story, lounged back casually on his chair. 'Who were these "Non-Productionists"?' he asked, his fingers again shaping the inverted commas in the air.

'They were a pack of . . .'

'They were a group of highly principled artists,' Garnet cut across Curridge, 'who objected to the gross commercialisation of the art-object, and decided, as a challenge to the orthodoxy of modernism and its complacent accommodation to post-war capitalism, to stop producing artworks altogether.'

'So what did they do instead? Get a proper job?'

Garnet missed the bait. 'Well, clearly, if you are not actually producing any work, there is a danger of your being overlooked amidst all the unseemly noise and self-promotion of the art world, and there is of course the difficulty of needing something to sell in order to make a living. So they chose instead to sell certificates which stated that the owner had not bought one of their works.'

'Had *not* bought one?'

'Exactly. They bought the certificate, *not* the work.'

'Except then,' Horton broke in from his corner where he was spooning instant coffee from an industrial-size tin, 'a breakaway group started selling certificates that said that the owner had in fact bought a *non-work* by the artist. So it got a bit complicated, and the artists started falling out with one another about what you could or couldn't do without losing your credibility as a Non-Productionist. Whether you were *not* producing art, or were *not-producing* art.' He handed Charles his coffee. 'Meanwhile some of the people who'd bought the certificates started trading them at a profit, and that really upset everyone. So then they fell out with the collectors as well as each other.'

'But they were very successful in their day,' Garnet chirped.

'Well, their first couple of shows certainly got a lot of publicity,' Horton conceded, 'but then other galleries began to claim to be showing Non-Productionist works when in fact they just had a gap in their schedule, and the market got flooded with unproduced works of art.'

In a rare moment of self-doubt Charles looked from Horton to Garnet, trying to detect a signal that they were making fun of him. But there was none.

'And speaking as an educationalist,' Curridge said severely, 'it is quite difficult to distinguish between an artist who is authentically and programmatically not producing works of art and some lazy so-and-so who can't be bothered to get off their backside.'

'But who does a good line in designing certificates,' Horton agreed.

'So what became of them all?' Charles asked.

'Oh, you know, they were all trying to make money out of empty crap,' said Horton, slapping Charles cheerfully on the shoulder and sloshing his coffee, 'so most of them ended up in television.' Charles did not seem amused. 'Some of them graduated to making pop videos, or running networking events.'

'Henry Holmes adopted a pseudonym, Harry House, and took up flower-painting,' said Garnet enthusiastically. 'So as Henry Holmes he carried on not producing art, but as Harry House he could make some money out of the tourists.'

'Bit of a comedown from cutting-edge, anti-orthodox art-warrior to flower-painting, wasn't it?' asked Charles.

'Well, he always insisted that his flower-paintings were ironic,' Garnet said apologetically. 'But yes, I suspect the irony was a bit lost of some of his customers. I think you probably have to know it's there to spot it.'

Meriton entered the room abruptly, with a verbal expression that might have been an apology for lateness or simply an acknowledgement that he was not alone. He was followed at a distance by Dave and Shunt in full gear. A few minutes later they were making their way up to the Painting Department, to which Curridge had earlier dispatched Marjorie, his secretary, with a curt instruction to ensure the students were looking industrious. In the studio Marjorie had been commandeered by Sheena for her portrait series and was now sitting in the usual spot next to the out-of-order computer, gossiping happily. Sheena peered at her through the viewfinder, giving her a verbal prod when the flow seemed to weaken. Marjorie stopped guiltily when Curridge entered, followed by Meriton. Behind them shuffled Dave and Shunt, who were already filming the drama of the double doors. Charles brought up the rear of the group, peering casually around the large space of the studio.

For the purposes of a documentary that would further his career, Meriton forbore to comment on most of the work on show, focusing only on a small and favoured selection, in which he could at least look interested and about which he could offer some sage advice. He passed without a glance at the Incredible James who was applying red paint to each tiny seat in his stadium, and came to Andreas, kneeling as usual amidst dozens of plastic trays of tesserae, meticulously graded by colour. The life-size poster of the Pollock on the wall beneath Kurt Cobain briefly inspired Meriton with warm memories of his optimistic youth. He was able to pose for the camera with a look of pleasant indulgence as he listened to Andreas, in his accented English, describing his progress so far, the dramatic, existential flicks of paint now re-experienced as a measured, courtly progression.

Crossing the studio, Meriton exchanged a few words with Sheena, and nodded approvingly as she, with some reluctance, brought out her series of portraits. She and Marjorie posed for Dave as if Sheena were taking more photographs. Meriton worked his way up the room, past Gary who was resting his head on his folded arms, and Martin, who appeared to be playing with dolls. In averting his eyes from Martin, his startled gaze fell on Paul, who was applying paint to a large cardboard box. Horizontal bands of red, straight-edged on three sides but curling like speech-bubbles on the fourth, had been applied to all four vertical sides, the word 'New!' reversed out in white on the upper bands. Although it was only partially completed, it was evident from the stencilling that the completed logo between these bands would say 'Brillo'. Struggling with his resolve to act well for the camera, Meriton paused, irresolute, looking across the distance at Paul and then, in disbelief, back at the box. Paul looked up and returned Meriton's stare hesitantly, but then defiantly. Meriton gathered himself together and strode past Paul and round the corner, where he happened upon Anand, who was working on a figure of an Asian child, crouching on the ground, head between its knees, hands behind its head, constructed out of discarded fashion shoes.

As Meriton stopped to talk, Dave and Shunt captured the exchange from one angle then edged round to take in a contrasting view. Charles lingered to run his finger idly round Nick's plaque, and then wandered to the end of the aisle. Martin slid quietly up to him, ostensibly taking an idle interest in the filming.

'You in charge of this crew?' Martin asked.

'Yeah. Charles Fairbright.' He automatically extended a hand, and Martin shook it perfunctorily.

'I hear he's doing a replacement work for that thing that got lost in the van?' Martin began.

'Yeah. Only this one's in glass, so he can't lose it.' Charles laughed unkindly.

'Are you not a fan?' asked Martin.

'Well, I'm making the programme, so yeah, I'm supposed to be loyal. But at the end of the day,' he lowered his voice, 'it is all a load of empty crap, isn't it, though don't quote me on that.'

Martin smiled: 'Gives a new meaning to art with "an air of significance", eh?'

Charles laughed and added quietly, 'And you sometimes wonder which end the air comes out of.'

'So, no chance of this one going astray, I guess?' Martin asked casually. 'Going to risk using the same van, are they?'

'Well, different van, of course. They're now saying the original one's still got the art inside it, so it's suddenly become really valuable and they've had to replace it. And no mime artistes this time, I hope. But otherwise, yeah, same routine.'

'Really?' said Martin unenthusiastically. He was quiet for a moment, but seemed to feel that out of politeness he should keep the conversation going. 'And you going to have to film that too?' he asked, as if it would be an unnecessary burden.

'Oh, you bet. Wouldn't miss that. Just imagine if something else happens.'

Martin smiled indulgently. 'Yeah, that would be fun to see. Is that soon? Can't be long before the show opens now, I guess?'

'Oh, we've got a few weeks. Some time after Easter, I think. Press Office are handling the details.'

Martin nodded abruptly as if this really was as far as he was willing to go with small talk, and continued to stare at the top of Meriton's head as he advanced down the next row of students to another safe bet.

✎ ✎ ✎

The consensus in the cafeteria was that all future studio visits by Meriton should be televised. Students congratulated each other on their escape, whilst those who had been filmed had acquired a new charisma.

Martin and Gary were sitting with the other members of their gang, Eggy and Zapper, their heads very close together across the table. Paul stood in the middle of the room for a minute trying to spy a spare seat before sliding in at the end of Martin's table. Martin broke off what he was saying and looked up suspiciously. He registered that it was only Paul and returned to his conversation.

'They're bound to turn left out of his road and head for the town centre,' Martin explained.

'So we jump 'em at the lights?' suggested the diminutive Zapper, his spiky hair seeming to have caught the excitement of the moment.

'Yes, but what if the lights are green, dodo?' Gary snapped.

'We need a definite way of stopping them. Like roadworks,' said Martin.

'But there aren't any roadworks there,' Zapper objected.

'We create some,' Martin explained with heavy patience. 'There are some temporary lights on the way in from my place to college. If we go out tonight and borrow them, then all we need is a lookout at the end of his road . . .'

'But you need a generator for those things,' Gary objected. 'They're not solar-powered.'

'Well, what then?' Martin demanded angrily. He looked round and saw Paul again. 'Where's Nick?' he demanded.

'I don't know. Probably busy at home, as usual,' Paul said genially. A pause, and then he added: 'By the way, sorry I couldn't help overhearing, but if it's any help, I saw the gas people digging up the road last week, and they have those Stop–Go signs, that you just turn round to control the traffic.'

They looked at him as if he were a monkey who had learned to speak.

'Hey, that's good,' said Gary. 'We could just climb in their compound one night and knock one off, or borrow one from a lorry at lunch-time.'

'Is it urgent?' Paul asked.

'Dunno. Sometime after Easter, according to that Charles guy,' Martin explained. 'We just phone up the Press Office at the gallery, pretending we're him, and ask some dumb question, and get them to tell us. We've got time. Eggy, you make sure you get the video camera?'

Eggy nodded his heavy blond mane solemnly, as if he had single-handedly undertaken the most heroic part of the exercise.

'So, we keep it simple,' Martin explained. 'Eggy's at the end of the road with the camera. When he sees the van moving, he gives the signal, we nip out into the road with some cones and this Stop–Go thing. We stop the van, show them our . . .' – he dropped his voice theatrically – '. . . haul out the driver, pile into the van, and off we go.'

'Are we wearing balaclavas?' Zapper asked hopefully.

'Of course we're wearing balaclavas,' said Martin. 'We can't risk the driver identifying us, can we?'

'And what if some passer-by tries to be a hero?' Eggy asked.

'You've got the flipping camera,' Martin said in exasperation. 'You leg it from the end of Meriton's road to the hold-up, filming all the way. Then if anyone asks what's going on, you just laugh and tell 'em it's a low-budget film – which is true. When did anyone ever stage a daylight robbery and video it at the same time?'

Martin looked round to check if his voice had risen accidentally, but everyone else was still drinking to their success in escaping Meriton's censure. Martin nodded to Paul in the closest way he had yet come to acknowledging him as a fellow artist.

'Cheers,' he said.

'Yeah, cheers,' Gary agreed as he stood up. 'And keep going with those Brillo boxes. You've really got something there.'

Zapper and Eggy laughed unkindly, but Paul smiled and thanked them.

9

April

Meriton took breakfast up to Pam on a tray at eight-thirty, together with the newspaper.

'I'm off to the studio as soon as the physio gets here,' he explained. 'They want to start early and film the whole thing. Hoping for another disaster, I expect.'

'Well,' said Pam cheerily, 'watch out for speeding cars.'

Meriton grunted.

'Anyway, I shall be fully occupied. The physio said we'd try walking along the landing and back. That will be my masterwork for the day.'

Meriton smiled at her as he briefly emerged from his own thoughts. 'I hope . . .' He struggled for words of encouragement. 'I hope it goes well.' He bent over and kissed her.

'You too, dear,' she replied, as she sipped her tea and turned her attention to the front page.

✎ ✎ ✎

'Just like old times,' said Shunt cheerily, but Meriton did not reply. It was only the need to complete the documentary that compelled him to allow Charles and his crew back into the studio, and he was determined not to enjoy the experience.

Dave was adjusting the angle of the lights and Charles looked impatiently at his watch. He had another appointment and this looked too much like footage they had already shot.

'Right, are we ready to roll?' Charles demanded. 'Carry on in your own time.' Then, remembering how long this process had taken the first time, he went outside to make some phone calls.

Dave and Shunt focused on Meriton who set himself to inflate the new plastic cube. He settled himself for a minute, trying to put the crew out of his mind. The two of them seemed to catch the mood and stood motionless, recording the stillness. Meriton began to inflate the cube, the even sound of his breathing accompanied again by the creak of the plastic as it filled. Dave started out wide, taking in the glass cube as well as the flat plastic one, then gradually moving in until Meriton's nose and mouth filled the viewfinder. Meriton was lost in thought, meditating on life and creativity. As before, he had to break off periodically to counter the dizziness, clamping a finger over the mouthpiece. As the cube reached its capacity, Meriton gently closed the valve on the mouthpiece and sat back.

Dave found himself suddenly caught in indecision. Should he follow Meriton, for the human interest of his reaction, or focus on the cube? As a professional he knew he should stick with the human interest; but the mood of the event had temporarily overcome his agnosticism, and he kept the camera on the cube, now invested with sacral significance.

'You guys OK?' asked Charles, returning to the studio and finding them all in silent contemplation.

The moment broken, Meriton seized the plastic cube with a sudden energy and brought it closer to the glass one. He joined the two with plastic tubing, ramming the connectors on tightly at both ends.

'Ready?' he asked, as Dave and Shunt shuffled round for a good angle.

Dave nodded.

There was a sudden screech as Meriton turned the valve, and the plastic cube collapsed with the suddenness of disaster. But Meriton was smiling. The glass had misted up slightly as his warm breath met the colder surface, but he liked this extra detail: invisible as the contents were in the cube, this was evidence of their reality.

'Has the van arrived?' Meriton asked.

Charles went out to look. It was standing in the road, while the driver was peering into Meriton's Corvette.

'It's a shame about the car,' said Charles as he came back into the studio.

'What is?' asked Meriton brusquely.

'Well, it would be nice to have a shot of you turning up for work, you know, ready for a hard day's creating, sweating away over the . . .' – he gestured to the work bench – '. . . whatever. But the car's all wrong. If you were a Premier League footballer going to work, or a city whizz-kid, that would be OK. But it's really not people's idea of an artist's car.'

'But, as I have said to you before, it is an artist's car,' Meriton snapped. 'The truth, Mr Fairbright. Don't lose sight of the truth. Of reality as it is.'

Charles raised his eyebrows and pulled a face at Dave, as if Meriton had broken out in a foreign language. Charles was not inclined to bother with a translation.

'OK, we'll do the same as last time,' he announced more loudly than necessary, as if the room were thronging with noisy assistants. 'Out to the van, shot from inside. Back inside, and out to the van again shot from outside. Only no mime artists this time, right?'

Meriton said nothing.

'Just a man with a van,' Dave murmured.

'Let's get him in then,' said Charles.

As if anticipating further trouble, the driver had shaved his hair back to grade 1, balanced by a day's stubble on his chin. With him was a young lad, thin, pale and biddable. Between them they carried a large wooden crate.

'Taking no chances this time, eh?' the driver said with a dark grin.

'There has never been any question of taking chances,' Meriton answered dourly.

The glass cube was packed inside the crate, a task hindered by the need to allow a clear view of proceedings for the camera. The lid was put in place and tacked down. There then followed the pantomime of carrying the case out to the van, bringing it back into the studio, and carrying it outside again. At this stage Charles realised that the van doors were still closed.

'Cut!' said Charles.

'What?' demanded the driver.

'Van doors, still closed,' Charles explained briefly.

'Well, open them,' the driver barked. 'I want to put this thing down.'

'No. You'll have to take it back inside. I want a single long shot, like last time, all the way out of the studio and into the van in one long pan.'

'I'll give him one long pan,' the driver muttered to his unseen assistant as they edged their way back up the steps into the studio.

The driver deposited the box, went out and opened the rear doors of the van. Across the street, the panel beaters were resting from their labours, welcoming the return of free entertainment.

'OK, in your own time,' said Charles.

'My own time!' the driver continued to mutter. 'Think I'd be spending my own time on this?'

Dave and Shunt stood in the gutter and filmed the driver, his lips still shaping soundless invective, as he backed down the steps. As he passed out of sight, the camera found his assistant nervously feeling for the last step. They crossed the pavement into the road, and finally edged up and into the van. As Dave and Shunt stood behind the van, the driver and lad jumped from the tailgate, folded the ramp into the vehicle and, with professional decisiveness, slammed the rear doors as forcefully as they could.

'Right!' said the driver, panting slightly. 'Are we done?'

'Not quite,' said Charles. 'Like last time, we'll shoot you going up the road from here. Then you'll need to stop and reverse down here again, and we'll shoot it all again from the other end of the road. And then we're done.' Charles smiled encouragingly. 'And, er . . . look out for cars in the side road?'

The driver narrowed his eyes but the presence of the camera constrained his actions. He strode round to the front of the van and started the engine, gunning it noisily to express his frustration.

There was a sharp knock on the driver's window. A figure

wearing a parka, whom the driver had noticed leaning against the wall by the car-body shop, had appeared next to the van.

The driver wound his window down. 'What?'

''Fraid Charles wants you again.'

'Who are you?' said the driver.

'Just a gofer. You know, watching out for the traffic. No more accidents and that, know what I mean?' The young man, his hood pulled up round his face, was looking towards the back of the van, as if afraid of the consequences of delay. 'Anyway, come on, he said he needs you again, before you go.'

'What's he want?'

'Dunno.' The minion sounded impatient. 'Something's not right, I suppose.'

The driver looked in his wing-mirror, but Charles and the crew were out of sight round the back of the van. The driver swore, opened the door, and got out.

The minion obligingly held the door for the driver, then leaned in to the cab and said to the boy: 'He wants you too.' The young lad eagerly jumped down and ran round to the back of the van.

'What now?' demanded the driver.

'Is there a problem?' asked Charles.

'What do you mean, "Is there a problem?"' the driver mimicked.

They looked at each other blankly, and then at the van as the engine revved, the gears crashed, and the van began to move, the driver's door still swinging open.

The driver shouted and began in pursuit along the cobbled road, but the van was already up into second gear. The panel beaters cheered and whistled.

'There is a problem,' said Charles calmly. 'Are you getting all this?' he asked Dave.

'Oh, yes,' said Dave quietly.

The van was already at the end of the road. It indicated right and pulled out of view. As it disappeared, Dave, still following the action through his camera, was surprised to see, staring directly back into his viewfinder from the other side of the main road, another video camera, a tuft of blond hair blowing beside it in the wind. For a moment they stared, like two snipers finding each other in their sights. Then, as Dave watched, the other camera swung to follow the rear of the van and then just as smartly swung back in the opposite direction, the user gesturing helplessly with his free hand.

'Get after him, someone,' shouted the driver, but Meriton had already reacted. Standing in his studio door waiting for the farce to end, he had not seen the hooded figure approach the driver's side. Nonetheless, it was obvious what had happened. He pulled his keys from his jacket pocket and fumbled the way into his car. He reversed dangerously fast up the road, swinging the back of the car into the side road in order to turn and set off in pursuit. But as he approached the junction, a small red Nissan, which the video later showed had lost its number plates, and which had been holding up the traffic in the main road, swung clumsily in a wide arc into the middle of Farlane Street, straddling the white line.

Meriton sounded his horn, and mouthed 'Get out of the way' at the figure behind the filthy windscreen. There was a moment of impasse. Meriton waved his arm, as if to push the Micra to the side of the road, and continued with his other hand to press the horn.

The penny seemed to drop for the other driver. He waved

vaguely, tried several times to engage reverse gear, finally succeeded, and backed cautiously, in another wide arc, out into the main road. As soon as there was space, Meriton pushed past him and, with a thunderous growl of the engine, swung into the traffic. But by this time the van had disappeared.

The red car seemed to think better of trying Farlane Street again, and this time drove straight on, past a group of underemployed navvies who were standing at the side of the road clutching traffic cones and a large Stop–Go sign, and looking at one another in confusion.

✎ ✎ ✎

Later that night the keys of the van were hand-delivered through the letter box of Clayforth Museum and Art Gallery, together with a page of a local map showing where the van could be found. Officers of Clayforth police, to whom the map was handed the following morning, were affronted by the implication that they needed help to find the van. They had already recovered it from a country lane four miles away. The doors were closed and locked, but the packing case and contents were gone.

The museum security cameras revealed only a figure wearing the same parka jacket with its large hood up over his, or her, head. There were no forensic clues on the map or the van, but the helpfulness of the perpetrators in returning the keys, and their self-restraint in not setting fire to the vehicle, were uncharacteristic of professional art thieves.

'Probably a student with a grudge,' suggested Inspector

Greenstreet, his mouth full of sandwich as he sat with his feet on the desk and idly watched Dave's video footage again on a monitor.

'No shortage of them, from what I hear,' said his sergeant, peering over Greenstreet's shoulder and nodding his head knowingly. He had recently arrived on a graduate training scheme, with a degree in film studies to his credit. Although his course had included a module on *film noir*, he was still struggling to find the right tone of world-weary gravitas with which to mask his youth and inexperience.

'But then again, it could be a particularly clever professional, pretending to be a student with a grudge.' Greenstreet sucked in air noisily as he drank his tea, and checked on his watch to see how much longer it was until home-time.

'But it's only a glass box anyway,' said the sergeant. 'Why bother to nick it? You could knock one up yourself in a couple of hours, if you were desperate.'

'Exactly. They return the van, which is by far the more valuable item. And we're supposed to divert our forces to look for a glass box? Meanwhile, all the murderers, drug dealers and estate agents of the town fill up the moral vacuum unhindered.'

Greenstreet swung his feet onto the ground, and leaned forward with a grunt. He put his finger on the screen: 'But who is this lone cameraman, I wonder?' rubbing his finger back and forth beneath the blond mop at the end of the street. 'That is very odd.'

'If he was on a grassy knoll, we'd have him bang to rights,' the sergeant said confidently.

Greenstreet looked round at him with distaste, as if he were a piece of litter that someone had left in his office, then returned to the video. Meriton was impatiently waiting for the red Micra to reverse.

'Nice car,' said the sergeant. 'Wouldn't mind one of them myself one day.'

Greenstreet gave him another look and sighed: at least one could get rid of other people's litter.

'And that red car,' the sergeant continued. 'Got so much muck on the windscreen, we could do him for reckless driving. Do you think he's in on it?'

'Very perceptive. But given there are about a million and a half Micras in the country, and half of those are red, we are not about to waste our colleagues' time trying to track down this particular one, when we could all be going home and having our tea.'

He stretched across the desk for a phone. 'Hello, love. Need to put out a statement about the glass box work of art thing. Just the usual: pursuing all possible lines of enquiry; anyone knows anything about it, or wants to own up to being a serial killer or liking the Pet Shop Boys, just let us know, blah, blah.' He put the phone down. 'Should hold them off,' he said hopefully.

But live coverage of the theft of a work of art belonging to one of the country's few internationally renowned artists was more valuable than that. Dave's film was already running on the news bulletins. Charles had been promoted from the 'And finally' section to become an expert source on art theft. And across the country people were even now trying to find Clayforth on the map.

10

May

Meriton strode through the hall, staring suspiciously at each of the students as they went about the many tasks preparatory to the degree show. Like the police, he had been trying to keep an open mind as to whether he had been the victim of a sophisticated art theft or a stupid student prank. There were certainly some in the college who fancied themselves as urban terrorists and lawbreakers, but he had never thought they had the guts to put their words into practice. Two weeks of police enquiries had uncovered only rumours and suspicions, and Meriton was inclined to start his own investigation.

Most of the main rooms and teaching spaces of the college had been cleared of furniture. Partitions had been brought in to create individual exhibition areas, and a coat of white paint had been applied to every appropriate surface. Some spaces were still empty, but others were already arrayed with the usual run of severed limbs, melted dolls, and collages of deformed human faces culled from tabloid newspapers and medical textbooks. Surreal objects, including a concrete football and a plate of exquisitely carved and polished wooden animal-droppings, were offset by thoughtfully chosen everyday items that, in Meriton's experience, proved more interesting than their accompanying artist's statements.

In the assembly hall, the Incredible James was bent over his model of Highbury Stadium, which had suffered substantial damage in the wake of Arsenal's traumatic exit from the FA Cup. In an expressive and cathartic act James had brought his not inconsiderable fist down on one of the stands, and dozens of small figures were now urgently erecting scaffolding and carrying in supplies for the rebuilding project. But as, with the healing passage of time, despair had begun to give way to reluctant acceptance, James was now delicately placing the tiny figure of Ryan Giggs, waving his shirt as he continued to run round the pitch in front of the now empty stands and blank scoreboard, in permanent celebration of a moment when skill and chance had combined in a moment of triumphant beauty, albeit one James would have preferred not to see.

Further along, an almost bald mannequin's head was having its last vestige of hair removed by a very small lawn mower, which had been glued to its pink surface. It was accompanied by a canteen of brightly shining stainless-steel cutlery, and a heart-breakingly long explanation. Another student was adjusting the tracking on a video that showed her having a tooth drilled. The shape of her mouth filled the screen, the drops of water and fragments of tooth gradually obscuring the camera lens. On top of the video was a photograph of the screaming woman from *Battleship Potemkin*. On the wall behind it a text of several pages mused on the universality of teeth and human suffering. In the next space, behind his child made of shoes, Anand was displaying a series of watercolours of the college buildings: it was not immediately obvious whether they were ironic or not, and Meriton was not inclined at this stage to find out. He was looking for guilty faces, and no one was catching his eye.

He went upstairs into the Painting Department where, on a table next to the computer desk, Sheena was connecting a stack of video monitors, arranged three across and three high, to an accompanying pile of nine video players.

'Where are these students?' Meriton asked Bridget, indicating a pair of spaces on the other side of the aisle. One was occupied only by a name holder, 'Nick'. The other displayed two large boxes, painted like cardboard cartons for packs of Brillo soap pads. Across the top of each face, in blue capital letters was written '24 Giant Size Pkgs.' At the bottom it boasted: 'Shines Aluminium fast'.

Bridget paused in the middle of nailing up a photograph of Tony Blair, from which she had digitally removed all the facial features.

'They said they were going to put their things up at the last minute,' she said with a shrug. 'Although it looks like Paul's done his already.'

Meriton grunted: 'Yes, no need to ask who this inventive genius is. And presumably the other student is holding off displaying his work to prevent him from copying that too.'

Bridget pulled a face behind Meriton's back and reached for her photograph of him, which had been grafted onto a large print of Caravaggio's *Salome and the head of John the Baptist.* Meriton's face was grafted not only onto that of the unfortunate John, but also that of the executioner who was holding it up by the hair for display.

Meriton came upon a student who was struggling to persuade a sewing machine and an umbrella to remain balanced on what was presumably intended to be a dissecting table, beneath a sign saying 'Some chance'. Meriton glanced down at the accompanying text:

> As an artist I am dealing with images in a purely visual sense. The visual idiom allows a nonverbal dialogue with the viewer that helps me to express and find my own identity.
>
> As an artist I am constantly challenging my tools and materials, pushing them beyond the boundaries of what is possible, to create new techniques and processes which are as important as the piece itself.

Meriton shook his head and went to leave the studio. As he reached the swing doors they opened towards him and he was obliged to hold one open as a trolley, borrowed from the kitchens, was propelled through, pushed by Paul. On the trolley were two more very large Brillo cartons, their fresh red and blue paint gaudy and stark against the white background. Behind him came Nick carrying a roll of wallpaper and some paper-hanging equipment.

Meriton looked at Paul as though he were a swatted wasp that refuses to die.

'Surely, this is not your offering,' Meriton began.

'It's OK,' Nick called out with a broad smile. 'He knows all about Warhol.'

Meriton started at the sight of Nick.

Nick saw his discomfort and continued: 'But there is much more here than Warhol. I assure you, this work questions our most fundamental beliefs about the nature of art. When you look closely at this work, you will think Warhol a mere Sunday painter, a conventionalist of the deepest water. Though I say it myself, and it is not my work, this will quite transform your way of looking at even your own work – although, of course, I appreciate that not all your work can be seen anyway.'

He smiled in his most friendly fashion and added pleasantly: 'For a variety of reasons.'

Meriton scowled back and went through the double doors, still hunting for guilty faces.

Nick helped Paul to arrange his Brillo boxes in a pile on his table, and then Paul assisted Nick in covering his section with wallpaper that was patterned like exterior brickwork. On one partition Nick mounted his memorial plaque: 'Borough of Clayforth: Nick Thompson worked here 1996–99'. However, he had at the last moment proved unable to contain his creative instincts and, at the risk of undermining the arguments for his plaque, had produced a second work. He mounted it, slightly askew like a fly-poster, on the opposite partition, an A0 sheet on which was printed, in the large, severe letters of a newspaper hoarding:

IS THIS A JOKE?

Martin gave them a curt nod as he sped past, bent double, to speak to Bridget.

'Oi, Bridget,' he whispered, crouching even lower by her table.

'What's the matter? What are you doing down there?'

'The police are after us,' he said urgently. 'Someone shopped us.'

'What? You mean the Meriton thing? You didn't actually do it, did you?'

'No. But the police think we did. They've got Eggy, and now they're looking for me and Gary. I don't know how they found out, but I guess we're just going to have to talk to them.'

'Well,' said Bridget, dropping her voice to a loud whisper, and bending down towards Martin's level, 'I have to say, we didn't think you were actually going to go through with it.'

Martin was offended. 'We were. And we tried. We were all set up for it, but the van went the other way, and some other tosser nicked it.'

Bridget clapped her hand to her mouth to contain the laughter.

'It's not funny. Now, listen. I need you to do something for me.'

Bridget recovered herself. 'Well, I'm a bit busy myself at the moment, as you can see,' indicating her photograph of Curridge whose face was superimposed on a nineteenth-century engraving of King Canute vainly instructing the advancing sea.

'No, it's for Degree Day. Gary and me – if we can get away from the police – we're going to do a kind of joint Happening, only we can't do it here, it has to be somewhere else. So on the day, about ten o'clock, I need you to open this.' He offered her a large, sealed envelope. 'There's a piece of paper inside, just, you know, telling people what's going on. In case it goes wrong or anything, could you pin it up in my space?'

Bridget looked at the envelope suspiciously. 'Why don't you just pin it up now?'

'Well,' said Martin with a grin, 'let's just say that surprise is part of it.'

Bridget continued to study him.

Martin went on impatiently: 'Look, all I'm asking you to do is to pin it up. That's all. You're not implicated.'

'Implicated? In what?'

'Oh, come on. It'll be all right. It's just a wheeze. Just put the piece of paper up, will you?'

'Well, all right,' she conceded. 'Are you sure it's going to be OK?'

'It'll be fine,' said Martin, already scuttling, bent double, towards the door. 'In fact, it will be amazing,' he called back. 'Rembrandt, eat your heart out. Van Gogh, cut your ear off.'

'It's been done,' Nick called, but Martin was already running.

✎ ✎ ✎

The sudden influx of journalists to Clayforth, commandeering taxis from Leeds and Bradford airport and arriving at the central police station expecting news, had compelled Inspector Greenstreet reluctantly to install a police presence at the college, a visual implication that all avenues of enquiry were indeed being pursued.

Half the police presence was in the atrium chatting to Miss Grimm as Martin attempted to slide by, looking fixedly in the opposite direction, keen to complete his preparations for Friday. Miss Grimm, whose loyalty to college and students had run dry many years before, enjoyed the opportunity to identify the suspect and the constable was able, half an hour later, to march him triumphantly into the police station. In traditional fashion Martin loudly protested his innocence, although, in a departure from the standard dialogue, he also insisted that he needed to be getting on with preparations for his exhibition.

Inspector Greenstreet, whose lunch had already been delayed by journalists who could not find the art college for themselves, was less than pleased to be further kept from his food by an art student who needed to be interrogated. The resulting communication of his displeasure to Martin was so effective that the latter made a spontaneous and reasonably full confession of the gang's plans to intercept the van, although he passed over any reference to replica guns or the borrowing of a British Gas Stop–Go sign. He repeatedly insisted that the van had turned right and not left, as seen on television, and therefore, he and his friends had committed no crime.

'So, if you wouldn't mind,' Martin concluded in what he hoped was a winning but not too presumptuously matey way, 'I've still got a lot of work to do before our degree show opens at the end of the week, and you want your lunch.'

Greenstreet continued to stare at Martin suspiciously. 'Any ideas who might have done this, if it wasn't your lot? Any other students into lawbreaking and petty crime?'

Martin laughed. 'Well, everyone's into lawbreaking of one kind or another. That's what they teach us to do. That's what art is all about now. But no, no one's been talking about nicking stuff. That was our idea.'

'Looks like someone nicked your idea!' the sergeant said a little too forcefully, from his perch on a desk in the corner of the room. For the first time in their acquaintance Inspector Greenstreet looked at him as though he might be human after all.

11

Final Show

Paul had been awake most of the night and got up early. There was no going back now; no time for rethinking. Three years of struggle now culminating in one display. On this he would be judged.

Jan, as Paul had hoped, had not slept well either. The baby, following its own clock, had kicked and wriggled most of the night, and Jan had rolled from side to side trying, without success, to get comfortable. Fortunately, she had already started her maternity leave.

'I'll get you a cup of tea,' he said. 'You stay in bed.'

'No, I'll get up now and come down with you to college. I'd like to be there when it starts.' Students had the morning to finish arranging their exhibits before the examiners set to work at noon. Then in the evening there was the Private View for family and friends.

'No, you really ought to get some rest. Otherwise you'll be hanging around for hours while they do the judging in the afternoon. You come down at six-thirty for the Private View.'

It was one thing to shock people with art, he thought as he went downstairs. But premature labour would be an outcome too far, even for Horton.

✎ ✎ ✎

As he got off the bus Paul felt unusually alert, confident, focused, the order of events clear in his mind. On the pavement he met Nick, who had parked at some distance from college. Nick was staring at graffiti that had appeared overnight on the front wall by the college gates. It was not the usual offerings from the youth of the town, but a series of slogans: 'This is public art.' 'We believe in art.' 'Art will set you free.' 'Art thou the Son of God?'

'Who do you think?' asked Nick.

'What?' asked Paul, whose mind was on what lay ahead.

'Whose do you think this is?'

'No idea. Gary, maybe?'

'No, too understated for him. My money is on . . .' He searched to pluck a name from the air. 'Hannah.'

Paul smiled. 'Come on. Things to do.'

✎ ✎ ✎

In his first-floor office Julian Curridge was on the phone to a firm of industrial cleaners. He twirled part of his remaining hair in his fingers and tugged at it anxiously.

'Yes, it is very urgent. Don't you have an emergency call-out system? I have the mayor coming later on, and graffiti again all down the front wall. I've told the students time after time, if they want to do graffiti, they should use the pottery shop, but they refuse to comply with even the simplest rules.'

'I'm afraid none of our operatives have any free time today,' said the friendly but firm voice on the other end, 'or, let me look, no, not till Tuesday. Is Tuesday any good?'

Curridge clucked his tongue, unable to explain the budgetary implications of the mayor's arrival when students had vandalised what were still commonly regarded as municipal premises.

'Or you could try the council. They have what they call "graffiti-busters".' She said it slowly and deliberately, like an item on a foreign menu. 'They might be able to pop out for you. Though I think you will still have to pay for it.'

Curridge gave a curt 'Thank you' and slammed down the receiver, forgetting that it was a push-button handset. Pressing the little on–off button was too minimal an action to assuage anger. How could he call the local council to remove the graffiti when it was them he was trying to impress?

Outside his office, three figures in camouflage fatigues and balaclava masks were converging on his door, silently sliding along the wall, guns held professionally at the ready, pointing at the floor. Along the corridor behind them, a fourth figure, similarly clad, was also advancing, although he was armed with nothing more than a video camera.

The three figures glanced round at each other, the leader nodded, gave a number of signals with his clenched fist, and they suddenly sprinted forward to take up positions either side of the principal's door. As they steeled themselves for the final assault, the door to the next office opened and Marjorie stepped out, clutching a cardboard box file.

By the time she caught sight of the hooded figures one of them had swung round and was already aiming his gun at her midriff.

She paused and groaned: 'Not again.'

'Grab her!' whispered the tall figure by the door.

The figure covering her with his gun dashed smartly up the corridor, pushed the muzzle of the gun into her back, warned her to remain silent, and propelled her, unresisting, towards the principal's office.

Curridge was still looking distractedly at the cracked face of his handset when the door was suddenly kicked open and two masked and armed figures darted into the room.

'Don't move!' one of them yelled. 'Keep still!'

'This is a stick-u. . .' the other shouted. 'This is a . . . You are our prisoner!'

Marjorie was bundled into the office by the third hooded figure, closely followed by the cameraman. The office felt suddenly full.

The principal blinked at the intruders, and then looked at the splintered wood of the door frame.

'The door wasn't locked, you know,' he said plaintively.

'Shut up!' said the first gunman.

'You could have just turned the handle. Here we are trying to persuade the council to increase our funding, and you destroy a perfectly good door frame, when you could just use the handle like the rest of us.'

'Shut up!' repeated the gunman, moving round behind the

principal's chair, and thrusting the gun into the back of the principal's neck. 'You are our prisoner, and you will do as we say.'

The pressure of the gun forced Curridge forward, until his head was lying on the desk gazing sideways, his limp hair dangling down, and his glasses pressed askew against his nose.

'This is quite uncomfortable,' he protested. 'Could you just let me have a list of your demands, and then we can get on with the day?' he suggested. 'I really am very busy. We've got the mayor arriving . . .'

'Shut up!' barked the second gunman. 'We are in charge now. There'll be no horses in here unless we say so.'

Everyone looked sharply at the gunman, but irony is difficult to assess where the speaker is wearing a balaclava. The principal sighed. He had repeatedly spoken to the governors about the lamentable state of political awareness among students, but the chairman of governors, who had already been quite old in 1968, maintained that it was best to leave it that way.

'Our demand is that you give us our degrees,' barked the third gunman, still menacing Marjorie, who was standing in the corner of the room, tapping her foot.

There was a pause.

'Is that it?' asked the principal.

'What do you mean?' demanded the first gunman, still aiming his pistol into the principal's now rather sweaty neck.

'Is that all you want? Just the one thing? No demands for the posthumous release of the Baader–Meinhof gang, or repeal of the TV licence fee? Are you not even going to ask for extra funding for the homeless, or more kidney dialysis machines? Really, this is a most selfish generation. Are you really just demanding that we grant your degrees because you are doing so at gunpoint?'

'Yeah, you got it,' barked the second gunman, oblivious to the burden of the principal's concern.

'Well, and the video,' added the videoman, a tuft of blond hair poking out of one of the eyeholes of his balaclava. 'The video is part of it.'

'Oh, well,' said Curridge, evidently disappointed. 'Now that we have established your demands – or demand, I should say – do you think I might be permitted to sit up? I'm beginning to get a crick in my neck, and the chiropractor is always booked solid for months ahead.'

The first gunman looked nervously at his colleagues. They nodded uncertainly and he gradually withdrew his gun.

The principal sat up, arched his back, and then twisted his neck left and right a few times.

'Well, now there's a couple of preliminaries to sort out,' Curridge began pleasantly. 'First of all, are you planning to get the police in?'

The gunmen looked at each other blankly.

'It's just that some students have thought it would help give an air of authenticity to proceedings, to have a real . . . er . . . stand-off, I think the word is, with the police. But it did get rather ugly once when a kind of locum bobby, who was not familiar with this area and our . . . traditions, called in his armed colleagues without checking with the local station. They had a kind of shouting match: "Throw down your weapons." "Not until we get our degrees." And then we found ourselves on the receiving end of a couple of stun-grenades. It was quite interesting, really. They got their degrees, of course, but afterwards, when the police had finished with them, they all reverted to more traditional media. One of them shows quite regularly at the RA.'

'Er, no,' said the first gunman. 'No police.'

'Good. That makes things a lot simpler. In any case, even if you phoned them up, they generally leave us to sort out this kind of thing now, in-house as it were.'

The gunmen looked at each other suspiciously.

'What do you mean?' asked the second one.

'There's someone coming,' said the third.

'See who it is,' replied the first.

'Get down on the floor,' the third gunman hissed at the secretary.

'Oh, for goodness' sake!' she exclaimed. 'Is this really necessary?'

'Do it!' he barked and pushed her downwards by the shoulder.

'There's no need to be rough,' she said. 'Really, this is not in my contract, you know, all . . . this.' She gestured helplessly, as she lowered herself to her knees, and slid sideways to sit on the floor. 'At least the last lot let us sit down comfortably. They even offered us a cup of tea, if I remember correctly.'

'Oh, don't remind me,' said the principal. 'Student cups of tea! I think I prefer the pistol-whipping.'

'Will you shut up!' hissed the first gunman, as the third one cautiously put his head round the doorway.

In an art college devoted to conceptualism there are many unusual sights to be witnessed on most days. But neither Paul nor Nick, hurrying towards the Painting Department, was prepared for a face in a balaclava peering, at knee level, out of the doorway of the principal's office. The three eyed each other in a long moment of indecision. Then, with a neat forward roll over his shoulder, the masked figure was standing in the middle of the corridor, pointing his gun at the two students.

'Get in there!' he said quietly but fiercely, gesturing towards the open door.

Paul and Nick hesitated.

'Gary?' said Nick.

'Is that a real gun?' asked Paul.

'Shut up and get in there,' repeated the figure, advancing on the pair. Under the influence of the gun, and uncertainty about its ontological status, the pair moved towards the office doorway. The gunman pushed them in the back to hurry them inside, and closed the door as best he could in its broken frame.

'Ah, more students,' said the principal genially. 'Are you part of this great work too? I simply ask because it is beginning to get a little crowded in here, and that always makes it harder to assess individual grades.'

'We were actually just on our way to the studio,' began Paul.

'Shut up and lie down,' said the first gunman from behind Curridge.

'Martin!' said Nick. 'They let you out?'

'Shut up! We do not reveal our identities until we have a written guarantee of our final grades.'

'Look, Martin,' said Paul. 'I don't want to be difficult or get in your way, but we have got stuff of our own we need to do in the studio. If you could just let us carry on our own sweet way down the corridor, we won't mention anything we've seen.'

'We're not bargaining. Like you said . . . or as someone told me you said,' he added hastily, 'it has to be authentic, huh? Got to be prepared to go through with it. Hostages, threats, everything. Nobody does anything till we get our signed statement saying that we have all passed, or things will begin to get difficult.'

'Ah, well now,' interjected the principal. 'That's very easily done. What we generally do in these circumstances . . .'

'What do you mean, "generally do"?' demanded the second gunman. 'Sounds like you're always getting held up.'

'Oh, but we are,' said the principal. 'Tell them, Marjorie.'

'About once every three years,' Marjorie agreed wearily from the floor. 'Someone comes barging in dressed like terrorists and demanding something or other.'

'You were, I deduce, under the impression that you were being original,' said Curridge, as if teasing out the details of a particularly interesting construction. He looked round sympathetically, and even with the balaclavas, the eyes and the tilt of the heads looked slightly dejected.

'But don't worry,' Curridge added brightly. 'We can't all be totally original all the time, can we? Don't tell anyone but I sometimes wonder if originality is a bit overrated these days. Dr Crippen was original, and that wasn't altogether a good thing.' He looked round expectantly, but the balaclavas were expressionless. 'Authenticity is important, of course, and you certainly seem to mean business. And then there's your own particular brand of directness. None of this namby-pamby, liberal-minded shilly-shallying about the world's poor and the righting of injustice. It's goodbye to reason and morality, and just "Give us our degrees, or else."'

'Schopenhauer,' said the third gunman in a low voice, nodding thoughtfully and stroking his gun.

'Not very attractive, but certainly clear and direct. Very contemporary. Very . . . post-Thatcher. Yes, in fact, on reflection, I think that particular touch does seem quite original.'

The gunmen seemed to take heart. Their heads tilted up again, and they gave each other a quick look in the eye to encourage themselves.

'Now, as I was saying, what we normally do in these circumstances is to come to a kind of gentleman's agreement. I agree to give you your degrees, but you have to agree to stay mum.'

'What?'

'Yes. I'm sorry, but you see it really is necessary. If it ever got out that people got a degree by bursting in here waving guns, we'd never get any work done. And we wouldn't get any funding either. They really are very conservative in their tastes. Oh heck, talking of money, the mayor!'

Curridge looked at his watch and, behind his benevolent smile, a mean mind calculated. 'Look, lads. We've really got to wrap this up. We've got graffiti all across the front of the college, and I've got to get it scrubbed off before the mayor arrives at five.'

'But that's a work of art,' Nick called from the floor. 'You can't just wash it off. That's iconoclasm.'

'Maybe so,' said the principal firmly. 'But, as you've been told more than once in your career here, if you want to survive as an artist, you have to keep a clear eye on where the money is coming from. Art may be a cosy little world, but liquidity is what keeps it in orbit. Now if you would be so kind as to pass me a piece of headed paper . . .'

He gestured towards a tray against the side wall.

The principal wrote rapidly for a minute and then showed it to the gunman standing behind him. The gunman read it carefully, then his eyes smiled.

'Hey, guys,' he exclaimed. 'We passed!'

They gave each other high-fives, before peeling off their masks. Martin seized the principal by the hand and shook it warmly. 'Thank you, sir. Thank you very much.'

Gary and Zapper slapped each other on the shoulder.

'Hey,' said Gary to Paul and Nick still spread-eagled on the floor, 'we passed. How about that?'

'Does that mean we can go now,' asked Nick impatiently. 'The fate of some of us is still hanging in the balance.'

'Oh, sure. Off you go,' said Martin. 'Sorry to hold you up. Nothing personal. Just business, you know.'

'Now, Martin,' said the principal as Paul and Nick left, just a hint of steel in his pleasantness. 'I wonder if, in view of my cooperation over your degrees, you might do me a small favour in return.'

Martin looked round at him uncertainly.

'As I explained,' Curridge continued, 'I have a rather urgent problem in getting the graffiti removed from the front of the building. As you have already secured your degrees, and have nothing further to do for the day, I wonder whether you might pop down to the caretaker's glory hole, find whatever you can, and get to work scrubbing it off. I would be most frightfully appreciative.'

The four graduands gaped at the principal.

'You see,' Curridge explained patiently, 'although I am a man of my word as far as your degrees are concerned, I do have other considerations as well. It seems to me that you and your friends are in possession of a number of offensive weapons for which you almost certainly don't possess a licence.'

'You don't need a licence for replica guns,' Gary said, rather more forcefully than was respectful.

'And art or no art, you must have broken at least three local-authority by-laws relating to the taking of hostages, making demands with menaces, etc., etc. All this has been preserved on what, I am sure, is your own excellent video. But it has also been captured on my own CCTV cameras, which you may, at your leisure, try to locate. It would be very bothersome for me to have to send this material over to the police, especially when I understand that some of you have met them only recently, and we know their taste in art is so hopelessly passé. In fact, they have at times come across as actively unsympathetic to contemporary forms. On the other hand, I do need the graffiti off the walls in short order.'

'But that's someone's work of art,' Martin protested. 'Like Nick said, you can't just destroy it.'

'And as I said to him, I can and I will. We all have our own concerns to see to, and mine is a painless, trouble-free and, hopefully, lucrative visit from the mayor at five o'clock. And if you won't do it, I shall have to get someone else who will . . . after they have dropped the tapes off with the constable in reception.'

He stared into Martin's eyes.

Martin looked down at his gun, disappointment welling up within him. For all his bombast it was not authentic. The guns were not real. There was no terror. The threats would not have been fulfilled. Each one knew that, and knew that everyone else knew it.

Like schoolchildren caught smoking in the bushes, they were being sent on punishment duty – their punishment being that they would be seen destroying the work of one of their fellow students.

Curridge, sitting with his hands neatly folded on the desktop, awaited their reply.

12

Unveiling

Paul and Nick ran along the corridor and into the painting studio. It was echoing with the confusion of conversations shouted over the noise of power tools and hammers, as students completed their displays.

Paul assured himself that no one had interfered with his area. He took a moment to enjoy the pristine, matt finish of the paint, which he had meticulously applied so that it was evenly absorbed into the cardboard. Against this background, the Brillo logos, copied from library book illustrations, were stark and brash, but had a certain fragility in their handcraftedness. Passers-by still gave him pitying looks, although some smiled at what they took to be obvious irony and began to talk knowingly about Neo-neo-Dadaism. Having a few minutes to spare, he looked briefly over the accompanying text on the wall. It blathered about quoting the quoted, hand-reproducing the hand-reproduction of the mass-produced, pushing back the boundaries of what counted as art about art. It then progressed to a second line of argument, that these identical copies of Warhol's works were transformative of the nature of western art, problematising the assumption that, to be authentic, a work of art must be the artist's personal and original creation. Paul's work therefore violated the taboo that artists should not plagiarise the work of others.

Paul was not sure whether he believed it not. However, it would do for now.

✎ ✎ ✎

Charles approached the reception desk. 'Stephen Meriton?' he asked.

'They're in the staffroom,' said Miss Grimm, without indicating the direction.

Charles motioned for Dave and Shunt to follow him, and he ambled along the way Curridge had led him before. He considered for a moment whether to knock and wait, but decided to walk straight in.

The room was unusually busy. Garnet was by the row of filing cabinets earnestly informing Horton about her ambitious travel plans for the summer. Curridge was in the centre of the room, talking loudly and confidently to the external examiner, a stern-faced woman in her forties with short hair and a very blue suit. She was holding a cup and saucer and taking occasional, reluctant sips.

Meriton was slumped in a chair, waiting for the assessment to start. At the sight of Charles, however, he was on his feet in an instant.

'What the heck are you doing here?' he demanded.

'We've come to film your degree show.'

'Who told you to come?'

'You did,' Charles countered in surprise.

'I did not. I've seen more than enough of you for one lifetime.'

Charles was at a loss. 'I was told you left a message on Monday, and another one yesterday. I've had to reorganise my whole schedule to get here. Said it was very important that we get some shots of you judging the students' final show.'

'Garbage. There was no message. You think I want you trailing around with me for another day, sticking your camera into everything I do?'

Charles looked surprised but slightly pleased. 'Well, someone phoned. My boss sent it down on Monday. Told me to get on to it. Phoned again yesterday when your reminder came in.'

He looked round at Dave and Shunt, who had pressed into the room behind him. They shrugged, to agree that they knew less than Charles.

He smiled and said quietly to them as he turned away from Meriton, 'Well, somebody wanted us here.'

Curridge, glancing up from his conversation, almost jumped with pleasure at the sight of the camera crew. He seized the external examiner by the elbow and drove her across the room to meet Charles.

'This is excellent,' he exclaimed. 'I had no idea you were coming. Well done, Stephen. You're going to be filming us doing the assessment? That's splendid. How about some coffee before we set off?'

Meriton cast his eyes to the ceiling and turned away.

✎ ✎ ✎

Paul was idly adjusting the position of his Brillo boxes by millimetres to left and right when Nick came past and said quietly, 'They're here. In the staffroom.'

Paul set about reorganising his display. He took down his artist's statement from the wall, and replaced it with a longer one. Then he removed the smaller Brillo boxes and pushed them under the table, where they were hidden from view by a large cloth draped over the front.

Nick returned from his space with a video camera that he had signed out from the college, and began to record. Paul produced a Stanley knife and began slitting around the top of the single large box that remained on the table. Catching sight of the sudden burst of activity, students nearby gradually ceased their final activities and came near to watch.

Paul removed the top of the box and leaned it against the back of the table. He began cutting slowly down one of the corners of the box and removing the remaining sides. There was a sharp intake of breath.

'*You* nicked it!' exclaimed Bridget, her voice a mixture of surprise and delight and admiration. She bounced up and down, clapped her hands, and embraced a surprised student next to her.

Paul had determined to play it cool. There was more at stake here than mere street-cred. He lifted Meriton's cube fractionally and indicated for one of the onlookers to pull out the sixth face of the Brillo box. Then he settled the cube down again on the table, and adjusted it neatly parallel to the edge of the table.

Within moments, it seemed, the watching group had become a crowd, as news of the exhibit radiated through the room and down the corridor. As they heard it, every student knew instantly that they had been upstaged. In the studio, and then in the adjoining rooms, and across the rest of the building, they abandoned their exhibits and ran along the corridors to look and wonder.

Meriton, hearing his name shouted down the corridor, strode from the window and flung open the door. From answering calls everywhere it was apparent that his cube had reappeared. He set off in the same direction as the crowd with a measured but furious pace, followed by all his colleagues. Charles, grinning broadly, elbowed his way along in practised fashion, closely followed by his crew.

They arrived in the painting studio and began to push through the throng. Seeing Meriton, the students obligingly let him past. As he got towards the front, he saw Paul standing on a chair behind the glass cube. In his hand was a hammer.

'Don't come any closer, please, Mr Meriton,' said Paul loudly, and raised the hammer threateningly over the glass cube. Around Meriton the crowd now seemed to push together, as if, with a single will, they offered their support to Paul.

Meriton, who was taller than most of the students, eyed Paul furiously across the tops of their heads. 'What is this?' he demanded. 'Is this . . . is this . . . ?'

'A joke?' asked Paul. 'No, that's next door.' He motioned with his thumb towards Nick's space, and was rewarded with a laugh from the crowd.

'What is this?' Meriton demanded again. 'What's going on?'

'This is my work of art,' Paul announced simply.

'What? Nonsense. Where did you get it from?'

'Well, it could be described as a "found object", but I am

presenting it here as an original work of art by myself. My glass cube. My work. My signature on it.'

The onlookers stirred. Dave had manoeuvred round the back of the crowd, and found a chair to stand on. Beside him, Shunt looked fearfully between the heads at Meriton. Charles, having taken one look at the cube, had pushed his way out of the crowd again and was calculating sums as he pressed numbers on his phone.

'Is that my work?' Meriton demanded loudly.

'Well, as you will be aware, the concept of "my work" is now recognised as being a little . . .' Paul made a play of looking for the appropriate word: 'A little tawdry and simplistic.'

Meriton flinched.

'And in some quarters, quite oppressive,' Paul added.

'Foucault,' said Gary to himself in the crowd, with a grudging nod of respect.

'On what basis do you claim it is yours?' Paul asked rhetorically. 'Can you prove it? And does it matter? I'm not sure it does. I think the best we can say is that technically, this *was* your work of art, but now it is mine. It has my name on it now.'

'Duchamp,' Gary nodded in approval.

Paul looked round to address the wider audience. 'This work, among its many interesting qualities, problematises the claims of authorship. It questions the nature of authenticity. It even questions our ability to be sure of our own history, and therefore our own identity. You might like to read the accompanying statement,' Paul added politely, indicating the new manifesto he had pinned on the partition.

Meriton stared malevolently at Paul and then at the cube. The external examiner, possessed by her professional duties, forced her way through the crowd and began to read through Paul's statement.

Charles had finished his phone call and, like a surfer patiently watching the smaller breakers wash by, could feel the oncoming thrill of fame. He called from the back of the crowd: 'Why don't you read it out so that we can all hear?'

The public nature of the event, the large crowd and the two cameras, seemed to rob the examiners of any remaining authority. Garnet obediently took down the manifesto, turned round and read to the assembly:

> This is a multilayered work dealing with many of the most fundamental questions in art today.
>
> First, it evokes human life at its most fundamental – the breath of life, captured and preserved. Pure and simple and yet rich in constituents, invisible but powerful to sustain human life, with all our wealth of imagination and creativity.
>
> Secondly, it dissolves the distinction between art and reality: it is reality itself, displayed for contemplation and reflection. It has no intrinsic aesthetic value, but it is still rich in meaning, or at least in paradox, for those with the skills to play the game.
>
> Thirdly, it problematises the nature of art by questioning the assumption that an authentic work of art must be original to the artist, and that the work of art should be attributed to the person who made it. But why should this be so? Who dictated that a work of art must be original in order to be

authentic? By what authority do they seek to restrict our artistic freedom in this way?

'That's my line,' Nick muttered to himself, trying to keep the camera steady. Garnet continued:

> Many works of the past have been collaborative. Many have been copied one from another. Where does originality begin and end?
>
> The tradition that says art must be personal to the artist or else be inauthentic goes so deep that it has not been questioned even by those who pride themselves on questioning traditions. But it is, as has been consistently taught in this college, the job of the artist to challenge received wisdom and taboos wherever they are found, and it is surely overdue that the artist should challenge the taboo against passing off other people's work as one's own.
>
> It is for this reason that this work, although originally made by Stephen Meriton, is now presented to you as the work of Paul Blythe. The work is mine because I am displaying it, and it has my name on it.

Garnet peered at the front glass panel and helpfully pointed to Paul's felt-tip signature in the bottom right-hand corner.

'Thank you,' said Paul politely. 'There is, however, one more part of the statement to come. If you could shuffle back a bit . . .'

He gestured for Garnet and the judges to move away from the display and, as if mesmerised by the performance and uncertain of their own authority, they complied. Meriton, however, exasperated beyond endurance, made to push his way to the front.

'Ah, ah, Mr Meriton, please,' Paul said loudly, brandishing the hammer again over the cube.

Meriton stopped.

Paul took a sheet of paper from his pocket and read:

> There is another taboo widely enforced in the art world: the taboo against damaging other people's works. Whenever a work of art is attacked, whether it is Winston Churchill burning a portrait of himself that he does not like, or an angry member of the public flinging ink over the portrait of a child-murderer, artists themselves are at the forefront of the condemnations. This degree of unanimity indicates the presence of another taboo, protected with an almost religious devotion. As taboo-breaking artists we should therefore be prepared to challenge it.

The audience stirred as it caught the implications of the statement. Meriton felt disoriented by the sudden succession of events. He had a sense of foreboding, but the compliance of the audience made it hard to prevent whatever was coming. There were too many witnesses, too many people who knew what he had said, knew that these were indeed the incitements that he and Horton had given to the students. There was also, round his face, down his arms and across his chest, a tingling awareness that he was caught up in something very real, authentic and significant.

But if he had had the will to intervene, he would not have had the time. For as the words of the statement faded and the audience tasted the ominous quality of the silence, Paul without warning crashed the hammer onto the top of the cube. The sound of the shattering glass filled the studio, drowning the sound of the spectators collectively drawing breath. Large, irregular shapes fell one upon the other inside the cube, the clashing beauty of their music muffled in the universal associations with undoing and despair. The reverberations died away, leaving only a faint tinkling as smaller fragments continued to break free and fall to the bottom. There was another, longer moment of silence as artist and audience eyed each other in fear and wonder. And then Paul raised his hammer again.

'No!', Meriton cried, but Paul had struck again, this time at one of the metal bars around the top. It dented under the blow, and in the same instant a crack shot down the side glass panel from top to bottom, and at a further blow it burst into fragments. Meriton tried to push forward, but the crowd tightened around him, collectively willing Paul to finish his work. Paul continued to flail with the hammer, the blows falling increasingly quickly, like those of one determined to press their advantage and ensure that their opponent will not rise again. He aimed the blows so that the shards of glass would not shower onto the viewers, but the front row nevertheless cowered in alarm. The room was ringing with the ecstasy of destruction as the last side panel imploded, the vertical members of the frame buckled suddenly, and the cube began to collapse from the top.

Paul's hammer fell still, as a stale smell spread from the cube across the room. There were isolated cheers from parts of the crowd, and someone began to clap. But silence fell over them as they contemplated the scene of ruin. They were transfixed by its novelty, by the drama of something that seemed like theatre but was real life. But they were also embarrassed: a deliberate solecism, a premeditated offence, had been perpetrated before them, and they did not know how to respond.

✎ ✎ ✎

Inspector Greenstreet was sitting with his feet propped on the edge of the desk, knees bent to just below his eye-line as he watched the one o'clock news on a television across the office. He worked his way in large chunks through a warm pasty as a po-faced spokesman for a firm of stockbrokers deflected suggestions of insider dealing, a reporter stood in front of 10 Downing Street to discuss the latest job figures, and the recently snatched artwork by acclaimed international artist Stephen Meriton was destroyed by one of his own students. Greenstreet's feet hit the floor as he started forward over the desk to stare at the screen. The camera panned across the gawping expressions of members of staff and lingered on a group of students smiling broadly as they stood on tiptoe for a better view. Opinion was divided, said the voiceover, as to whether this was a prank by an individual student, or a publicity stunt contrived to promote Meriton's imminent retrospective.

Greenstreet looked menacingly at the screen, put down the rest of his pasty on a file in front of him, and snatched up the phone, chewing vigorously to empty his mouth. After a minute he was connected to the college switchboard. A longer delay followed while Curridge was located and brought to a phone.

'Inspector!' said Curridge breathlessly.

'Mr Curridge,' Greenstreet replied ponderously, as if by a lengthy and rigorous process of reasoning he had identified the speaker. 'Is there anything you wish to tell me?'

'Tell you?' asked Curridge distractedly. 'Tell you about what?'

'About the missing cube?' Greenstreet proffered helpfully, his tone suggesting it was only one of a number of interesting subjects on his list. 'The one we're currently supposed to be looking for?'

'Oh that. My goodness.' Curridge was still panting.

'Only it's on the news at the moment, being destroyed in your college, with you apparently in the audience, and I wondered if you were going to get round to telling me that I could stop looking.'

'It's on the news already? Oh, my goodness.' Curridge tried to catch his breath and glanced at his watch. 'And the mayor's going to be here soon.'

'Well, that's delightful to know.' Greenstreet's tone was dangerous. 'Only I was thinking I might pop round myself, as you seem to be harbouring a miscreant who, it seems to me, should be under arrest. Perhaps we could arrive at the same time as the mayor and make a little party of it? Would that be convenient for you?'

'Arrest the miscreant? Ah yes, I see what you mean. And with the mayor . . . no, I don't think that would be a good idea. Not a good idea at all.'

'We are sure that this is the thing we're looking for? This is the . . .' – the words stuck in his throat – '. . . the work of art? He wouldn't just be pretending to have stolen it?'

'Oh, yes. I mean, no. No doubt about it. Young Paul is quite adamant that he took the van, and this is – or should I say, was? – Meriton's piece all right. I think we are all quite satisfied on that point.'

'You're satisfied? Well, that's a comfort. But there is one thing at present which remains unsatisfied, and that is the demands of offended justice.' Greenstreet's voice rose indignantly. 'I shall be with you in ten minutes to arrest him.'

'Ah, well. No, no, wait!' Curridge called. 'Just a moment.' He seemed distracted and still short of breath. 'It's . . . um . . . it's a bit complicated really.' His tone became confidential. Greenstreet could hear him smiling nervously. 'To be honest, we're not quite sure what to make of it. The judges are still conferring at the moment.'

'The judges?' Greenstreet exclaimed. 'What the heck have the judges got to do with it? This is a police investigation, not Torvill and Dean.'

'Ah, well, yes, that's why I say it is a little complicated. There are certain . . . nuances to this that, well, have us a little bit . . . um . . . how shall I say . . .?'

He paused, as if Greenstreet might explain the nuances for him.

'Mr Curridge. As you will know, we still have half the world's press on our doorstep, wanting to know what we are doing to find a missing work of art. And I do feel just a tad stupid shaking down every gangster, drug-pusher and antique dealer in Clayforth, looking for a glass cube, when everyone in the world except me knows that it has already been found.'

'Yes. Yes, I do appreciate your point, Inspector,' said Curridge, but his voice tailed off.

'In my view, the next thing to happen in this little drama is to remove this young hooligan for a grilling in the Lubyanka. Don't you agree? Your judges can carry on enjoying the fruits of their freedom to judge as they see fit; but I would be grateful if you would prevent this young man from leaving the building, introduce him to my constable at the front desk, and have him ready for collection in ten minutes. I will arrive with the blue light flashing to make the big arrest. Maybe then I can be on the telly as well, and have my own fifteen minutes of fame.'

'Ah, yes, Warhol again,' said Curridge, laughing distractedly. 'He does seem to get about.' Curridge laughed again, with the air of one barely holding at bay the seductive enticements of hysteria. 'I suppose it's a good thing . . . art influencing life. Although, to be honest, it still takes us a bit by surprise when we see it. Maybe one of these days we might get your colleagues to collaborate on a project, "Warhol and the exercise of jurisprudence". *Arresting art and the art of arresting . . .*'

But Greenstreet was in no mood for collaboration. He hung up and stalked out of the office.

✎ ✎ ✎

Paul sat in the interview room, hands together in his lap, his face pale, eyes concentrating on the table in front of him. If this was going to be his breakthrough work, the police interview needed to go well. The conversation had already completed three laps.

'Were you aware that this . . .' Greenstreet still struggled over the right noun.

'Work?' suggested Paul.

'This glass box belonged to Stephen Meriton?'

'Yes.'

'And that taking and destroying the glass box was an illegal act?'

'As I have already said, I am not sure that I am the right person to answer that question. Mr Meriton himself, or perhaps Mr Horton, would probably give you a better answer. According to their teaching this year, and that of other members of staff, it is the job of the artist to challenge taboos. There is certainly a taboo against damaging other people's works of art, but if it is the job of the artist to challenge taboos, then my actions are *ipso facto* a work of art, and I don't see that I have done anything wrong.'

'And as I've already said, I don't give a damn about Mr Meriton's teaching. My job is to enforce the law of the land, not the highfalutin nonsense of an art college. And the law of the land is quite clear about what constitutes theft and criminal damage, and it is particularly precise in its disapproval of the unauthorised removal of, and damage to, works of art.'

'And as I have already said,' Paul continued patiently, 'it is perverse to describe what occurred today at the college as the destruction of a work of art, when what I did was itself the creation of a work of art.'

'And who says that what you did was a work of art?' demanded Greenstreet, thumping the wall.

'The college,' replied Paul quietly. 'Just ask the judges.'

Greenstreet threw himself into his chair and expressed himself with a sigh, a grunt, and the slamming of his hands face down on the table. He remembered the rest of his pasty, by now cold and congealing, grease seeping into the file on his desk.

✎ ✎ ✎

Jan was at home, feeling hot and uncomfortable, when her mother phoned. Jan groped for the receiver on the table next to the couch.

'It's on the news,' Jan's mother said excitedly. 'Paul's stolen that glass thing.'

A tone of satisfaction was clear in her disapproval, as she had never believed that Paul was a suitable husband for her high-flying daughter, and Paul's career so far had done nothing to persuade her otherwise.

'You know, that glass work of art thing that was on the news. Paul stole it. And he was on the news just now smashing it with a hammer. Yes, of course I'm sure. They showed him right close up. And they said his name.'

Jan was too angry to go into premature labour. She tried Paul's mobile but it was switched off. She struggled to her feet and waded across the room to hunt down a number for the college, muttering to herself about self-centredness, lack of awareness of her condition, and ridiculous sense of timing.

Half an hour later she arrived at the police station, together with Mark Bradley. The knot of reporters who had followed Paul from the college were rewarded for their patience by the opportunity to take poignant photographs of his pregnant wife toiling up the steps.

It irked Jan to have to call in Bradley but, as she was on maternity leave, she needed someone who would be in the office. Also, if she acted for Paul, she would be ethically restrained from hitting him over the head when they got home. She was obliged to fume in the waiting room, while Bradley took up their cause.

Bradley, in contrast, was enjoying himself with the novel possibilities of defence that Paul was developing in the interview room. He paused only to sweep his mop of straw-coloured hair from his face before launching in, his self-confidence combined with a tendency to speak extremely quickly, as if graciously ensuring that his clients got value for their money.

'It seems to me, Inspector,' he said, 'that if you consider that you have a case against my client on the grounds of either theft or vandalism, you should at least be considering at the same time a case against Mr Meriton and other staff at the college on the grounds of incitement to theft and vandalism, and, from the sound of it, to all sorts of other illegal acts.' He leaned as far back in his stiff chair as it would allow and added grandly: 'However, as my client has only done what Mr Meriton has himself instructed him to do, and no one has suffered any harm as a result other than Mr Meriton, I'm not sure what case you think you may bring.'

Greenstreet had already tired of this line of argument, and was regretting the current policy against police brutality. There was a smugness about these people that he felt would benefit from a short, sharp shock.

The phone rang and Greenstreet answered it, listened for a minute or two, and wrote himself some notes. He put the phone down.

'That's interesting,' he said pleasantly. 'Apparently, Mr Blythe, you have not only been nicking Mr Meriton's work and destroying it, but you also now seem to have been making death threats against him.'

'Death threats?' exclaimed Paul. 'That's nonsense. What are you talking about?'

'My colleague at the college,' Greenstreet said, gesturing to the phone, 'says there is video evidence, currently being played at the college, of you threatening to kill Mr Meriton.'

'That's rubbish,' said Paul.

Greenstreet was gratified to see the first signs of alarm. Paul unconsciously wiped his forehead, fearing that with this unforeseen element in the discussion he might be losing control over his work.

'I haven't threatened to kill anyone,' Paul said, adding weakly: 'I'm against murder.'

'I'm delighted to hear it, but how come therefore there is this video of you saying . . .' – he consulted his notes – '. . . "I'd kill Meriton."'

A vague memory echoed in Paul's mind, an impression of himself in the painting studio staring into a camera.

'Oh that. You mean when I was talking to Sheena? I may have said that as a joke, a long time ago, when we were just messing around. We were talking about whether murder could count as a work of art, you know, if there are no taboos.'

'I see,' said Greenstreet, suddenly all mildness and kindly warmth in case Paul might now be induced to confess to psychopathic tendencies.

'But she was only taking photographs of me for a portrait drawing. She wasn't doing a video. How did you get hold of a video of it? Has the college been spying on us?' Paul looked at Bradley for encouragement that the evidence might have been illegally obtained, and then added more plaintively: 'Anyway, if you see the whole thing, you'll see me arguing that we don't murder people, because murder is wrong. Some taboos are important. There are things that are just wrong – they are wrong because they are wrong – and we shouldn't do them, because they are wrong. There are some things we shouldn't do.'

'Like nicking other people's works of art and smashing them up?' Greenstreet snapped.

Paul flushed. This, he knew, was his weakest point, the aspect of the work that he had not reconciled in his mind. However he might arrange words and massage the college's own reasoning against itself, what he had done was wrong. It was because it was wrong that he had done it. And he knew that, in a deeper sense, that did not make it right.

'That's the whole point,' Paul said with attempted bravado. 'We all have taboos. We all believe some things are right and wrong. Even criminals have their own codes of honour, rules that they mustn't break.'

'I'm not convinced that you should speak of criminals in the third person, Mr Blythe,' said Greenstreet and glared at him in silence for a minute. But then he seemed to relax, and leaned back in this chair, stretching his arms up in the air, then folding his hands behind his head. 'But of course, you're right. Never ceases to amuse me that your far-out anarchist group, who like nothing better than to charge down the street throwing things at coppers, the moment someone breaks into their offices and nicks their computers – probably MI5, but never mind – what do they do but call us in, the very embodiment of the repression they despise, and demand that we nail the blighters and get their stuff back for them? Funny old world . . .'

He stared at Paul for a long time, trying to delay as long as possible the obvious conclusion that Paul, in his discomfort and embarrassment, was unlikely to be a provable psychopath. They could still prosecute him for wasting police time, but that might raise awkward questions about exactly how much police time had been spent on trying to recover a glass cube filled with someone's breath and spit. The case seemed more complex than it needed to be.

Twenty minutes later Paul and Jan emerged at the top of the steps. The crowd of reporters surged forward, cameras clicking loudly. On the advice of Bradley, who fancied himself an expert in public relations, Paul and Jan were arm in arm, smiling broadly, and waving happily.

Bradley stepped in front of them and read a short statement: 'My client has been advised to say nothing at this time, other than to confirm that he has not been charged with any offence and has been released pending further police investigations. Now, if you would let us through . . .'

He dramatically forged a passage through the reporters towards a taxi, which he had summoned, and the cameras followed Paul and Jan as they crossed the road and climbed in.

✎ ✎ ✎

By five o'clock the story had moved up to number two on the news. Paul and Jan sat at home in silence in separate chairs watching themselves on television, standing outside the police station, smiling inanely, waving like returning Olympic champions. After another viewing of Paul's destruction of the cube, a balding art critic with large, heavily framed glasses and a flowery, open-necked shirt told a reporter that art was about creativity and freedom, rather than the art-object itself, and as a total experience it could be critiqued in open-ended ways.

Jan was clutching Sylvester for comfort while attempting to formulate in her mind a series of questions to ask Paul. Why had he seen fit to plunge them into a crisis just at the point when she was focused on giving birth? What would happen to his career if he was thrown out of college? And how could she take up her career again as a lawyer with a convicted felon as a husband? But she was not sure she could say anything without screaming, and, as she could hear the reporters and cameras outside their front door, she presumed that they would hear her too.

Paul sat stiffly and in silence. He watched expressionlessly as the television showed him again beating down on Meriton's cube with the hammer. He knew he should be feeling elated. His work was a success. He was acclaimed by his peers and, thanks to the press, already famous. He could be counting the zeros on the handwritten notes thrust through the letter box and accumulating on the mat, as three newspapers conducted an auction for their story, Jan having finally unplugged the phone. But as he watched again the hammer blows falling, the metal buckling and the glass cracking and shattering, he could distinctly hear on the sound track the despairing tone of Meriton, a lone voice shouting simply, 'No!' It was an unusual sound from Meriton: not bombastic, sarcastic or condescending, but vulnerable and pleading. Paul felt no pride as he watched, no sense of achievement. The elation of the moment had dissolved into shame at his own self-righteousness. He was conscious of an ineluctable burden of responsibility, of guilt.

At seven o'clock, still clutching cold mugs of undrunk tea, they were interrupted by knocking on the front door followed by Nick's voice shouting through the letter box. He was smiling uneasily at the cameras as the door opened fractionally and Paul let him in.

'What've you been doing?' Nick exclaimed as soon as he was in the hallway. 'I've tried calling, but I can't get through. And you seem to have turned off your mobile. They're all waiting for you down at the Private View.'

Paul did not answer.

'You are coming, aren't you?'

The question expected the answer 'yes', but the silence suggested otherwise.

'Oh, come on, man!' Nick followed Paul into the living room. 'You can't let them down. You're a hero. They're all talking about you. You've got to come.'

'I don't know,' said Paul. 'I'm not sure it was a great idea.'

'Nonsense. It was a fantastic idea.' Nick grabbed Paul by the front of his shirt and gently shook him. 'You stuffed them. You nailed them. You pulled out their tongues and pinned them to the wall.'

Jan winced.

'Metaphorically,' Nick conceded. 'Artistically.'

'I'm not sure I can face them,' said Paul feebly.

'Oh, get over yourself,' said Nick impatiently. 'They love you. You're a star. Apart from Martin, of course. He may want to remove part of your liver, or gouge out an eye or something. But that'll be later on. Tonight . . . You've done something really new. Something brave and amazing. People recognise that. Now get out there and meet your public. Seize the moment!'

Paul seemed still to vacillate.

'Milk it while you can!' Nick insisted. 'You too!' he said to Jan sharply, gesturing with his hand that she should be on her feet and moving towards the door. 'He needs you too.'

Time seemed suspended as Paul and Jan walked through their small front garden towards the crowd of reporters on the pavement.

From watching television news and films he was familiar with the noise of chattering cameras, but to be the target of such relentlessly frantic attention was disorienting. They found their way to Nick's Micra, which was still shiny from a recent wash, and climbed in. Nick worked his way through the town centre.

The streets round the college were heavily parked by over-dressed parents who were now moving circumspectly through the alien environment of the art college to support their offspring in their moment of vulnerability and pride. Nick dropped Paul and Jan at the gates of the college and drove off in search of a space. They were instantly surrounded again by a press horde that had been tipped off to expect them, and others who had pursued them from their home. Hapless bystanders were elbowed unceremoniously into flower beds as the mêlée moved up the drive towards the main doors. Paul would have liked to have made a dash for it, but Jan clutched his arm as she made grim-faced progress towards the entrance.

In the foyer the drinks tables were already exhausted and abandoned. Dozens of used plastic cups stood forlornly in a shallow sea of spilt beer and wine, which was now dripping over the table edges and forming ponds on the grey lino. On the mezzanine, two large flat cardboard boxes, which had briefly been filled with savoury delicacies, offered only limp celery sticks and carrot fingers on a damp bed of paper napkins. Paul idly wondered if he could put a label on them and claim them as a work of his own: *Food for thought* and *Running on empty.*

The corridor upstairs was filled with students and parents, some looking at works on the walls, other standing in small knots, shouting to make themselves heard and laughing together nervously.

Paul and Jan began to work their way along the corridor but were obstructed by a throng outside Stuart's room.

From inside, and rising over the noise of conversation, came the chuntering sound of train wheels crossing points and then accelerating. Above this could be heard the muffled, gruff voice of the guard: 'Welcome aboard this Greater Scape train to World's End. We apologise for the late running of this service, due to washing on the line. The first stop on this service is . . .' A blast of static drowned the rest of the guard's words, and then the sound of the train resumed free of interference. 'A buffet service is available on this train, for therapy, light massage, and theological discussion of all kinds. The buffet car is situated at one end of this 24-car train.'

Over the door Stuart had erected a sign, stencilled in the timeless sans-serif font of the railway network, *Train of thought*, with an arrow pointing downwards towards the door. Paul and Jan paused at the edge of the crowd.

A smooth, formal, woman's voice came over the air, broken by further bursts of interference: 'Please ensure you have a . . . at all times. Anyone without a . . . may be subject to . . . or have their . . . . off.' A train-whistle blew and there was the faint sound of bleeping from a level crossing before the female voice resumed: 'Please do not leave your soul unattended on any part of the Greater Scape network. Any unattended souls may be removed and destroyed without warning.'

There were fifteen seconds of rumbling wheels, during which Paul and Jan tried to edge through the crowd, but more people were joining from the other side and it would not yield. Behind them, the corridor was filling with reporters.

The crackling suddenly stopped and, with a sharp click of the microphone, the guard's voice resumed more clearly: 'The next station stop is not Crewe or Manchester Piccadilly.'

The posh lady interrupted: 'Please note that smirking is not permitted on any part of this service.' But the guard would not be silenced and cut back in. 'Next stop and listen,' he insisted. The train wheels began to slow. 'This is World's End. World's End. All change here. Yes, you too. Wake him up, someone.'

As the soundtrack came to an end and the pressure towards the doorway eased, the noise of the press pack sounded more clearly. Heads turned and stared. Paul, looking bemused, and Jan, tired and irritable, forced their way between bodies towards the painting studio. Beyond Stuart's room the corridor opened up again, and they moved between more small groups of earnest conversation. In one clump Paul saw Hannah, and they both coloured as their eyes met. She was standing next to her exhibit, a giant model of a pineapple, its individual spirals picked out in rainbow colours. Along these designated paths crawled dozens of exquisite models of snails, each sporting on the side of its shell, like a veteran racing car, a large white circle marked with a Fibonacci number. Across the back of her display area was written the title, *Order! Order!* Hannah looked as though she wanted to say something but could not break away from her group. Paul, his stomach filled with disquiet, saw both the alarm and the accusation in her gaze.

As they came through the double doors, however, Bridget put two fingers in her mouth and produced a screeching whistle, which was followed by a pandemonium of shrieks, cheers and applause. Paul, having no previous experience on which to draw for such a situation, reverted to learned behaviour from the television, and waved and nodded politely in the manner of royalty on a state visit. Jan's glower softened slightly in the warmth of their reception.

The noise abated to be followed by an embarrassed silence as everyone watched Paul lead Jan through the room to the scene of the crime. Through the silence, from somewhere in the distance, came Paul's voice: 'I'd kill Meriton.' Paul looked round for its source but could not identify it before they reached his display area. In his absence it had been transformed. The broken glass had been cleared away, partly by individual students who, at first surreptitiously but then increasingly openly, helped themselves to the larger shards, holding them like sacred relics, and ones that might increase in value in the future. The caretaker had swept up the remains and disposed of them with less reverence. The buckled frame of the cube had been removed by the police, and Bridget had reinstated the other Brillo boxes to the table, so that it would not look too bare.

As they came upon the scene, they found Martin fixing to the partition behind Paul's boxes a poster that he had run off on the college's printer. In the same font as Nick's *Is this a joke?* it said:

I AM A FRAUD

Caught in the act, Martin glared defiantly at Paul, and then marched towards him as though he would exact revenge there and then with his fists. But he only thrust a stubby finger close to Paul's nose: 'I'll get even with you one day, you wait and see,' he snarled. 'We had a perfect plan, all worked out, and you ruined it. You're too dumb to get ideas of your own, so you just go and steal ours.'

Paul looked at him a little nonplussed, and said as if it were a question: 'But you were going to steal someone else's work.'

'Don't get smart,' Martin snapped. 'Stealing the work was my idea, and you should have left it to me.'

'I don't understand,' said Paul quietly. 'Are you saying that it is alright for you to steal from Mr Meriton, but not for me to steal from you?'

'Damn right, I am. And you'd better hope I don't catch you down a back alley any time soon, or I'll show you, and no mistake, who to steal from and who to leave alone.'

'And what did you do to my work of art?' said a voice from the audience. Martin looked round to find the speaker. It was Anand. 'I left my work on the front walls this morning, and then I watched as you and your mates came along and cleaned it all off again. What was all that about?'

Martin blushed in confusion and was silent.

'Just as well I used water-based paint,' Anand added, 'or you'd still have been at it now.' He turned to Paul and Jan: 'It was a challenge to the supposed artistic freedom that the college encourages us to indulge. But of course, they don't allow us any freedoms that inconvenience themselves. And Martin and his mates, who also claim to be in favour of artistic freedom, cheerfully collaborate in volunteering to wash it all off.'

'It wasn't like that,' Martin began gruffly.

'But not to worry, my friend,' said Anand more cheerfully. 'You got to star in my final submission – a video of you destroying my work. It's called *Hypocrisy*.'

Martin scowled at Anand and then at Paul, and barged past them into the crowd.

'What, by the way, was the title of your work?' Anand called after him.

'What work?' Martin asked, turning round.

'Your gimme-all-your-degrees stick-up job.'

'How do you know about that?'

Anand seemed surprised by the question. 'You describe it all in the statement pinned up in your show.'

Martin issued an inarticulate cry. In the agony of embarrassment of cleaning the walls, he had forgotten to retrieve the envelope from Bridget.

As Martin hurried off, his boots squeaking on the lino, across the top of the partition came Paul's voice again: 'I'd kill Meriton. I'd kill Meriton. I'd kill Meriton. I'd kill Meriton.'

Paul followed the sound to the end of the row. It was coming from Sheena's bank of monitors. On the wall beside them were nine hand-drawn portraits, angular, stiff and childlike, but clear enough for Paul to recognise himself, as well as Nick, Meriton and Marjorie among the others. On the monitors was a video loop of each sitter, talking quietly. Marjorie was chattering about Curridge, and when the loop came to the words 'He's a bit of an idiot' the film jumped back to repeat the words. Curridge was caught in a hellish cycle, endlessly repeating the words 'Her famous bum' with only something that sounded like a hiccup between iterations. Nick turned out to be discussing Paul's series of photographs, ending with a repeated refrain, 'I mean, what an idiot. I mean, what an idiot. I mean, what an idiot.' Meriton was talking in soft tones about his wife's accident, ending with an echoing phrase: 'After all, you do anything for the people you love. After all, you do anything for the people you love. After all, you do anything for the people you love.'

'Ah, you've found it,' said Nick cautiously as he appeared. 'Sorry, about that. She caught me off guard.' Nick pointed to a small label, fixed to the wall beside the monitors. It read: 'Sheena Crofton. *Out of order* (1998–9). Mixed media'.

'Apparently, the computer wasn't out of order after all,' Nick explained.

Paul picked up a laminated sheet on which Sheena had written her apologia:

Art is truth, but people tell lies.
How much of the truth should we tell?

Art is truth, but the truth hurts.
How much pain should we inflict?

Art reveals, but people want to hide.
How much should we show?

✎ ✎ ✎

Ralph Ellis looked around uncertainly as he entered the foyer. He nervously straightened his tie, gazed with distaste over the wasteland of the refreshment table, and approached the reception desk.

Sir George, away on business in Bradford, had been phoning Curridge's office repeatedly throughout the afternoon to initiate a crisis meeting. However, with the college surrounded by press and occasionally visited by police officers, the principal had decided to make himself unavailable while he attempted to recover his equilibrium and compose his thoughts. Sir George had finally phoned Ellis and sent him to track down Curridge in person.

Miss Grimm, annually displeased to be working on a Friday evening, confirmed that Curridge was in the building, but was not inclined to offer more guidance. Ellis edged his way apologetically between the knots of students and parents until, after some time, he spotted Curridge down a corridor, delivering a well-rehearsed monologue on broad educational goals to a pair of smartly dressed, discomforted parents. Their daughter, black eyeliner enhancing her glassy expression of boredom and unspecific resentment, was trying to stand on one leg and balance her empty glass behind her on the sole of the other foot.

At a break in Curridge's flow, Ellis stepped forward with an 'Excuse me a moment', a command rather than a request. He took Curridge by the arm and, with surprising determination, steered him towards a fire extinguisher in a dark corner, partially shielded by a pair of doors that had been propped open.

'What on earth is going on in your college?' Ellis demanded in a fierce whisper. 'Here we are, trying to establish Clayforth as a cultural centre of the north, and half the country is laughing at us for a town of hooligans, art thieves and vandals. What am I supposed to say to the press when your people are smashing up works from our museum? Sir George, as you know, is all for a bit of controversy to raise public awareness, but even he thinks this is ridiculous. Am I supposed to bring in armed guards in case next year's cohort of students decides they all want to rampage through the whole museum?'

At one point in the afternoon, to escape the frenzied circus of exactly these questions, Curridge had resorted to hiding in the Pottery Department where there was a modestly sized and little-used cupboard. Pausing only to make free with the pottery staff's coffee machine, he had shut himself in the cupboard and spent a fruitful half-hour of contemplation, weighing the possible arguments that could be advanced, and their financial implications. He was thus able to conjure up a tone of confidence and confidential warmth as he replied.

'Well, I think we need to take a broad view, and I am sure Sir George will concur. By my reckoning, our humble college, and by extension the town whose name your museum bears, have been continuously in the national news for the past . . .' – he ostentatiously consulted his watch – '. . . nearly seven hours at least. Those seven hours have done more to raise the national awareness of the town of Clayforth, and to link it in the public mind with cutting-edge contemporary art, high culture, and sheer bloody-minded adventurism, than all our marketing and recruitment strategies for the past seven years.'

Curridge leaned in confidentially and Ellis instinctively stooped to bring his ear closer. 'So, I would strongly urge that we refuse all talk of thievery and vandalism. Instead, we talk about art engaging with reality; about providing exciting, risk-taking, thought-provoking works; about daring to think the unthinkable; and – I always like this one as a kind of catch-all, get-out-of-jail-free card – "pushing back the boundaries of what counts as art". We deny any suggestion that this is a hotbed of vice and scandal and criminality, and we focus on Clayforth becoming, as the Americans would say, a very "happening" place, all vibrant and innovative and exciting. In comes the attention, and press, and – ahem – money, for the college and the museum. For us, it's thousands of pounds for every extra student who chooses us over some other, more tediously conventional art college, because we are suddenly hip, or groovy, or whatever the term of the day may be. And for you, with Stephen's retrospective about to open, if you point your press officers in the right direction, you could have half the art world of Europe coming through your turnstiles. They'll be putting on special trains direct from King's Cross.'

Ellis, anxious and bewildered, eyed Curridge silently for a moment, and then said hesitantly: 'Are you joking?'

'I am the principal of an art college, struggling to make the sums stack up. This is hardly the time or place for levity.'

'Do you seriously think people will accept such an argument?'

'My dear Ralph,' said Curridge, 'we belong to a different era. You and I still hanker for the days of definitive judgements. We used to declare confidently that Abstract Expressionism was passé, that Land Art or Happenings or whatever it was at the time was the Real Thing, and that pictures of doe-eyed puppies were kitsch. But now . . .' – he leaned in even more closely to whisper the heart of the secret – '. . . nobody knows. No one is certain of anything.' He straightened up slightly but still spoke conspiratorially: 'And as our French philosophers tell us – not that I've read them, but Eric says he has – in a world without absolutes, it's all about power. The person with the most powerful ideas, the person with the loudest voice, or, in our case, the person with the most powerful position in the establishment, wins.'

'The French have got a lot to answer for,' said Ellis glumly.

'In the meantime,' Curridge added, 'as you brought it up, it might not be a bad idea to put on a few more attendants next year. Just in case.'

✎ ✎ ✎

Meriton had no intention of attending the Private View. He had the excuse of needing to look after Pam, but in truth he had no desire to see any student or staff member ever again. The laughter and cheers that had accompanied the casual sacrilege against his work had hurt as much as Curridge's prevarication and the attempt by the external examiner to take Paul's actions as a serious submission for his degree.

At home, preparing the meal, Meriton as usual was listening to the evening arts review on the radio. As he had feared, his name featured in the opening headlines. The presenter delivered the outline of the story, with barely concealed amusement, and began to introduce responses.

'It's clear from the artist's statement,' a pundit was insisting, in a high, earnest voice, 'that this is a work that raises issues both about taboos and taboo-breaking, about the sanctity of the art-object, as well as about artistic originality.'

Meriton realised with a jolt that the 'artist' being quoted with such solemnity was the hooligan student, and not himself.

'You don't think he was just trying to be outrageous for the sake of it?' asked the presenter.

'Well, every time an artist does something new, people say he or she is just trying to be outrageous, and of course these days outrage is usually a part of it. But it's too easy to just dismiss it as outrage and not listen to what the artist is saying. I think you have to give this student, Paul Blythe, the credit of believing that he is being serious, and then see what issues that throws up. And of course, like any good work of art, that can be unsettling. I'm sure there are lots of artists right now about to lend their works to exhibitions, and wondering if one of their fellow artists is going to walk up and suddenly start destroying them.'

'So you think this could be the start of a new school? Could there be an entire movement of artists stealing other people's works, passing them off as their own, and/or then destroying them?'

'Well, not really. It would quickly become passé. The young artist here has made something original out of being unoriginal, but to do that again would be back to being unoriginal.'

'And if you were Stephen Meriton, what would you be thinking right now?'

'Well,' said the pundit, stretching out the vowel so that listeners could tell that he was thinking deeply, and probably steepling his fingers as he spoke: 'Meriton's work is disarmingly simple, but also deceptively so. He makes a very plain object, but he invites you to explore it in terms of physics, of geometry as a lived experience, of space as a metaphor of meaning. I think, if you look at what has happened to his work today, the notion of "dis-integration" – and you have to hear the hyphen there because it's about "undoing" rather than mere destruction – has a lot of potential, if he is minded to embrace it.'

'On the line we have Julian Curridge, the principal of Clayforth College of Art. Julian, quite a busy day you're having.'

'It's certainly been exciting,' said Curridge enthusiastically.

Meriton kicked the oven door, which slammed shut. He had not expected support from Curridge, but even so, he was disappointed.

'Which do you think is the more serious crime: stealing a work of art or destroying it?'

'Well, I think you have to choose your words with caution,' Curridge said in his friendly, earnest manner. 'The word "crime" is heavily loaded . . .'

Meriton switched the radio off. He felt isolated and betrayed. The moral sophistry exasperated him. He kept reliving the moments as he stood and watched his work being hammered to pieces. He wanted to meet fire with fire, violence with violence; to do to Paul what Paul had done to his work. But he was also disappointed with himself. He heard himself cry out and wondered why he had not fought harder to push forward and intervene. The crowd had seemed to tighten around him. The horror of destruction had frozen him, but so too had indecision and doubt. It was the doubt that was the worst. He felt eviscerated, emasculated, exploited.

13

June

Meriton, wearing a crisp, open-neck black shirt and black jeans, stood amongst his works and surveyed the display bleakly, his bald head gleaming in the spotlights. Museum staff occasionally passed through the halls, attending to details, while the cleaners repolished the floor in readiness for the guests arriving at five-thirty for the Private View. Across a corner of the room catering staff were laying cloths on tables, and ferrying in trays of glasses.

In contrast to the ludicrous funfair atmosphere downstairs where the gallery, despite his protests, had parked what was now known simply as *The van*, the exhibition upstairs had the stillness that he had envisioned. White drapes obscured the incongruous 1920s frescoes on the ceiling, Ellis having refused Meriton's request to have them whitewashed. A false floor of white laminate had been installed at a cost that still put the director off his lunch when he thought about it. The seven pieces had been positioned and repositioned until the staff complained to Ellis, but he merely shrugged hopelessly, after which the works were reorganised for a further two days.

Ellis had finally conceded three rooms to the show. The middle one had been sealed at both ends with a series of three airtight doors to protect *Strength*, which was suspended in the centre of the room, a few feet above the floor. Meriton still regretted the need for a frame on it. It would have been much more powerful stretched from wall to wall and up to the ceiling but, without a well-trained and obliging spider, that would require specially manufactured fibres and would lose its aesthetic impact.

Strength shared the space with *Doubt*, an octagonal box the size of a medium-sized room, admitting one visitor at a time. Each of the internal surfaces, including the floor and ceiling, was covered by a single mirror, and with the help of small spotlights the viewer could scrutinise themself from several angles simultaneously, fragmented and multiplied, disappearing down infinite corridors.

In the centre of the first room, on a low platform, was the *Sounding Bell*, a glass container, ten feet high, bulbous like a vinaigrette holder with a long, straight neck and a fluted opening. It had been manufactured for him by a firm in Italy for a Documenta exhibition in Kassel. High above the floor, its mouth was filled with a large cork bung, which Meriton had made himself. The heart of the work, however, was inside the jar. Through a set-designer friend he had arranged for the Royal Opera House to lend him their orchestra and leading trio to perform Mozart's *Soave sia il vento*, the three soloists directing their voices straight into the mouth of the jar, which had then been sealed. Periodically, the rich waves of the music now played through speakers high up in the corners of the gallery, as if literally descending from heaven, three minutes of ethereal and beautiful hope and fear, longing and acceptance of loss. The soft undulation of the orchestra's opening line offset the melody of the sopranos, which seemed to float on the breeze that they prayed would accompany their lovers safely across the sea. Meriton especially enjoyed the contrast of innocence and guilt as, after two minutes, the music built briefly to a climax of longing, a sustained high note from the trusting, guileless women allowing prominence to the climbing and falling of the bass line from the duplicitous Don Alfonso, before they united in a final, slow descent of heroic stoicism, a sudden final brave emotional forte, and then the orchestral resolution. If the viewers co-operated, there followed a silence in the gallery so profound that, at the time of its first exhibit, it had earned Meriton the soubriquet of 'the John Cage of the art world', as all stared into the glass jar, seeing in its emptiness the exquisite poignancy of beauty and happiness, experiencing the gnawing desire to hold on to them, and the heroism that accepted their passing, as the invisible music played upon memories and imaginations.

Meriton had intended to pair this with *Breath of life*, each attempting to embody some appreciation of the reality and potency of life with a recognition of its passing, a recognition that became more intensely real with age. But instead there was only an empty plinth.

The artist had held out against sustained, three-pronged pressure to create yet another replacement work. Ellis was not keen to have an empty plinth in the exhibition, in case visitors felt they had been short-changed. Sir George was eager for the news value of a replacement, whilst Curridge was still attempting to divert Meriton from any lingering thoughts of legal action against student or college.

'You can style yourself as the new Duchamp!' Curridge had boomed with what Meriton recognised as uncharacteristic heartiness. 'No one minds that the *Large Glass* is a replica, and that the urinals aren't the original. In fact, it adds to the interest: the sense of history that gives the work a kind of authority. Helps to distract from the fact that they're not really saying anything.'

'And you are thinking the same would be true of my own work?' said Meriton in a level voice.

'Well . . . No, no. Just the sense of history. It's OK, it won't matter not being the original. People will be interested . . .' His voice tailed off.

'Whatever that young vandal may claim, originality and authenticity do matter. Even if one can't rationalise the reasons, remaking the work will not be the same, and I have no intention of doing it.'

Sir George had joined the chorus by phone: 'The world is watching. Out there people are talking about you, about us. People are talking about Clayforth. For once, they know where we are. Right now, *Breath of life* is the most fizzingly famous work in the country. People want to see it. You've got a real chance to put us on the map, and make yourself the most fizzingly famous artist in the country at the same time. You're not going to turn that down, are you?'

But as Meriton had skulked at home, periodically stirring himself to help Pam negotiate the stairs or hobble over to her workshop, he had kept returning in his mind to the students' degree show. He pictured Paul with the hammer; he heard the laughter and cheers. The baby face of Charles kept floating back, with his uninformed condescension and mockery. Meriton could reconstruct the work without difficulty. It would have some kind of authenticity, inasmuch as it would be a real object, with real breath in it. But why would people come to see it? Not because of the significance of the work, but because of its history. There would be no quiet contemplation of life, breath or even the perfection of a rational shape, but a ragged scrum of tourists having their photographs taken in front of it, paying no more aesthetic attention to it than they did to the *Mona Lisa*, ticking it off as one more site to be visited, one more celebrity to be spotted. Everyone would always know that this was not the original: that somewhere in the world, in a landfill site or recycled into a chrome and glass table in the foyer of a chrome and glass building, the fragments of the original work still existed, destroyed in an act of defiance by a mere student. The history, the story, would always dominate the aesthetics. Paul's intervention would always trump Meriton's meaning.

Reality was against him. Destruction could not be undone, time could not be reclaimed, and originality could not be forged. Reality, beyond his control, had destroyed the purity of his idea. And as the music once more descended from its peak towards silence, Meriton was aware of its echo in a bottomless sense of powerlessness and regret.

The plinth stood empty. Nearby, on a neat, white pedestal, was a small display board on which Meriton's text was printed:

> This space had been reserved for the work entitled *Breath of life*, a cubic space containing the artist's breath. Tragically, the work was recently destroyed in an act of vandalism.

14

July

The midwife turned a page of the *Jamaica Times* without looking up and resumed reading. It was three o'clock in the morning and Jan was dozing again. At the other side of the bed Paul sat on a stiff, metal and plastic chair.

There had been a flurry of excitement the previous evening around nine when the contractions had speeded up and Jan had begun to dilate. But it had gone quiet again and the staff had drifted away. He had been left alone with the midwife who seemed intent on reading every word of every article. Paul thought she was on page twelve now.

Jan's face, lying sideways on the raised pillows, was very pale. Two tubes had been inserted into the back of her left hand, much to Paul's distress. Apart from the misadventure with his sculpture, he had never suffered anything worse than a sprained ankle, and the sudden reality of medical intervention on this scale made his body seem even more fragile than he had appreciated.

In these quiet hours his mind had kept returning to Meriton, and the injustice Paul had caused him. Paul had not dared to go to Meriton's exhibition, although it had been widely and enthusiastically covered in the national media, and was attracting crowds from around the country and abroad. Paul feared that, if he were recognised among the visitors, he would be pre-emptively arrested. But also, when he closed his eyes, he still heard the plaintive 'No!' from Meriton; and every time he replayed the hammer blows, he flinched at the brutality of it. Paul remembered the shattering of glass in the first impact, and the buckling of the metal frame with the second, followed instantly by the shooting crack down the side pane. And, as other images and sounds reappeared in his mind, Paul had to stop himself from yelping out loud in embarrassment and regret.

Meriton appeared to have accepted the situation with high-mindedness, and was not pressing for action against Paul. The police had been sufficiently unsettled by Paul's defence that they had decided to hide behind Meriton's charity and let Paul off with a warning. But it would have been easier for Paul if Meriton had tried to take revenge: the necessity of mounting a defence would have enabled him to focus on reasons by which he might justify himself.

Paul remembered Hannah at the bus-stop, apparently willing to absorb and forgive the rudeness of Horton and others at the group crit. At the time it had seemed like weakness, but now he was less sure. He did not imagine that Meriton had forgiven him, but Meriton's refusal to take action, his choice to accept the pain and injustice and not to fight back, made Paul feel more thoroughly exposed, pinned up for examination with no defence against the accusations that sprang from his own conscience.

He had his degree, and the blustering support of the principal, as well as the long-desired admiration of his fellow students, but he could find no satisfaction in what he had done. For all the brilliant diversion that words could spin, they could not alter the fact that what he had done was wrong. And his motives, he knew, were not pure: neither morally nor artistically. He had been angry and frustrated; he had wanted revenge. And all Meriton's bile and contempt did not in the end seem to weigh enough to justify the hurt that Paul had inflicted in return.

The room was very still. The clock ticked; the baby's heart monitor flashed; an occasional footfall echoed in the corridor. The hours had passed surprisingly quickly, with the midwife periodically checking Jan's dilation. 'She's about seven centimetres,' she had said matter-of-factly last time, before returning to a closely written report.

At least they were financially secure for a year or more, while he sorted out his next move or Jan went back to work. While Paul had vacillated, Nick had engaged an agent to market his Degree Day video of Paul, and the two of them were sharing the proceeds that were now accumulating from around the world. In the meantime, Paul had sold an exclusive interview to one of the tabloids, and, given the threadbare nature of their immediate job prospects, Jan had agreed to a photo shoot with the new baby.

Jan suddenly stirred and cried out, and struck out with her right arm across the bed. The midwife briskly folded her paper and stood up to check her patient.

'I'd say she's nearly nine centimetres,' she said without any hint of excitement. 'I'll call the doctor to check.'

The stillness of the past hours was roughly banished as the room filled with people: the midwife returned with a doctor, followed by a junior doctor and two nurses pushing trolleys of equipment. Behind them trailed a group of medical students clutching clipboards. Paul remained at the bedside but felt suddenly excluded. Jan cried out again, and Paul handed her the gas-and-air mask, thinking vaguely that at least it had the benefit of stifling the noise.

The doctor worked his hand inside Jan. 'Yes, I can feel the top of the head.'

Jan yelled again, inarticulate but convincing, but everyone's attention was at the other end.

'Yes, I can feel it coming. Tell her to push.'

The midwife conveyed the message, but it seemed to Paul that Jan could not hear anything in her pain.

'Keep pushing,' called the doctor, as he squatted at the foot of the bed.

'Remember to breathe,' said the midwife. 'Big breaths . . . deep . . .'

Jan gasped and clutched at Paul's arm. Her nails dug into his flesh and hurt him. There was no reason, he felt, for him to suffer as well, but he said nothing, and mopped her forehead with a damp cloth, murmuring whatever encouragement he could think of.

And then his attention was caught by exclamations at the other end of the bed. He transferred Jan's hand to his own hand, so that he could edge along the bed to see what was happening. From out of Jan was coming something huge and round.

'They didn't say it was going to be a breech birth,' Paul thought, as the large pale form slowly emerged.

Paul stared with fearful anticipation.

'Keep pushing,' said the doctor. 'Nearly there.'

The noise seemed to intensify as Jan shrieked and writhed at one end of the bed, and everyone else edged closer together to witness the moment of revelation, talking with increasing excitement to whoever was listening. And Paul suddenly recognised it. It was a head. It was so huge, he had thought it must be the backside. But now, silent and impassive on the doctor's hand, for a single intense moment it lay in regal state, impassively self-contained, possessing the room. In that instant, there was nothing else in the world. Tears of wonder sprang to Paul's eyes. And now it was he who was hurting Jan's hand as if he would crush it out of an inability to express himself in any other way.

Then, with a sudden slithering rush and mess, it was all there. Pale, thin arms and legs, tiny tummy, its backside in reality hardly noticeable. Slimy with blood, squealing with need, it was rapidly placed on Jan's stomach, as she groaned and fell silent. There was a bustle of cleaning and organising at the foot of the bed, as Paul stared transfixed at the child. Coming to the hospital the previous day, he had of course known, as an abstract concept, that the baby would be born. But he realised that he had not been emotionally prepared for the reality that now, at the end of the process, there was another, entirely separate, living person in the room.

Jan put her hand gently on the child, rubbing its head with her thumb, and smiled wearily. The baby was quickly bundled up in a towel and taken away by two nurses into a corner of the room to be checked for the essential signs of health.

Jan turned her head to Paul and smiled again faintly. Paul smiled in return, but could find no words, and Jan became blurred as tears again filled his eyes.

✎ ✎ ✎

Half an hour later the room was as it had been. The doctors and nurses had disappeared as unceremoniously as they had arrived. The sheets were changed, the floor washed, the trolleys wheeled out. The midwife had efficiently arranged the room, folded her paper and said goodbye. Jan was fast asleep. Paul sat in the stiff chair by the bed, staring down at his daughter in the crook of his arm. She was cocooned tightly in a white, hospital blanket, sleeping fitfully as she recovered from such a rude removal from the world she had known.

The head no longer seemed large, much smaller than the head of the soft, blue velveteen rabbit that Paul had placed in the corner of her cot to act as guardian and friend. But the power of that moment of misrecognition remained. Paul sat awestruck by the power of the small person he was holding. Try as he might, it seemed impossible to comprehend the reality of what was there. He recalled his previous visit to hospital with his injured hand, when he had thought to grasp after reality through the variety of its details. But this new life in front of him seemed to inhabit a different dimension of wonder: the very fact of her existence, beyond the safe control of his own thoughts, was difficult to accept. He thought of the drawings in his own blood, when he had wanted to introduce the shock of physical reality into graphic work; and yet now they seemed only dry, sophisticated games. He thought, more fondly than usual, of Hannah with her daft, busy hair bobbing from side to side as she talked over-enthusiastically in the seminar room about art being worship of God who was himself the greatest artist. For the first time, he began to sense what she was trying to say.

As he sat in awe of this small form, not beautiful by conventional standards with her thin hair matted and face blotchy and wrinkled, hardly moving with the breaths that she took, worship was exactly what he felt, a deep sense of all the worth that this creature embodied. He was astonished at her reality, her identity separate from himself, her own life. And yet he also sensed their visceral connectedness. He remembered a phrase from the old translation of the Bible that they used to read at church, a phrase that always used to make him laugh: 'his bowels yearned upon him'. What Paul felt was nowhere near the heart; it was indeed deeper down. He felt that yearning he had known for so many years and which had seemed to seek satisfaction in art; and yet also now he sensed a kind of satisfaction, a sense of oneness in the physical embrace and yet of the separation which had already begun and which would gradually deepen as the child grew.

He placed his daughter very carefully in the cot, her head nestling against the foot of the rabbit, whose startled expression made it seem quite as overwhelmed by its new responsibilities as Paul was by his. Paul fumbled in his jacket, which hung on the back of the chair, and found his blue bound notebook in the inside pocket. From the side pocket he produced a pencil and began to draw.